Voices Carry

For Rick,
"Enjoy!"
[signature]
2005

Front/Rear Cover Design by Robert Howell
Copyright 2005
Carolina Moon Publications

ISBN 0-9712737-1-5

Printed in the United States of America

To order additional copies, please contact us.
BookSurge, LLC
www.booksurge.com
1-866-308-6235
orders@booksurge.com

Booksurge Publishing
5341 Dorchester Rd Suite 16
North Charleston, SC 29418

Voices Carry

A NOVEL

Robert Howell

Carolina Moon Publications
2005

Voices Carry

This book is for anyone who loves to be frightened as much as I do, for my family, and for anyone else who ever thought I had a strange imagination.

Thank God, you were right.

PROLOGUE

Sumter, South Carolina
November 12th, 1914

They were dead; all of them except him.

As he lay there against the cold, wooden floor, the first rays of the morning sun crept through the small doorway. Tears formed in his swollen eyes as they tried to adjust to the brightness. He winced in pain as they rolled across his cheeks, the salt stinging the open cuts that covered his face. Slowly, his vision began to focus. Just beyond the sun-lit doorway, he could see the gray fields rolling off into the distance. The tops of the pines stretched for the sky at the field's edge. Though his entire body ached with the slightest movement, his senses were somehow extremely intact. So intact, that he could hear the horses in the south field as they played. The sound of birds chirping came from above him in the rafters. The aroma of drying tobacco was rich in the air, intertwined with the smell of dust and rat droppings.

The coppery taste of his own blood was on his tongue. His mouth was filled with it. Beneath him, the floor was stained with it.

He knew that he was dying. . .just as the others did last night.

Laying his head back down, he closed his eyes and felt thankful that they had not suffered as he had; that they were dispatched quickly and with some degree of mercy. Though he prayed for his end to come quickly as well, it was not to be. He was told that he would be taught a special lesson; that his pain would be greater. Once the *lesson* began, it was as horrible as promised. At some point in the midst of it, he lost consciousness. That was all he could recall until he opened his eyes to the morning.

Oddly, he found himself thinking less of the torture he had endured and more of the fact that he was now all alone in the world.

The risk he had taken had been for nothing. No one from town had come to help him or the others. Perhaps today would be the day that they came. Even so, it was too late. They were all gone, never to return. Soon, he would be gone too.

Somehow, he had crawled here to his hiding place last night. Knowing that he had been left for dead, he had waited until darkness fell before starting his painful journey. Staggering part of the way, and then dragging himself the rest with one good arm, he felt that he would never make it. There was so much pain; too much pain. It crept through his body and stabbed at every muscle, seeped into every bone, the slightest movement sending him into spasms. His skull felt like it would surely burst. Twice, he had felt as if he would be sick, yet he had no food in his stomach to expel. The last leg of his trek called for him to climb. With only one hand and the injuries he had sustained to his legs and feet, it proved to be almost impossible, yet somehow, he made it. Delirious and spent, he had found himself sprawled upon the floor in what he hoped would be a place of refuge.

Now, he lay in a quite cramped and uncomfortable space. He felt as if his entire body had gone numb from lying in a prone position throughout the night, but he welcomed the numbness over the pain. It was almost relaxing. He knew that if he tried to move about too much, the pain would return. That was the last thing he wanted. Maybe he would just lay right here until someone from town came to help him. It would feel so good just to go back to sleep. There would certainly be no pain then.

The sound of his name being called aloud from the yard below jolted his eyes open and caused his labored breath to catch in his throat.

"Conner?" the voice cried.

He was being searched for. He knew it would happen. The call came once more, louder this time.

"Conner?"

He would not answer. He would stay here, where it was safe. No one could find him. He was tired and wanted to sleep. Soon, he knew all his suffering would be over.

"You'll not hide long, worthless runt!" cried the voice.

But he would. He would hide right here. Slowly, he closed his eyes once more and felt himself drifting away, the shouts becoming distant echoes that faded into nothingness as sleep came for him.

Ninety winters passed.

PART I

AWAKENINGS

CHAPTER I
Sumter, South Carolina
July 14th, 2004

The sounds always came at night.

For weeks now, five-year-old Jonathan Fowler had been hearing things from the darkened hallway just outside of his bedroom door. Scratching sounds, like that of an animal trapped within the walls; like a monstrous rat attempting to gnaw its way into a boy's bedroom and feast upon him while he slept.

Sometimes, they seemed to come from within the hallway bathroom, or even as close as within his own bedroom. Either way, they always came from a point somewhere in-between Jonathan and the sanctuary of his parents' bedroom, which was just beyond the stair landing about eighteen feet away. To Jonathan, it may as well have been a hundred miles. During the daylight, a journey down the hallway was not threatening in the least, but when the night came, things were different. Every dark corner seemed to host a waiting beast which would leap upon him the second it had a chance. Just beyond that darkness were his parents, sleeping peacefully in their bed. The urge to rush to them was almost over-powering, but that meant exposing him-self to whatever nightmarish creature was making the noise. Such a risk was not to be taken, so Jonathan remained in his bed where he knew he was safe.

It was as if the nightly visitor was *daring* him to make a run for it.

Tonight, the sounds jolted Jonathan from his sleep around eleven thirty. His light brown hair was sticking in every possible direction from his pillow and his eyes were bloodshot from being asleep. Usually, it was one or two o'clock in the morning when he heard the hidden thing come to life. For some reason, tonight it had started early.

Sitting upright in his bed, Jonathan clutched the sheets to his small frame and wondered what he should do. Feeling the urge to cry, he did his best to fight it off. Perhaps he *should* try to make it to his parents' room, racing down the hall as fast as his small legs would carry him, risking life and limb...but then he remembered what his father had told him once before. He had slept in the same bed with them the first few weeks after they moved here, and he knew his father wanted him to be a *big boy* now and sleep in his own room. Even so, he had still called out to them when he first heard the sounds, and they came to comfort him every time. His mother had even slept with him some nights when he was particularly frightened. On those nights, there were no strange noises. They only came when he was alone, just like he was tonight. Perhaps he would call to them and they would come, silencing the sounds in the dark.

Jonathan knew that a *big boy* would not call for help. He also knew that they would probably not believe him.

Being a child with all the typical "boogeyman" fears, Jonathan had informed his mother and father many times of something lurking in the darkened hallway or bathroom at night, only to be told that *"There are no monsters or goblins"* waiting for him in the darkness. His father was quite stern in instilling the ridiculous adult belief of a world without monsters; a world where no beasties lay waiting for the opportunity to spring on an unsuspecting five year old and devour him.

Jonathan *knew* better.

Outside, a pale sliver of moon hung over the tree-tops. Jonathan could look right out of his second floor window and see it. The tops of the pines moved gently in the night breeze. Every once in a while, he could catch a glimpse of headlights traveling Highway 76 in and out of the town of Sumter.

His father's job at the bank had brought them here. They had moved here from their home in Camden about a year ago, when Jonathan was only four. He had loved their old house - largely because he was right next door to his grandparents and that there were other children to play with in the neighborhood. The night his father and mother told him that they were moving to a nicer house, he had cried for hours. To Jonathan, it was un-imaginable to be up-rooted from the world he knew. To top it all off, the thought of moving more than five minutes away from his grandparents had terribly upset him. As time passed and tears were shed, he eventually came to terms with the idea of his new home. He even began to feel a bit excited when his mother explained that he would have new friends, a new school, and a big back yard to play in. The house in Camden had been fairly small, but the new house in Sumter was big; a two-story log cabin style home, it was located two miles east of Sumter sitting on about six acres of land just off Highway 76. Jonathan was thrilled to see that he did indeed have a huge yard to play in now and a much bigger bedroom than he had in Camden. He was nearly as excited to find out that he would be living near the Coca-Cola Bottling Plant and that Shaw Air Force Base was only a few miles away. Surely that meant that he would never run out of soft drinks and that he would get to watch the big jets fly overhead.

He loved his parents and knew that they seemed much happier now. He often overheard them talking about what a *"good deal"* they had gotten. To make things even better, he found out that he would still get to see his grandparents almost every weekend. Sometimes he would go visit their house and sometimes they came to see him at the new house. In the end, Jonathan was happy.

But the sounds in his bedroom had begun almost a month ago, and that's when things began to change.

Now, as he sat there in his bed listening to them, he wished he was back in Camden where things didn't try to come into your room and eat you alive at night.

Quickly, he reached for his nightstand and fumbled with the top drawer. Pulling it open, he kept one eye on the hallway and began feeling around for his Sponge Bob flashlight. After what seemed like forever, his small fingers fell across the familiar cylindrical shape of the lights handle. He flicked it on with his thumb and returned to his position sitting upright on the bed, casting the lights beam directly into the center of the hallway facing him.

The scratching suddenly stopped. There was nothing there.

Slowly, he directed the beam toward the left side of his room, letting the brightness wash over his closet door, then onto his dresser, then into the corner where his dirty clothes hamper sat.

He saw nothing.

Moving it to his right side, he scanned the small table where he kept his action figures and comic books. Then, he let the light pass across his bedroom window, briefly illuminating the shear curtains and giving them the appearance of two hanging ghosts.

Still nothing.

He pulled his legs up underneath him and sat on his knees, directing the light back into the hallway, determined to spot any ominous figure that may come lurching toward him out of the dark.

He still saw nothing.

Though he was too young to think about it or understand why, even the smallest sound seemed amplified a thousand times at this hour of the night. Jonathan suddenly became aware of his own heart beating in his chest. The tick of the clock above his window seemed thunderous. From downstairs, he could hear the air conditioner unit humming to life and roaring like a monstrous wave. Above his head, the ceiling fan blades cut through the air at what seemed to be a deafening level. The icemaker in the kitchen dropping a fresh load of ice into the freezer tray sounded to him like a pile of human bones being tossed into a wooden crate.

Then...the scratching started again.

Nearly dropping the light, Jonathan swiftly pointed it back to the left side of the hallway and across the bathroom door.

It grew louder...and it was coming from the bathroom.

Jonathan noticed that the bathroom door was completely closed. Whatever was in there would have to use the doorknob to get out...or eat its way through.

Then, as abruptly as it started, it stopped.

Sudden silence; it was almost worse than the scratching.

Jonathan noticed then that the flashlight beam was growing dim. He realized that the batteries were almost dead. He shook the light in a futile effort to make it brighter, but it began to fade more and more with each passing second. He felt himself start to sweat.

There was still total silence in the hallway...but for some reason, he felt like someone was there.

Like someone was watching him.

Suddenly, Jonathan lost all interest in being a *big boy*. He felt his lungs fill with air as he drew in a breath and prepared to call for his mother and father. They would make it all go away as they always did. His lips moved to form the cry for help and he forced the air back out of his lungs, waiting to hear his own voice break the horrible silence.

It never came.

The words lodged in his throat, and he realized he was too frightened to scream.

His small fingers tightened around the flashlight in a vise-like grip, tighter and tighter with each passing second. Had he not been so terrified, he would have felt the pain in his hands and noticed his knuckles turning a ghostly white.

Something creaked in the darkness. Something was in the hallway... and it was moving.

Jonathan had heard the sound before, when his father had pulled up the hall carpet to check a spot in the flooring. The same creak had been coming from that spot beneath the carpet every time someone walked across it. Though it had been fixed twice in the past year, the creak always seemed to come back. The problem was that someone usually had to walk across it to produce the sound. Weight had to be applied to it.

There was no one there...yet the board creaked just the same way it did whenever his parents or anyone else approached his room.

As Jonathan looked frantically back and forth between the dying beam of light and the unseen presence, a sound rolled forth from the darkness; a sound unlike anything that he had ever heard in his young life.

He wished he was not hearing it now.

It was like a thousand whispering voices, building from a distance and growing in intensity. It was above him, beside him, all around him. It seemed to come from everything and everywhere. Even the night breeze that danced through the pines outside his window seemed to be a part of its horrifying, yet fascinating chorus.

Then, with a clarity that was unmistakable, the rising crescendo of sound reached its peak...and a voice called out Jonathan's name.

He felt the flashlight fall from his hands, and then the warmth of his own urine as he wet himself.

CHAPTER 2

"Damn!"

Neal Fowlers exclamation of pain broke the silence of the quiet Saturday morning.

"Tiffany, bring me a rag, quick!" he shouted, looking toward the kitchen window. "I cut myself!"

Neal stood on the brick patio behind their house, a couple of sawhorses in front of him that supported a sheet of plywood. The wood's yellow surface was dotted with crimson. Holding his left hand up in front of him, he watched the blood slowly begin to run down his forearm, stopping at his elbow and dripping onto the brick below.

So much for the back nine this afternoon he thought.

He had wanted to wrap up his project early and go play a little golf later, but now that was out of the question. He had been cutting the plywood to make a small ramp for his storage building, but the new skill saw he was using had sliced through the wood a bit easier than he had figured and damn near took his left index finger off. The blade had bitten into him before he knew it. Luckily, it stopped before it went deep enough to hit bone, but it still had left an ugly half-moon cut between his first two knuckles.

He sat in the resin chair by the patio door and removed his safety glasses. Even they had a couple of spots of blood on them. He wiped them on his shirt and put them in his pocket. Tiny drops of blood had trailed behind him as he walked across the patio, and there was also some on his yellow polo shirt. He felt about his face and forehead, checking for more. There was none - just sweat on his forehead and a day's worth of stubble on his jaw. Tiff would be all over him if he didn't shave tonight. He ran his uninjured hand through his dark, but slightly graying hair, then sat back in the chair, feeling like an idiot for cutting himself. He knew better than to do something so stupid.

Tiffany stepped out through the sliding glass doors, her tennis shoes and sweats on. Her long brown hair was thrown up under an Atlanta Braves baseball cap. She was holding a first-aid kit in her hand. Neal thought she was beautiful, whether she was dressed to the hilt or just "bummed-out" in jeans and an old shirt. As she walked toward him, he smiled. She still looked just as young today as she had when they first met back in college.

"Really, Mr. Fowler," she said, smiling and shaking her finger at him. "If you're pushing forty and *still* don't know how to operate power tools, maybe you should give them up for good."

Neal laughed a little, holding his injured hand out to his side so that he didn't continue bleeding all over himself.

"Yeah, yeah, yeah, just c'mon and wrap me up, Florence Nightingale," he said. "I guess your husband is all thumbs."

She knelt in front of him and wrapped a wet piece of cloth around the cut to clean it up. Neal winced and she heard him catch his breath when she applied pressure to it. Removing the rag, she took a good look at the cut.

"Keep *this* up and you won't have any thumbs left," she said with a concerned look. "Looks like you did a pretty good job of trying to mutilate yourself, hon. I believe you could probably stand to get a couple of stitches."

Neal looked at her like she was crazy.

"Stitches for a little boo-boo like this? C'mon, it's not *that* bad."

She looked at him and gave him the smirk she always did when she felt she was right. Neal knew it well.

"Oh, so are we a medical expert now? Should I address you as Doctor Fowler?"

Neal pretended to ponder the idea. "Well, it's never too late for me to take up a career in medicine."

"Remind me to never get sick if you do," she laughed. "All kidding aside, this is definitely stitch worthy, baby."

"Don't like stitches," Neal said, shaking his head. "Don't like hospitals either. I'll get a few butterfly bandages from the cabinet under the sink and I'll be fine. I've had cuts plenty bigger than this."

"Hard headed to the very end," she replied. "Okay, macho-man, but we still need to wash it off a little better."

She stood up and stepped over to water-hose that lay coiled in the pine straw by the house. Turning it on, she rinsed the cut with the cool water. Then, she took some anti-biotic ointment from the kit and gently applied it.

"What would I do without you?" Neal asked.

Lightly wrapping the cut with gauze, she lifted the bandaged digit to her lips and gently kissed it.

"All better, but this is a temporary fix," she said. "Really, Neal, between you and Jonathan, I don't know who bangs themselves up the most around here."

"Looks that way," he chuckled. "At least *he's* not using power tools on himself yet."

Tiffany closed the small plastic kit and gave Neal a hug.

"No, but his sleepless nights are almost just as bad."

Neal knew what she was talking about. He veered from the topic, knowing that it would lead to a long and upsetting discussion as it had so many times before.

"Well, in the future I will do my best to keep all my fingers and toes away from any moving machinery," he replied. "Deal?"

She looked flustered. "Okay, it's a deal."

Neal knew that a *"but"* was coming…and it did.

"But, I want you to go inside and put those butterfly bandages on good and tight. I'm going to the gym for about an hour. Jonathan's parked in front of the television watching cartoons. I'll grab you both some lunch on my way home."

Neal gave her a peck on the forehead.

"Sounds good," he said. "Looks like golf's out for me today. I'll be right here being a couch potato."

"Please consider the stitches," she said. "If that bleeding isn't any better by the time I get back, I'm going to knock you cold and drag you to the doctor."

"Get outta here." he laughed.

"I love you."

"Love you more."

With that, she headed back inside. Neal could hear her grabbing her keys off of the kitchen counter, followed by the front door opening and closing. Then he heard the Durango crank up, and she was gone.

Neal had always thought that he and Tiffany had a great marriage. He had met her in his last year at the University of South Carolina. Having moved to Columbia from Spartanburg, Neal never really dated a lot while at school, largely due to the fact that he was majoring in Business and actually studied instead of partying all the time. He opted not to play any sports either, knowing that it would take his focus away from why he was there in the first place. Neal was well liked and made several friends, but most were classmates. Outside of school, he really hadn't met a lot of new people.

Tiffany Anderson, as she was known then, did not attend USC. She lived in Camden with her parents and made the drive back and forth to Coker College in Hartsville. She had started going to a few USC football games with her father, an avid fan and season-ticket holder. Eventually, she crossed paths with and got to know some of Neal's friends. One thing led to another and before either of them knew it, they were set up on a blind date.

Hesitant at first about going out with someone he'd never met, Neal almost backed out. At the last minute, he decided *what the hell* and went through with it, agreeing to meet her at a small party at a friend's house. Of course, on the actual night of the party all of his buddies enjoyed toying with him, trying to convince him that Tiffany was buck-toothed and ugly as sin. One of his classmates even tried the old *she used to be a man* routine on him. Neal was nervous enough as it was without everyone ribbing him so hard. When the doorbell rang and his friends rushed to see her in, he had no idea what manner of woman or beast he was about to meet.

Then, she walked into the room...and he fell in love with her right then and there. The two of them became inseparable.

After that it all happened very fast.

School came to an end and real life began. Neal took an apartment in Columbia and landed a job as a loan officer with Carolina Trust Bank. Tiffany still lived in Camden, but worked just outside the city of Columbia as a legal assistant. She met his parents and he met hers. They lunched together every day and usually saw each other four out of five nights during the week. On weekends, they were always with each other. After about a year, Neal proposed to her. She gladly accepted.

As luck would have it, a small house in Camden not very far from Tiffany's parents' home went on the market one week after he gave her the diamond. It was located about two miles from Interstate 20 in a quiet housing development. Neal made an offer on it and the seller accepted. Six months later, after Neal and Tiffany went in and re-painted, re-carpeted, and re-decorated it from one end to the other, they were ready to move in. All they had to do now was get married, which they did in a small but very sweet ceremony on the first day of March in 1991. Tiffany's mother insisted that it be held in her back yard and no one disagreed. It went off without a hitch, just a few close family members and friends present. Neal drove into Columbia to work at the bank every day and Tiffany stayed on at the lawyer's office. Both of them were happy, and it seemed that the world was close to perfect. Only one thing was missing; a child. So began the long period in their lives leading up to the day they were blessed with Jonathan.

Tiffany and Neal were both in their late twenties when they first decided to have a baby. It was the first real emotional crisis they had to deal with. The doctor had informed Tiffany that she may have trouble conceiving due to a cyst that had been surgically removed from her ovaries while she was a teenager. The fear was that her uterus would not be strong enough to carry a baby to full term. Her doctor then informed her that it may be a concern that she would not be faced with, as he didn't think she would be able to conceive anyway. It devastated her. She had cried on and off for weeks, feeling that she had let Neal down. He did his best to let her know that he loved her regardless, but he knew that it did nothing to ease her pain. As the months went by, she thought about it less and less. The tears eventually stopped, for which Neal was grateful. The only time he ever noticed her get misty-eyed was whenever they were around other couples who went on and on about the joys of parenthood. Every once in a while they would bump into friends with infants or toddlers and Neal could see it getting to her. He knew that it was killing her inside, but she was trying her best not to show it.

Then, life did what it does best. It surprised them.

She skipped a period that very next December. She had been due the week before Christmas and you could normally set your watch by it. The days ticked past slowly and she kept the secret of her disrupted schedule to herself. She didn't want to get Neal's hopes up for something that might be a false alarm. Christmas Eve came and went. On Christmas day, she decided to tell him. Neal was immediately ecstatic when he heard the news and rushed right out of the house to go and get her a home pregnancy test from the local drug-store. Upon his return, she retreated to the bathroom with the small blue and white box he had brought her. After about five minutes of letting Neal pace around the bedroom, she opened the bathroom door, smiled, and said, "Congratulations, Dad."

Eight and a half months later, on September twenty-first, Jonathan Lee Fowler was born in the Camden Hospital. Both baby and mother came through just fine. Jonathan was a beautiful child. He had his mother's blue eyes and thick, brown hair. About the mouth and nose, he was pure Neal, who became so excited that the doctor offered him some Valium to calm him down. Neal politely refused, opting to bask in the joyous emotions that came with being a new father.

They brought Jonathan home on a Monday afternoon and settled him into the nursery. Preparing the room had been a labor of love for both parents. They opted to go with a nautical theme and it turned out wonderfully. Neal had painted the walls light blue and airbrushed white clouds in certain places. Tiffany had added seagulls, lightly sketching the birds in with a pencil and then hand painting them. Her mother and father, eager to start spoiling their new grandchild right way, paid to have Tiffany's old crib re-finished and surprised them with it.

Jonathan took his first steps on the front lawn of the house in Camden at the age of eleven months. He got his first stitch when he was two and fell chin-first into the coffee table while playing. He rode his first tricycle in the driveway, had his first birthday party in the backyard, and was stung by a bee for the first time while sitting on the front porch. All the wonderful and sometimes not-so-wonderful pleasures of being a child were his.

Neal knew that was why the move had been so tough on the little guy.

It was the hardest thing he had ever done the day he had to tell Jonathan that they were re-locating. He had loved the house himself, but the money that Carolina Trust Bank had offered him to work at the Sumter branch was just too hard to turn down. He tried commuting between Camden and Sumter for a while but soon grew tired of it. Even though it was a shorter drive than the commute to Columbia that he used to make every day, he wanted a home closer to his work. Being closer would allow him to get home to Tiffany and Jonathan a little earlier in the evenings and sleep in just a bit later in the mornings.

He had spotted the house while it was still under construction. It was located just out of the city limits, one mile east of the overpass where Highway 378 wound around the city of Sumter. He immediately discussed it with Tiffany. After much talk about property values, schools, taxes, and what seemed like a dozen other issues, they both decided that it would be a good thing. Besides, they had just about outgrown the eleven hundred square foot home in Camden. Sumter seemed like a good place to be. With a population of about 40,000 people, it wasn't as annoyingly large as Columbia had become, yet it wasn't as "small-town" as where they were currently living.

Now, here they were. Though the move was a pain, as moving usually is, once they settled in, they were fine. His new salary made it possible for Tiffany to stay at home with Jonathan and decorate the new house to her liking. Jonathan certainly didn't mind his mom being with him during the day, especially since he was in a new place and had not made any new friends yet.

Neal considered himself a very lucky man. He was thirty-five years, had a decent job which paid him well, and was blessed with a family he couldn't imagine himself without. Tiffany was his best friend and greatest comfort. They still flirted and kidded with each other as if they were teenagers.

Then there was Jonathan. He was the light in both of their worlds.

If only the nightmares the boy was having would stop.

Reluctantly, Neal stood up from the resin chair he had been sitting in. The cut on his hand was throbbing like hell, but he still wanted to cut that sheet of plywood, injured finger or not. Tiffany would object to his finishing the project if she were still here so he decided to get it done and sweep off the patio before she returned. Then he would take it easy and hang out with Jonathan until she came home.

Neal suddenly realized it was getting warmer outside and that he was very thirsty.

Making sure he held his bandaged hand up at his shoulder level so that the bleeding would ease off, he slid open the glass doors on the patio and stepped directly into the kitchen. A glass of iced tea seemed like a good idea before he got started again. A cold beer would be even better, but it was still before noon. As he walked over to the refrigerator, he could hear the sounds of the television coming from the family room. The volume must have been at full blast. Neal could hear loud crashes and comical sound effects intertwined with music. Saturday morning cartoons always were the best. As a boy, Neal himself recalled being glued to the television on many a Saturday morning. Sure, they had the Cartoon Channel now, but there was still something special about Saturday.

"How's my little man doin' in there?" he called out.

Jonathan didn't answer, undoubtedly involved in the cartoons.

Neal opened the refrigerator door and removed the pitcher of tea that Tiff had made last night. As he lifted a clean glass from the dish strainer next to the sink, a high-pitched sound split the air.

It was the skill-saw roaring into life outside.

"Jonathan, no!" he heard himself shout.

The glass fell from his hand, shattering into pieces on the tile floor as Neal ran for the patio.

When Neal reached the glass door he saw Jonathan, still in his Disney pajamas and bare feet, holding the saw by the handle. It still rested in the slot that had been cut in the plywood. Jonathan was depressing the trigger and watching the blade spin.

"Jonathan, stop it!" Neal shouted, startling the child. Jonathan quickly let go of the saw as if it were smoldering hot and jumped back, facing his father with a look of guilt on his face. The blade spun on for a few seconds and slowed to a stop.

Neal walked up to the boy and knelt before him. He held him gently by both shoulders, knowing he had frightened him.

"Haven't I told you, little man? It's not safe to touch dad's tools."

He popped Jonathan lightly on the behind, not enough to hurt him but just enough to let him know that he meant business. Jonathan winced and his lower lip began to protrude as it always did when he pouted. Neal could see tears forming in his eyes.

"But I wanna saw *too.*" he piped up.

Neal smiled at him.

"I know you do, Jonathan, but you could cut yourself like daddy did just a little while ago. See this?"

He held up his bandaged hand for the boy to observe. The blood had soaked through the cloth, making it look twice as bad as it really was.

"Your mom even told me to be careful with the saw too," he said. "So if a big guy like me has to be careful, little fellows like you don't need to play with saws."

Jonathan regarded the bloodstained wrapping with mild interest. Still, he had his sulk face on. He was stubborn to the very end when he wanted to be. Neal and Tiffany always argued over which side of the family he got it from.

"I won't cut myself. I wanna saw too. Why can't I? I don't ever get to saw!" he exclaimed.

"Because it would hurt your mom and me both if something ever happened to you," Neal replied. "We both love you very much and certainly don't want you to hurt yourself."

"But I won't hurt myself," Jonathan shot back. "I wanna saw like you!"

Neal hated it when the child did this, because he knew he would have to be even sterner with him.

"I said no and I mean no," he said, louder and firmer this time. "That's it. You can play with your toy tools but you mustn't touch your dad's until you get bigger? Understand?"

Jonathan looked in every direction except for into his father's eyes. He said nothing, his lower lip still holding pout-position.

"Jonathan...I asked you if you understand what daddy is trying to tell you. Do you?"

Jonathan looked down at his own bare feet for a minute and then mumbled an almost inaudible reply.

"Yes."

Neal leaned forward, as if struggling to hear. "Was that a yes?"

Jonathan nodded his head up and down.

"Yes what?" Neal asked.

"Sir." the child said, finally meeting his fathers gaze.

Neal stood back up and wiped Jonathan's long, brown bangs from over his still glistening eyes. "Okay, little man, back to your cartoons so daddy can finish working, okay? I'll be in shortly and we'll play a game or watch cartoons together. Sound good?"

Jonathan sniffled and nodded his head again. A faint smile touched the corners of his mouth and the pout went away.

"Okay, move it out." Neal said, patting him on the shoulder and veering him toward the house. Jonathan hurried off, through the patio door and kitchen, then vanishing behind the counter as he headed for the living room.

Neal went back to his project feeling slightly guilty, even though he knew that there was no reason to feel that way. He loved the boy with all his heart, but it had always killed him when he had to scold or punish him. Tiff could handle it better than he could. Part of the responsibility of being a parent was discipline and he knew it, but it still didn't make him feel any better. He wondered if his own father ever felt this way after taking a belt or switch to him as a boy.

The nightmares were weighing heavily on his mind too.

Jonathan's nightmares, or night *terrors*, as Tiff called them.

They had been going on for over a month now, and Neal was growing more and more concerned. When they had started, they were dismissed as simply bad dreams, but they had seemed to intensify as the weeks passed. The boy would wake up calling for help, swearing he heard things bumping or creaking around in the hall. Neal explained to him that sometimes houses settled after they were built and that the noises he was hearing were probably no more than a few boards groaning. He even pulled up the hallway carpet and fixed a spot in the wood flooring beneath that actually did creak when you stood on it. Tiffany would sometimes sleep with the boy to calm him, or allow him to come and sleep with the both of them in their bed. That seemed to be the only time the child truly rested, but Neal knew that they couldn't allow him to sleep with them all the time.

The bed-wetting had started a couple of weeks ago. It only seemed to happen on the nights that Jonathan was in his own bed. It was not a nightly occurrence, but Tiffany had changed his sheets no less than five times since then. To make matters worse, he still claimed to hear things at night. He was convinced that something was *in* his room *with* him on several occasions. Neal had tried his best to vanquish the fear of a lurking presence in the dark, checking the bathrooms and closets for signs of a mouse or anything else that would possibly make noise. He never found anything, yet Jonathan still believed.

In fact, the child insisted that he was telling the truth.

Tiffany hoped and prayed that it was just part of growing up. Nothing more than the fear of things that go "bump" in the night. All children had them in one form or another. Perhaps Jonathan's was simply more intense. Neal wanted to believe that too, especially since he himself had to go through a similar rite of passage when he was a child. He was quite a scaredy-cat after his father or mother turned out the bedroom lights. On one occasion, he had fled from his bedroom and out the door onto the back lawn because he was dreaming that the Wolfman was after him.

After that night, he was not allowed to watch any more late night horror movies on channel thirty-six.

It seemed like a logical thing to blame having bad dreams on, but there was only one problem; Jonathan never saw any scary films or programs. The weirdest thing Neal had ever caught him watching was Barney.

For most of the previous week, Jonathan had not been waking them up or crawling into their bed anymore. Maybe he was trying to be a big boy like Neal had asked him to and tough it out. On those nights, both Tiffany and Neal thought that things were getting back to some degree of normalcy. Neal was sure that this period in the boy's life would pass. He just hoped that it wouldn't get any worse. Nightmares could be a very traumatic experience for a child, especially repetitive ones.

Such a possibility led him to ask Tiffany if she thought that they should take Jonathan to a doctor, or maybe even a therapist. It was the only option they hadn't tried.

If things stayed the way they were, Neal didn't know what other choice they had.

Inside the house, Jonathan sat with his legs crossed Indian style in front of the blaring television. He had been watching cartoons when he heard the sawing outside on the patio. When he went to investigate what was going on, his father had told him not to touch the skill saw and scolded him.

He had told him he was "not allowed" to play with it.

Tears formed in his eyes again and rolled across his cheeks. He began to rock back and forth on the floor, angry that his father would not let him do as he wished. All he had wanted to do was pull the trigger and watch the saw run. He wanted to watch the big silver wheel with teeth turn around and around. His father had said no. Jonathan did not think it was fair. He wanted to play and his father had stopped him.

He didn't want to be like the dead boy that had been speaking to him in his room for the last two nights. He had not been allowed to play either.

CHAPTER 3

Tiffany arrived back at home around one o'clock to find her husband fast asleep on the living room couch. She didn't see Jonathan.

Probably out in the back yard she thought.

Neal had obviously passed out while watching television. He still had the remote at his side and his bandaged hand resting on his chest. It appeared that he had put the butterfly closures and wrapped it with fresh gauze. She still wished that he wasn't so macho about getting a couple of stitches.

She had picked up a bag of sub sandwiches for the guys. After placing them in the refrigerator, she headed upstairs for a shower. Pulling her hair down from beneath her cap, she paused on the stair landing to glance out the window overlooking the back yard. She didn't see Jonathan anywhere. He obviously had retreated to his room to watch his Disney tapes or play with whatever action figures he could dig out from under his bed. He could occupy himself for hours playing. There were times when she couldn't even tell if he was even in the house or not because he was so silent. Often she found him on the floor between his bed and the bedroom wall, silently acting out battles with G.I Joe, Batman, or his Transformers. Sometimes he would draw. He had never been a child who had constantly needed to be entertained or to have a playmate. Tiffany thought that it was wonderful that he could be that way, but yet it worried her at the same time. In Camden, he had kids in the neighborhood around his age to play with. Now that they had moved to Sumter, he had *no* playmates. They lived right off the highway outside the town limits, not in a neighborhood, so it wasn't as easy for him to come in contact with other children. Maybe when school started he would make some new friends.

She hoped that it would make his nightmares end as well.

As she reached the landing at the top of the stairs, she saw that Jonathan's bedroom door stood open. She stepped down the hall to check on him. She didn't hear the television so she figured he must be on the floor with his drawing pad or toys.

"What's my favorite boy doing?" she asked aloud as she stepped into the room.

Jonathan was nowhere in sight.

"Oh, behind the bed again, are we?"

She walked across the room and peeked behind the bed.

No Jonathan.

Getting on her knees, she lifted the bed skirt to see if he had crawled under the bed to play. She saw nothing but toys and board game boxes strewn about. A Mickey Mouse glass lay on its side over near his nightstand and a few candy wrappers were wadded up and tossed here and there. She knew one little boy who was going to have to clean up under his bed.

The closet was where she checked next, but he wasn't there either.

"Jonathaaan?" she called, looking back out into the hallway.

No response.

She stepped out into the hallway and noticed that Jonathan's bathroom door was closed.

"There you are." she said softly to herself as she approached the brown wooden door and reached for the antique brass handle.

Then, she opted to lightly knock instead of just bursting in. She certainly didn't want to surprise her son as he was doing his business. He had gotten a little funny about people being in the restroom with him over the past year.

"Jonathan?" she called, gently knocking.

No one answered. She knocked again.

"Jonathan, are you in there, honey?"

The response was quick this time.

"*Sshhh.*"

A whisper came immediately afterward.

"*Quiet, mamma.*"

Tiffany pondered over her child's response.

"Honey," she said, putting one hand on the knob. "I just wanted to see if you were okay. Is your stomach hurting? Do you feel sick or anything?"

"*Sssssshhhh, mama.*"

Tiffany stood back from the door. What the hell was he *doing* in there? He was way too young to be playing with himself, and why would he want her to be quiet for that? There were times when Neal had told her that sometimes he needed to concentrate when he was on the toilet, but he was

22

a grown man. What did a five year old have to be secretive about when it came to the bathroom? You do your thing, flush, and go back to playing or watching videos or whatever you were doing. At that age, Jonathan surely couldn't be relishing the experience of taking a *fine dump* as her dad used to say.

With one good twist of the knob, Tiffany stepped into the bathroom.

"Jonathan, what's going on in….?"

She stopped before completing her sentence, staring at her son curiously.

Jonathan was sitting on the floor between the toilet and the bathtub. He was still wearing his pajamas from the night before, which was odd. Usually he had thrown on his shorts and a t-shirt by this time of day. Spread out in front of him was a pile of comic books. In his lap was the Polaroid camera that he had somehow gotten out of the top of the hall closet. Sitting atop the closed toilet seat was Jonathan's set of Rock- Em', Sock- Em' Robots, a toy game that once belonged to his dad that had never been thrown out. Neal had taken it down from the attic and given it to Jonathan to play with this past summer.

The child looked at her, a serious look on his tiny face. He placed his finger in front of his lips and said *"Ssshhhhhhhhhh."*

Tiffany surveyed the odd assortment of items that her son had chosen to bring into his bathroom. She looked at Jonathan and spoke soothingly to him, kneeling down in front of him to look him eye to eye. "Honey, what's with the *sshhhh* stuff? What are you doing?"

Jonathan glanced around the room and across his mother's shoulder, as if he were trying to get a peek at someone standing behind her. Then he turned and pulled the shower curtain back, looking to make sure no one was hiding in the tub. Frustrated, he turned back and faced Tiffany, seeming like he could cry at any moment.

"Mom, you probably scared him away." he said, obviously upset over her intrusion.

Tiffany sat on the floor in front of him. She reached out, stroked his bangs from his eyes and then placed her hands on his.

"Who, sweetie? Scare *who* away?"

Jonathan wondered if he should tell his mother about the child-thing that had spoken to him at night. Maybe she would laugh and tell him it was all a dream…that there were no such things as phantoms that lurked in bathrooms or hallways eager to talk to little boys.

"Nobody." he mumbled, his head hanging down so he would not have to meet her gaze.

Tiffany knew something was up now. To be in here in the middle of a perfectly beautiful Saturday afternoon when he was usually playing outside was uncharacteristic for her son. Why he would bring in the camera and the Robot toy was also puzzling.

"Jonathan," she said, gently squeezing his small hands in hers. "There's a reason why you're sitting cooped up in here. Now, I want you to tell me *who* you thought I scared away."

The boy fidgeted on the tile floor and pulled one hand from his mother's grasp, placing it across the Polaroid in his lap. Still, he kept his head hung down as he spoke.

"It's a boy, I think. Last night I thought I heard him in here. I wanna take a picture of him so you and dad will *believe* me."

Tiffany knew he was talking about his dreams and the lectures he had been given.

"Sweetheart, that person is in your dreams. Dreams aren't real," she said. "You can't take a picture of something that isn't there."

Jonathan looked up, his eyes beginning to glisten with the moisture of welling tears.

"He *is* real," the child sobbed. "He comes at night and he tells me about the things his daddy wouldn't let him do and about how bad he got treated."

Tiffany didn't know what to say as the child went on.

"He says he never gets to play so I brought him the robots. I was hoping he would show up and I would let him play with them. Dad won't care if I let him play with the robots, *will* he, mom? I know they were his when he was little, but he wouldn't mind another little boy playing with them, would he?"

The boy's mother reached out and wiped the now freely flowing tears from his small cheeks. "No, baby. He wouldn't mind at all," she said softly. "All little boys should be able to play."

Jonathan wiped his nose with his arm, a habit that Tiffany would normally have corrected him for. This time, she let it slide. She reached around and pulled a piece of toilet tissue from the roll which hung just behind her, using it to further clean the sad little face.

"What is this boy's name?" she asked as she wiped. "Did he tell you?"

Jonathan shook his head vigorously from side to side.

"He won't tell me his name…and he talks funny."

Tiffany wrinkled up her nose at his reply, not sure what it meant.

"You mean he talks funny like one of your cartoon characters does?" she asked.

Jonathan shook his head again.

"No, not like that. He just talks different from us. His words come out sounding funny. He sounds like…sort of like Mary Poppins."

Tiffany almost felt relief that the boy was relating his experience to a movie. At least that meant there was a reason behind this. Jonathan had seen Mary Poppins at least a dozen times. Maybe it was as simple as cutting out some of his television.

"Jonathan," she asked. "Have you actually seen this boy?"

"No. I just hear his voice. Sometimes he makes my curtains or my toy cars move. I wish I could see him so I could play with him."

He paused for a few seconds, then:

"But I know you don't believe me," he burst out. "I know that Daddy never does either. That's why I didn't want to tell you about the boy. You won't believe me and you'll spank me or yell at me or maybe even hurt me like he got hurt."

Tiffany was stunned at how quickly the child was almost in a state of panic.

"No, baby, we would never…" she began, but Jonathan interrupted her.

"I don't have any other friends to talk to here," he sobbed. "He's the only one, and I promise I'm not making it up, mom."

For just a second, Tiffany was at a loss for words.

What do you tell a child after he gives you a story like this?

All the child-rearing books she'd ever read must have skipped right on over the solution to this particular problem.

"Honey," she said. "We love you, and we want you to have all the friends in the world. I know that you miss the place in Camden and this is all new to you, but there may be *real* little boys and girls nearby who you haven't met yet and who would like very much to play with the robots and let you take pictures of them."

Jonathan hung his head again and spoke between the sobs.

"When will I meet them? When school starts?"

"You sure will, and you only have three weeks until that day. Just think of all the friends you'll make then."

The child frowned.

"They probably won't like me," he said. "What if they pick on me or tease me?"

"They won't, sweetie. I promise."

"How do you know?"

"I just do. Besides, I won't let them."

Tiffany wanted to pick the boy up and hold him, to comfort him, but she maintained her position in front of him and let him continue.

"This morning, daddy told me I couldn't play with his saw. The boy who talks at night told me his daddy never lets him play either. And he beats him. He beats him with a whip. He beats him until he bleeds. Is daddy gonna beat me until I bleed, mom?"

Tiffany found that her right hand had instinctively shot to her lips to cover her mouth after it fell open with shock. Jesus, where was the kid *getting* this stuff?

"Honey, honey, absolutely not. Your father and I would never hurt you like that, no matter what you did."

She reached for him, only to have him pull away.

"His daddy beat him." the child went on. "He beat him and he wouldn't let him play, and he wouldn't take him to the fair or nothin'. His mamma was mean too, but not as mean as his daddy. He said his mamma would be nice sometimes, but if his daddy found out he'd hurt her bad."

Tiffany could not believe her child was reciting this nightmarish fable. She sat and listened, letting the boy get it all out of his system.

"He had brothers and sisters, but his daddy hurt them so bad they died. They didn't get to play and they got beat and they didn't have toys. Is that what you'll do to me?"

Tiffany moved forward again, scooping the boy into her arms even as he struggled to resist her.

"No we will not, Jonathan," she said, holding his head to her shoulder as she had when he was a tiny thing. "We would never, ever, in our whole lives do such a thing. We love you, baby, don't you believe that?"

The child sobbed as she sat cross-legged on the floor and rocked from side to side, holding him as tight as she could to her. Though he had his nose buried in the material of her sweatshirt, he still kept talking.

"Daddy wouldn't let me play this morning."

She stroked his hair and smiled.

"That's because your father and I don't want you to play with things that can hurt you."

"But I wanted to play with it." Jonathan told her. "I wanted to and he wouldn't let me."

Tiffany suddenly heard the Rolling Stones in her head.

You Can't Always Get What You Want.

"Baby, just because you wanted to doesn't mean we should let you. It's dangerous. It doesn't mean we don't love you or that we are going to punish you. Look at how old your daddy and I are and *we* don't get to do everything we want to either."

He raised his head and looked at his mother, his face red and puffy. Tiffany kissed him on the forehead.

"Mom. I don't want to be like that boy." he said.

She gave him a big squeeze. "Don't worry about that, baby. You won't be."

"Mom, I don't want to be like him because he's dead."

The statement caught Tiffany off guard. It was as if she had been slapped in the face.

Sweet Lord she thought to herself. *What are we going to do?*

"Hush, now, "she said, stroking his hair as she did when he was an infant. "I've got you now and everything will be okay, I promise."

She sat there and held him in her arms, gently rocking back and forth as the afternoon sunlight fell upon them through the bathroom window.

CHAPTER 4

That night, Tiffany tucked Jonathan in around nine-thirty.

The boy didn't seem to be as frightened as he usually was at bedtime. In fact, he gave her no problem at all when she told him to put away his coloring book, brush his teeth, and put on his pajamas. He surprisingly bounded up the stairs and did as he was told. Tiffany followed behind him to make sure he actually used toothpaste instead of just water, as he had done before on several occasions. Though he may have been acting skittish and unusual lately, he still never missed a chance to get one over on his parents. She found him vigorously brushing as he stood on his wooden stool in front of the bathroom sink. He was too short to see himself in the mirror without it. Still on the bathroom floor were his comic books and camera from earlier today.

She hoped that the talk she had with him in here this afternoon had helped.

Jonathan leaned across the sink and spit his toothpaste out, then reached for the bottle of mouthwash on the counter next to him. Unscrewing the cap, he turned it up and filled his mouth with it, gargling as loud and long as he could. Tiffany knew Neal had taught him that, among other little "cute" things that could become annoying after awhile.

"Okay, enough with the gargling, kiddo." she said. "Let's get you into those PJ's."

Jonathan spit into the sink one last time, jumped down from his stool, and raced to the bedroom. Tiffany didn't know quite what to think. He seemed to have gone from being terrified of going to sleep to actually looking forward to it.

Following him to his room, she saw him pull off his clothes and grab his pajamas from the bottom dresser drawer. He always insisted on dressing himself in the mornings and before bed. Tiffany had placed all of his play clothes, underwear, socks, and pajamas in drawers low enough for him to open. Tonight he had pulled out what Neal called the *Have a Nice Day* PJ's. Solid white and covered with yellow smiley faces, they were one piece with footies made into the bottom. They were Jonathan's favorite ones and he usually wore them until Tiffany told him they were too dirty to wear another day. Sometimes she had to sneak them out of his room just to wash them.

Buttoning his sleepwear up the front, he crawled onto his bed and underneath the dark green covers. Tiffany walked over to him and brushed his hair back out of his eyes. He needed a haircut badly. Maybe she would take him into town this week and get it trimmed up. He was as cute a child as she could have ever wished for, especially now with the comforter pulled all the way up to his chin. He looked up at her and smiled.

"I'm not scared, mom."

Tiffany couldn't help but feel relieved. She asked, "You sure? This is a sudden change."

"Yeah, I'm sure," he replied. "I can stay up here by myself."

"I'll sit with you a while if you want me to." Tiffany said.

He shook his head no. "That's okay. I'm a big boy and big boys don't ever get scared."

"Well, I'm very glad that you aren't scared, sweetie," she said, sitting down on the bed next to him. "There's nothing to be scared of. Besides, your father and I would never let anything or anyone hurt you. Not in a million years."

He yawned, the smell of his peppermint toothpaste reaching Tiffany's nose.

"Jonathan," she said. "I hope that when we talked today...in the bathroom...that you understood what I was trying to tell you."

"What?" he asked, still lying with the covers up to his small face. "You mean about the boy I talk to just being a bad dream and about me making new friends and going to school and all that stuff?"

"Yes, all that stuff," Tiffany replied. "I just want you to know that even if you do have bad dreams and even if you do have an accident in the bed, your dad and I love you very much. We used to have bad dreams too when we were your age. A lot of children do. A lot of us saw boogey-men that were never really there, and we heard things that were nothing at all."

"What did you do when you got scared?" he asked, a curious look on his face.

"Well, sometimes I ran and jumped in the bed with Grandpa and Grandma. Sometimes I called to them, just like you call for us. And just like we do now, they always came and they always made me feel better. Pretty soon, I realized that I was safe. I realized that no matter what kind of sounds I heard or dreams that I had, that that's all they were - just dreams and sounds. Nothing was going to hurt me, just like nothing is going to hurt you now."

Jonathan seemed to think about her statement for a moment and then asked "Did anyone ever talk to you like the boy who talks to me?"

Tiffany paused, not sure what her reply should be. As a child, she had never invented any phantom playmates or heard voices in the night, but that didn't mean that other children didn't have such experiences. She thought it through and gave him the best answer she could.

"Different people have different dreams and get scared by different things," she said. "No, I never had anybody who I couldn't see talk to me in my bed at night, but I saw plenty of make-believe monsters, heard lots of scary noises, and imagined things that were never there."

Jonathan looked toward the hallway, a faint touch of uncertainty crept into his eyes.

"And no dead boys? Did you see a dead boy?" he asked.

"No and neither have you," Tiffany replied.

Jonathan frowned. "Yeah, I can only hear him. He won't let me see him."

Tiffany knew they needed to quit talking about the subject before the boy *did* start to get frightened. He had been doing so much better tonight that she didn't want to blow it.

"There are no dead boys or creepy-crawly critters after you, baby," Tiffany said, noticing that he was looking toward the bathroom. "Nothing's going to get you. Besides, they would have to come through *me* first and I don't think any boogey-man is that brave. I'll bop him right across his big green, pimply nose."

The boy smiled and she leaned over, planting a big kiss on his forehead.

"You sleep tight and remember what I told you, okay?"

He nodded his head, the smile still on his face.

Tiffany stood up and stepped over to the door, reaching for the switch.

"Ready for lights out?" she asked.

He nodded again.

"I'm leaving the hall light on, okay? Your dad and I are right down-stairs if you need us. Get some sleep, baby. I love you."

"Love you, too." Jonathan said.

Tiffany flipped the switch, darkness surrounding the small face that peered from atop the covers. She pulled the door only partially shut so that the comforting hallway light would fall through Jonathan's doorway, then turned and headed for the stairs.

Neal was standing in the kitchen in his flannel lounging pants and a t-shirt when Tiffany came back down from Jonathan's room. He had just put a pot of decaf on the stove and its fresh aroma filled the downstairs.

"Oh, coffee, good," Tiffany said with a smile. "I knew I married you for some reason."

Neal put his hands on his hips and looked at her in mock resent-ment.

"And here all these years I thought it was because of my wonderful personality," he said. "You really know how to hurt a guy, hon."

She laughed gently as she grabbed a fresh mug from the cabinet. "Well, I guess your personality isn't too bad either. A lot more than I can say for your skill with handling sharp objects."

Neal held up his bandaged hand and wiggled his fingers in front of his face.

"Hey, it's not as bad as you thought. Actually it feels a heckuva lot better," he said. "I think as long as I keep it butter-flied up for the next couple of days it'll be as good as new."

She stopped in front of him as she walked to the coffeepot, leaning up and giving him a quick kiss across the mouth. "I love you anyway, even if you are clumsy and stubborn."

"Same here," he replied.

"Oh, so I'm clumsy and stubborn too?" she asked.

"No, just stubborn." Neal replied with a smile.

"Watch it, Mr. Fowler," she said jokingly as she poured her coffee. "I wouldn't want an injured man to have to sleep downstairs on the sofa tonight."

Neal laughed. "Well, I guess that injured man you're speaking of bet-ter behave himself."

"Exactly," Tiffany replied, doing her best to sound bossy. "You keep thinking smart like that and you'll go far."

"Yes, my Queen." Neal said.

"We need to talk, hon." replied Tiffany. "Get your coffee and sit down with me."

"Oh, so dramatic all of a sudden," said Neal. "Everything okay?"

"I think...or rather, I hope so."

Neal grabbed a clean mug from the dish drainer and poured himself a cup full of the fresh coffee. As he stirred in some sugar and cream, Tiffany took her cup and sat down on a stool at the marble-topped island in the center of the kitchen. She lifted her mug to her lips and sipped lightly on the hot liquid.

"I had a strange encounter with Jonathan today," she said. "I need to tell you about it."

Neal pulled up a stool and sat across from her. "Strange? How so?"

"Well, first of all...did you have to scold him this morning?"

"Yeah, sure did. He was on the patio with his hands on the skill-saw. You know how I've told him to be careful and not to touch any of my tools."

Tiffany took another sip of coffee. "Well, you weren't extremely harsh on him were you?"

"Tiff, I popped him on his bottom once and used a firm tone. If anything, I wasn't harsh enough, but you know I never am. Why, did he tell you I did anything different?"

"He just seemed to over-react to it a little," Tiffany replied. "But... there was more to it than that."

Neal's eyebrows went up and he stopped his mug just before putting it to his lips. "More how? Something related to his bad nights?"

"Yes."

"Okay, so tell me."

Tiffany took a deep breath and sat her mug down. "I found him sitting on the bathroom floor with some of his toys and a camera. He said that he was trying to take a picture..."

"Of what?" Neal asked, picking up on the pause in her statement.

"Of a dead boy. A dead boy that he says has been talking to him in his room at night."

Neal's surprise was evident in his expression. "So we've gone from strange noises and bedwetting to ghosts now?"

"Looks like it. I don't know if you've noticed or not, but he hasn't been wetting the bed for the past couple of nights like he was."

"Yeah, I had noticed."

"And he also seems to not be as afraid of being in his room by himself anymore."

Neal took a sip of coffee. "Well, that's good news, isn't it?"

"Yes, but for all the wrong reasons," Tiffany replied. "It just seems to be too much of a sudden turnaround. Something's just not quite right about it."

"I agree with you on that," said Neal, nodding slightly. "So what do you think? The therapy idea still floating around in your head?"

"I hate to say it, but yes it is."

Neal could tell that she hated the idea of sending their five-year-old to a psychologist more than anything in the world - but she knew it needed to be done.

"What did you say the name of the woman was?" she asked him.

"The therapist?"

"Yes, the one that you said was recommended to you when you asked around at work."

Neal thought for a moment, sipping from his mug again before he spoke.

"Grayson, I think," he said. "She's got an office over on Liberty, not too far from where Jonathan's going to be going to school."

Tiffany reached beneath the counter and opened one of the small drawers there. After a few seconds of digging around, she came up with the telephone book. Placing it on the counter in front of her, she immediately flipped to the yellow pages.

"What would she be listed under? Should I look under Medical? Psychologist? Mental?"

"Slow down, hon," said Neal, holding up his bandaged hand, palm open. "I want you to be absolutely sure about this before we take such a drastic step. I mean, is it possible that Jonathan is starting to work through this thing on his own? Maybe this boy he's telling you about is just something he's made up to get him through this or to make himself feel safe. I know plenty of kids who develop imaginary friends or talking animals. It's not all that uncommon."

Tiffany looked up at him. "But a *dead* boy, Neal? Why would he dream up a dead person instead of a living, breathing boy or girl? Hell, why not an invisible bunny, a cartoon character, or a fairy? Why not something normal like that?"

Neal saw the faintest glimpse of a tear forming in one of her eyes. He gently reached across the counter and placed his hand on top of hers.

"Sweetheart, I wish I knew. All I'm saying is let's just give him a few more nights and see how he does. I don't want you to put yourself through any undue stress with this therapy thing, especially if it's fixable right here at home."

She wrapped her fingers around his and squeezed, wiping her eye with her other hand.

"So...what do you know about this Doctor Grayson? I'd like to know just in case we decide to do this."

"Well, from what I've heard, she's great." Neal replied. "She's written a couple of books for kids and served on the City Council. Has a pretty high success rate with a lot of children."

"Did someone from your work take their child to her?" asked Tiffany.

"Yeah, one of the managers named Bob McKnight."

"What was the problem?"

"His wife had recently passed on from cancer and his son, Daniel, just withdrew from everything and everybody."

"How old was...I mean, is, Daniel?" Tiffany asked.

"Second grade. Probably around eight, I guess. He's a bright kid but Bob claimed he wouldn't eat, wouldn't talk to anyone, wouldn't even watch television. He just stayed cooped up in his room with an old photo album of his mother for weeks after her death."

"That's so sad."

"Yes, it was," said Neal. "But it seems that the sessions with Doctor Grayson brought the little guy back around. Last time I saw him with Bob, he looked as happy as he could be. He even waved to me."

"Did he start eating again?"

"Well, I saw them in line at McDonald's so I assume so." Neal said, laughing softly.

Tiffany smiled, giving his hand one more squeeze. "That's good to know."

Neal lifted his mug, taking another swig of the decaf. "Yes it is...and it's *also* good to know that she's there if we decide we need her."

"So. . .you think we should give it a few more days?"

"Let's try it," he said. "Remember, school will be starting soon and he's got a birthday coming up too. Maybe the excitement of all that will help get his mind off all this stuff."

She let go of Neal's hand and retrieved a pad and pen from the drawer, taking a long sip from her mug as she did so.

"Okay, I'm worrying entirely too much. We'll give it a bit longer," she said. "But I'm going to write down her name and number and put it on the fridge."

Neal laughed again. "That's fine, hon. In case of an emergency, right?"

"Right," she replied, as she began flipping pages again. "Aha, here it is, under Psychologist; Melissa S. Grayson – PHD – Licensed Clinical Psychologist – Specializing in Families and Children - 1214 Liberty Drive."

She began to scribble the number down on the paper. When she finished, she ripped the page from the small pad and tossed it back in the drawer. She rose from the stool and walked over to the refrigerator, clamping the paper to the door underneath a bright orange ladybug magnet.

"Done." she said, turning to face her husband with a look of satisfaction.

Neal finished his cup of coffee. Sitting the cup down, he stood and gave her a stern look "I hate to be the bearer of bad tidings, Mrs. Fowler, but there seems to be another emergency at hand that needs your attention immediately."

Tiffany looked at him questioningly.

"And what would that be, Mr. Fowler?"

Neal stepped from around the counter and up to his wife, placing his hands around her waist and giving her a gentle kiss.

"Your husband needs to fool around with you as soon as possible. Doctors' orders."

She looked up into his eyes and gave him the same sly smile that had driven him crazy since college. "And if I don't comply with your doctors' orders?"

Neal kissed her again, this time on the forehead.

"The results could be fatal." he said.

Tiffany reached down and popped open the top few buttons of the long, silk pajama top that she was wearing.

"Well, we just can't have that, can we?" she asked, playfully.

"No, we sure can't."

She took his hands in hers, smiled, and led him to the stairway.

CHAPTER 5

"Jonathan"

The voice had come from almost directly next to the bed.

Jonathan eagerly sat upright, his pillow falling to the floor as he tossed the covers away from his body. He looked at the clock. It seemed that only a few moments ago his mother had been tucking him in for the night. That had been around nine-thirty.

Now, it was a quarter after one in the morning.

"Where are you?" Jonathan asked. "Please let me see you."

Silence - awful silence. It was the only thing that scared Jonathan about the voice - when it wouldn't answer him. That meant that it could be anywhere in the room, maybe even right beside him in the bed.

Unable to stand it a minute longer, he called out to it again.

"Where are you?"

The silence continued. Jonathan peered around his dimly lit room but saw nothing. The light from the hallway diminished before it reached the darkened corners on all four sides of him. Perhaps the boy hid there?

"Are you there?"

When the reply came, it came so suddenly that it made Jonathan jump.

"Yes, I am here, Jonathan."

Jonathan, though startled, was grateful for the response. He sat cross-legged in the bed now, leaning forward in anticipation of catching a glimpse of the dead boy with the odd voice.

"I tried to tell my mom about you today, but I don't think she believed me."

Silence, then:

"It is best that you tell no one I was here."

Jonathan did not understand why it should be such a big secret. "Why not?"

"Because most will not believe you. The word of a child is often looked upon as ridiculous. I know, for my words have gone unconsidered as well."

"How old are you?" asked Jonathan.

"*Eleven.*"

"That's six years older than me, but I'll be six next month so that means you'll only be five years older than me."

"*Jonathan. . .I want you to know that I do not intend to hurt you. I promise you that.*"

Jonathan had already figured out that the boy was no monster, but still felt relieved to hear such a promise. "That's okay. . .I know. So, why can't I see you?"

"*Because no one can see me. I exist on another plain from you.*"

Jonathan was confused by what the boy had said.

"What do you mean, "plane"? On an airplane?"

"*A plain is like another world, Jonathan — an unseen world that spins and thrives alongside you each day. You simply cannot see me.*"

Jonathan screwed up his small face in puzzlement.

"But I can hear you." he said.

Silence, then:

"*Because I allow you to.*"

"Why just me? Why won't you let my mommy or daddy hear you?"

"*Because you are special. For one, you are a child like I am- and because you are a child, your mind is open, more so that the mind of any adult. You are. . .easy to reach.*"

Jonathan wasn't sure what the boy was saying. He pulled the covers back up over his legs as he felt a chill. "So do you talk to other children too?" he asked.

"*I have tried to reach many, but failed. You are the first.*"

"The first one you ever talked to? Me?"

"*Jonathan. . .I have waited for years to find someone that would allow me to make my voice heard in this world. You are the only living soul that I have ever reached out to that has been receptive. I am sorry that you had to be so frightened in the days before I could speak to you, but my journey has been a painfully slow and hard one. It took me many nights to be able to come as far from the other side as I am now. It will take me many more to be here as fully as I wish.*"

"Why do you want to be here so bad?"

"*There are things that need putting to rest.*"

Jonathan still was not sure what the boy was saying to him, so he rapidly changed the subject.

"Why do you talk funny?"

"*I do not intend to. It is simply how I was taught in my homeland.*"

"My daddy told me I couldn't play today. He yelled at me like your daddy did."

The voice went silent. Jonathan continued on.

"He told me I couldn't play with his saw and he spanked me and he made his voice all loud and stuff."

The voice was still silent.

"I was afraid when he yelled at me," Jonathan went on. "And I thought about what you said your daddy did to..."

"*It is not the same, Jonathan,*" the voice interrupted. "*The Father I speak of was as cruel as the day is long. The scars of his whip adorn my flesh and his words still ring in my ears.*"

"But you never got to play either and you didn't like it."

"*As I told you before...I was made to work, but I did what I had to in order to survive.*"

"Your brothers and sisters..."

"*They were my adopted family...and we all worked...from sunrise to sunset.*"

"And you really never had toys?"

"*We were not deserving of such pleasures.*"

"If you came and lived with us, you could play and have toys..."

"*But I cannot live with you...nor can I truly die...not yet.*"

Jonathan was now rocking back and forth on the bed, anxious for the next words to come from the darkness. "What do you have to do?" he asked. "Can I help?"

Silence, then:

"*I intend for you to, Jonathan. There is much to be done, but there are things I have to show you. Some of these things are not meant for the eyes of a child. Some things, you may be afraid of.*"

"Will you be with me?" asked Jonathan.

"*Yes.*"

"Won't you be afraid? You said you were only eleven?"

"*I fear only one thing — the one who pursues me. I fear that he may...*"

The voice trailed off into silence.

"Are you okay?" asked Jonathan.

Silence, then:

"*Yes. I will not think of such things now. I must deal with the task at hand.*"

"Will you be with me when you take me to show me these... things?"

"Yes. I will not leave you."

"Well…if you go with me…I won't be afraid."

"Soon, there will come a time when the doorway from my world to yours swings open wide, Jonathan."

"So can I help you come through the door?"

"You will help me the most when that night comes, Jonathan. That will be the time when I do what I must through you. You will know my thoughts, and I yours. We will be one. It will only be for a short while…and then I will be gone."

"So what can I do now?"

"There are things I could show you…so that you understand."

"When?"

"Tonight, if you wish it."

"What do I have to do?"

"You must do what I ask of you."

Jonathan kicked the blankets from his body once more and reached for the lamp on the bedside table. "Before I do anything, I've got to tell mom and…"

"NO," the child-thing's voice abruptly cried, causing Jonathan to retract his hand away from the lamp as if it were a hot stove. *"Do not wake them. They will only interfere with our contact."*

Jonathan was becoming slightly frightened now, yet his fascination with what was happening kept him transfixed on the voice.

You must not speak of me to anyone, Jonathan. Until the night I have told you about arrives, I will do my best to help you understand why I am here.

"Okay," said Jonathan, his voice trembling just a little. "What do you want to show me?"

"Listen and you shall soon see."

As the child-thing spoke on, Jonathan listened intently. Outside of his bedroom window, a night void of stars wrapped itself around the world.

CHAPTER 6

The sound of a horn blaring loudly on Highway 76 startled Tiffany awake at about two o'clock in the morning.

"Just great." she mumbled to herself as she sat up in the bed and looked toward the window. "Honey, did you..."

She cut herself off in mid-sentence, knowing that there was no need to ask Neal if he heard the horn. He was still asleep, snoring at what was sure to be a record-breaking decibel level. She'd be lucky to wake him up with a shotgun blast.

Quietly, she slipped on her silken top and buttoned it up to her breasts. She did not see her bedroom slippers anywhere so she stepped out of bed barefoot onto the cold hardwood floor, tip-toeing over to the window to see what was going on. She pulled back the sheer curtains and parted the blinds, looking toward the highway.

Tail-lights were disappearing to her right toward Sumter, most likely those of the horn blower. There appeared to be no other cars on the road into town or headed in the opposite direction toward Lynchburg. She wondered to herself what the hell there could possibly be to blow your horn at this early in the morning.

Then she saw something that nearly made her heart stop.

Vanishing into the trees across the darkened road was a small figure clad in white pajamas adorned with yellow smiley faces. Had it not been for the light color of the material, she would have never noticed.

It was Jonathan.

Oh God, Oh God, Oh God, Oh God.

The thoughts turned into a scream.

Oh God, Neeeaaall! For Gods sake, get up, Neal, get up!"

Neal bolted upright in the bed and saw Tiffany standing there at the window, hands grasping her face in shock. She turned and faced him, her eyes wide and filling with tears. With a trembling hand she pointed out the window into the darkness.

"Jonathan's out there! I just saw him run into the woods on the other side of the highway! Jesus, Neal, I think a truck almost hit him!"

Neal managed to exclaim a quick *Oh, shit* and was in motion. As he frantically pulled on his lounging pants and slippers, Tiffany opened the window and began to scream her son's name.

"Jonathaaaaan!"

The tiny figure was no longer visible in the darkness beyond the highway. The darkness of the trees had swallowed him up.

"Oh God, Neal, I can't even see him anymore!"

Mere seconds passed before Neal hit the already dew-moistened front lawn at a run, flashlight in hand and shirtless. Tiffany's cries of "Jonathan, Jonathan" filled the warm night air above him as he bolted toward the road.

No headlights from either direction. Neal never even broke his stride as he crossed the asphalt and hit the tall highway grass on the opposite side. The ground dropped off slightly toward the tree line and he almost fell as he made the transition from running on flat ground to sloped, then back to flat again.

"Jonathan, come here!" he shouted as he reached the trees and slowed his pace.

He was trembling and already starting to perspire in the humid air. A light sheen of sweat was appearing across his shoulders and his breathing became rapid, almost as if he were about to hyperventilate. Realizing that he had gone from a peaceful, almost dead sleep to a panic-filled, wide-awake run in a manner of seconds, he slowed to a full stop.

You are in some kind of shitty shape, Fowler he thought to himself, leaning over and resting his hands on his knees. He knew he had to catch his breath and regain his composure in order to think clearly.

After a few seconds that seemed to last forever, he caught his wind. Standing back up, he aimed the light toward the trees.

He could see nothing there but the night.

The flashlight beam jittered in his still shaking hand as he swept it left and right through the pines. He walked forward into the brush, high stepping briars and the other various growths that lay beneath his feet. About twenty feet in, he paused and called his son again.

"Jonathan! Come on, son, come to Dad!"

The shout echoed through the forest. There was no reply.

From back across the highway, Neal could hear Tiffany still calling him too.

"Jonathaaaan! Please, baby, answer mommy!"

Neal turned back to the blackness that lay beyond the trees and was very still. Maybe he could hear something if he just stood here. Surely the boy couldn't have gotten that far in such a short time. After all, he was only five years old and his little legs only moved so fast. That's it, he would stand here and try to zero in on some sound, any sound.

None came.

Neal never knew the night could be so quiet. The crickets were not even singing.

The darkness gave up no sounds of lost little boys.

Neal began to get frightened as he waited - frightened for Jonathan and for what might happen to him - frightened for Tiffany and himself if their child was taken from them. The scenarios had already begun to play themselves out in his head as he stood there, peering into the dark.

We found your son's body, Mr. Fowler.

Or maybe:

He fell into a drainage culvert, Mr. Fowler. There was nothing we could do for him.

Or even:

There weren't many remains after the animals got to him, but we identified him by this material from his pajamas...

"No, no, no." he said to himself under his breath as he broke into a run, heading deeper into the woods.

Jonathan heard his dad calling him, but he wasn't ready to answer yet. He was almost to the place that the child-thing had told him about. He knew if his dad caught him, he would take him back home and put him to bed.

Maybe he'd even get yelled at or spanked...just like the boy he could not see.

He ran onward even faster. His feet were protected from the brush by the footies that were a part of his pajamas. The material was soaked from the dew-strewn ground, but the thin plastic soles did at least keep the bottom of his feet dry. In the darkness, he was nothing more than a tiny white and yellow figure, bobbing ghostlike through the trees.

Jonathan looked up and saw the fields ahead.

He was almost there.

The trees had thinned out and the woods gave way to an unplanted tobacco field that lay on old Stuart Weatherford's property. On the far side of the field, Neal could see a crumbling old structure with a rusted tin roof. It was overgrown with vines and surrounded by waist high weeds. Apparently, it was an old tobacco barn. A huge oak tree stood off to the right behind the structure, its menacing limbs stretching out like gigantic gnarled fingers into the night sky. Old man Weatherford had moved a long time ago. He probably hadn't cropped tobacco in ten years. The whole place looked like it was about to rot into the earth.

Places like that were death traps for curious children...and Jonathan was halfway across the field and headed straight to it.

Neal broke into a run, kicking up gray dirt as he did so and feeling his slippers fill with it. The flashlight in his hand created a madly dancing white zigzag on the field's surface. Stinging streams of sweat rolled into his eyes.

"Jonathan, stop!" he yelled as he ran. "Come here right *now!*"

The child halted for a second and looked back. Then he turned and began to run for the barn again.

Neal had absolutely *no* idea what was wrong with his son, but he knew that after tonight, this had to stop.

"Jonathan, stop!"

The boy kept going. Neal had never seen him move so fast...not even when playing.

"I won't tell you again, Jonathan," he shouted in his best scolding voice. "Your mother and I are going to give you a good spanking after this!"

Jonathan slowed down and stopped. Neal couldn't believe it. The oldest threat in the book had actually worked.

Jonathan stood with his back to Neal for a few seconds and then turned to face him. For the next couple of minutes his attention constantly shifted from his approaching father to the darkened barn. He still appeared to be torn between staying put and making another run for it.

Then he began to cry at the top of his lungs.

By the time Neal reached him and dropped to his knees in the dirt to look him eye to eye, the child was screaming and hysterical with tears.

"No, Daddy, no, no, no, no."

The sobs were coming so violently that he could hardly speak. His father reached out and pulled him to him, holding him tight and running his hand through his hair.

"It's okay, it's okay, it's okay, Daddy isn't gonna hurt his one and only boy. I just said we would spank you to get you to stop."

The child cried on.

Neal didn't know what in the hell to do. Surely he shouldn't punish the child now since the "spanking trick" had worked. It was puzzling to him, however, why the boy reacted so severely to it when usually he just pouted a bit.

"Don't put me in the tree." Jonathan sobbed, burying his head on Neal's bare shoulder. "I don't wanna swing. I don't wanna."

Jesus, what is he talking about?

Neal didn't know what to think. *What* tree? *What* swing?

"Jonathan, what are you saying?" he asked, cradling the boy's head on his shoulder. "Daddy doesn't understand."

Jonathan sobbed on and on, his entire body beginning to tremble.

Neal's mind was racing. Maybe the boy was talking about the oak that towered out behind the barn. As he rocked the child on his shoulder and stood up slowly, he stepped a bit to his right to get a better view of the tree.

It was across the field about twenty to thirty yards from the rear of the barn. From a distance, it had appeared closer, most likely because of its massive size. Though he could barely make out where the tree ended and the night sky began in such blackness, Neal was able to make out a moving shape that caught his attention.

An old swing was hanging from one of the oak's lower branches. It rocked gently to and fro in the night breeze.

I'll be damned, he thought to himself.

It wasn't a regular wooden seat swing or tire swing. It was one with a wooden circular seat with a hole right in the middle. The rope passed through from above and was knotted beneath. The swing's occupants would sit with one leg on each side of the rope or "straddle" it, as Neal's father used to say. This manner of swing was designed so that children could stand up on it and hold the rope and spin wildly around and around whether they stood or sat as they rode it. Hell, Neal himself played on one as a boy.

But swings were playthings to be delighted over for a little guy like Jonathan. They brought joy, not fear.

So why was Jonathan almost in a state of shock?

Puzzling as it was, it concerned Neal less than the fact that Jonathan seemed to think he and Tiffany were out to harm him, something he should know they would never do.

"It'll be okay, little man," he said softly to the boy. "It'll be okay."

Neal stood there in the darkened field and held Jonathan close, realizing that he felt very much like a confused little boy himself right now.

CHAPTER 7

Jonathan turned six in September.

The summer passed, replaced by the cold, crisp mornings of fall. Afternoons were still a little warm, but nowhere near the hot and humid temperatures that had lingered through previous months.

The first day of school at Willow Drive Elementary was easier on Jonathan than Tiffany had expected it to be. Surrounded by kids his own age for the first time since the move from Camden, he seemed happier and more relaxed than he had in months.

She stood in the doorway with a few other parents who had remained to watch their little ones' first day. A smile touched her lips as she watched Jonathan in the corner of the room looking at a Sesame Street alphabet poster on the wall with classmates. Perhaps this is just what he needed all along; interaction with others.

Therapy with Melissa Grayson seemed to be helping a lot too.

After that night in the field a few weeks back, Neal and Tiffany felt they had no other alternative. It was a mutual decision that Jonathan needed to go. Tiffany had pulled down the number from the fridge and called to set up an appointment the very next morning.

Melissa started seeing him on Tuesdays and Thursdays for an hour each time. Though hesitant at first about going, Jonathan had really warmed up to her quickly. He would always return from his visits with her in high spirits and eager to tell his parents about his visit with *"Doctor Melly"*. Melly had been her childhood nickname and she had let Jonathan call her by it, much to his liking.

His nighttime awakenings had been less frequent occurrences as of late, yet still they went on. Visits with Doctor Melly had been a fantastic tool to take the child's mind off the problem and she had done a wonderful job of easing his fears that his parents were going to harm him. In the beginning, the child was terrified that Neal and Tiffany would go to great lengths to punish him violently if he misbehaved. Such dramatic fear of punishment usually went hand in hand with child abuse, but Doctor Melly had seen the boy's medical records. She knew he had never had any unusual bruises or breaks. There was no reason to expect that the Fowler's would harm their son. Besides that, they appeared to be perfectly normal and delightful people, as well as good parents. She had prescribed a mild dose of Thorazine to help him deal with such irrational beliefs, which seemed to work very well. After a few weeks, she had substituted Ambien in lieu of the stronger drug to aid with his anxiety and sleeping.

Doctor Melly was in her early forties and rather thin. She maintained herself very well, was quite attractive, and could easily have passed for younger than her age. Her shoulder length auburn hair was normally pulled back from her face and she wore glasses while working, reading, or watching television. Though she smoked, she was in good shape. Tiffany had picked on Neal by saying that Doctor Melly carried her age so well because she had never been married and lived alone. Neal would smile and say, "Very funny."

As she stood there watching Jonathan socialize with his classmates, Tiffany realized how glad she was that "Doctor Melly" was now a part of their lives

Melissa Grayson had been living and working in Sumter County for the past twelve years. She was born and raised in Augusta, Georgia, where she had lived with her mother until her death from cancer in 1991. Her father had left them when Melissa was only seven years old, choosing to blow his brains out with a semi-automatic rifle on the back porch steps of their home. When Melissa had asked her mother why her father would do such a thing, she received an answer that was partially responsible for her choice of careers.

It seems that Albert R. Grayson had been suffering from severe depression for most of his twenty-nine years. After drifting from one dead-end job to another ever since Melissa was born, he finally couldn't take it anymore. The struggle to make ends meet in an over-priced world proved too much for him. It had been a gorgeous Wednesday afternoon and Melissa had just gotten home from school on the day he pulled the trigger. Luckily, it happened while she was inside the house watching television. All that she got to see was his body sprawled backwards against the porch rocker, a white sheet stained with red thrown across what was left of his face.

Melissa didn't really know what depression was at that age, but she knew that her father had died because of it. Someone that she loved was no longer here. That made her curious. As a result, she asked many questions. Though her mother, a practicing nurse, tried her best to explain it to her, it would still be another seven or eight years before she grasped the true meaning.

She was twelve when she saw her first abused child.

His name was Cody and he lived two houses down the street. He was eight years old when Melissa first met him. She would see him playing in his front yard when she took her afternoon bicycle rides over to the local park. Some days, she even stopped and talked to him. He was very small and quite timid, but he had the most angelic smile she had ever seen. It was around the 4th of July when she noticed that he suddenly stopped wearing shorts and tank tops outside, opting for long sleeve shirts and heavy jeans instead. She thought this was unusual, especially since it was in the mid-nineties and extremely humid this time of year. One day she decided to stop and ask him why he had changed his normal play attire, but he would not answer her. That seemed even stranger than his choice of clothing.

It was the afternoon that she attended her friend Barbara's pool party when she finally figured it out.

She had invited Cody to go along. He arrived in his swim trunks with a long sleeve t-shirt on. He refused to remove it, even while he was swimming. Eventually, Melissa and some of her girl friends became involved in a playful in-pool-wrestling match that Cody was unfortunate enough to wind up in the middle of. In the midst of the splashing water, laughter, and flailing arms and legs, his shirt was pulled from over his head — and that's when Melissa, along with everyone else at Barbara Elaine Thompson's pool party saw that his arms and back were covered with massive bruises.

Once again, Melissa was curious, but angry too. Angry at the very thought that someone would do such a thing to Cody.

Almost immediately, she climbed out of the pool and went inside to get Mrs. Thompson. Cody cried and cried when they questioned him about where the bruises came from, but he eventually admitted that his dad had been drinking badly in the evenings and taking all of his problems out on him. It seems that Cody's mother had abandoned him and his father about six months prior to the beatings, running off with an electrical supply salesman from Albany. The rage that Cody's dad felt was directed at the one person he had left in his life who was still there and who loved him more than anything - Cody himself.

Cody was sent off to live with his aunt and uncle in St. Augustine, Florida. His father was a guest of the State of Georgia for quite a while after that, having to serve a twenty-two month prison term for the abuse of his son. Once his time was up, he returned to the same house that he and Cody had lived in. Rumor had it that he gave up the bottle completely. As Melissa grew older, she often wondered if Cody would ever come back and visit him. Years passed and holidays came and went, but she never saw Cody walk through the front door of that house again.

Her curiosity sparked by what she had experienced, first with what happened to her own father and then the incident with Cody, Melissa graduated high school and majored in Psychology at the University of Georgia. She was interested in all aspects of it — child, adolescent, and adult. Finishing with scores at the top of all her classes, she soon found herself at Emory Hospital in Atlanta. It was there that she performed her first six months of residency. She was twenty-three years old at the time.

Her mother passed away five years later. Melissa was working on her own at the time as a resident psychologist at the Augusta Child and Family Center. She had passed away peacefully in her sleep, finally losing her three-year battle with bone cancer.

After her death, Melissa needed a change. Augusta seemed to have nothing for her anymore. She wanted her own practice and her own patients. She wanted independence.

One day at the Child and Family Center, she heard through the grapevine that the Sumter Wellness Group in South Carolina had just lost one of their more notable family psychologists to a large hospital in Baltimore, Maryland. The news got her attention. Sumter was only a short drive from the State capitol of Columbia and about an hour and a half from Myrtle Beach. It seemed to be the perfect small town to live and work in. After giving it much thought, she applied for the position in Sumter and was almost immediately given the job. Arriving in town in late 1991, she assumed the position of family psychologist at the Sumter Wellness Group. Within the first two years of being in town, she had saved enough money to make a down payment on her own home and was able to open up her own independent practice. Before long, she gained a very commendable reputation and made many friends. She also became a prominent figure on the Sumter City Council. Through the Council, she became involved in a several community projects. To the surprise of many long-time residents, she soon grew into a well-spoken authority on the city and its history. Her knowledge even led to her assisting other Council members in the writing of a small book about the town, which sold very well regionally. She was respected in her chosen field as well, having seen many a troubled child in her day. She had broken children from bedwetting, sleepwalking, tantrums, nightmares, and a whole variety of problems.

The afternoon that Neal and Tiffany Fowler brought in their son, Jonathan, she sensed that she was about to encounter something different.

She just didn't know what.

Tiffany Fowler was still smiling as she watched Jonathan play with his new classmates, but her thoughts were still lost in one of her last conversations with Doctor Melissa Grayson.

On the spur of the moment just a few days ago, Tiffany had stopped by to visit her in the office after five o'clock. When she walked in, she found Melissa looking over a file by the light of a desk lamp.

"Hello, Tiff," Melissa had said, closing the file and taking her glasses off as she looked up. "How's my little patient doing? Everything okay?"

Tiffany sat her purse down next to the chair in front of Melissa's desk and took a seat.

"Yes, thanks, he's fantastic," she said. "You are doing an absolutely wonderful job with him, Melissa. Neal and I can't thank you enough."

Melissa looked at her intently, seeming to be trying to figure something out. "Okay...I can already tell something's bothering you. Spill it."

Tiffany felt embarrassed.

"Can't fool you, can I?" she laughed.

"Nope," replied Melissa. "Sure can't. So let's hear it."

Tiffany seemed uncomfortable in the chair, fidgeting a little as if she were having therapy herself. "It's really nothing, but it's been on my mind."

"Well, then it's something. I'm waiting," Melissa said, smiling. "Relax, Tiff, this is what I do. Just talk to me."

Tiffany crossed her arms and settled back into the chair. Still seeming a little embarrassed, she spoke.

"When you first met us, you told Neal and I that you thought there was something unusual about Jonathan's particular situation. Something different."

"Yes, I did. I remember that."

"Well, it just boils down to the fact that I really...respect what you do. You've been more than great for Jonathan, and being that I value your medical opinion the way that I do, I wanted to ask you one thing. Why do you think Jonathan's case seems so...different?"

Melissa cocked her head to one side and twisted her lips into an odd little smirk. Her eyes left Tiffany for a moment and she seemed to stare at nothing in particular. Tiffany knew that look. It meant she was thinking.

Focusing on Tiffany once again, Melissa said, "Okay. I'll tell you. I just don't want you to worry so much, okay? Now I feel like you did before you asked me *your* question. It's probably nothing."

"Well...I still want to hear it."

Melissa seemed to hesitate for a moment, and then she began to speak.

"It's normal for a child to have a fear of the dark or of sleeping alone. We all know this because many of us ourselves have experienced it. It's also normal to fabricate wild stories, imaginary friends, and monsters that aren't there. Jonathan's fascination with this "voice" just seems...more genuine and believable than most stories I get from troubled kids. This ghost-child is very real to him. He even says it sounds *"funny"*, like Mary Poppins did."

"Neal and I discussed that," said Tiffany. "He watches the video all the time. Don't you think maybe it's just fueled his imagination?"

"Imaginary or not," replied Doctor Melly, "it's certainly original. I can tell that Jonathan *believes* what this supposed child is saying to him. I think that's why he believes that you and Neal are going to hurt him if he makes the slightest step out of line. A mere slap on the hand or a raised voice is extremely threatening to him and he fears that he's going to get it even worse. How often do children make up this kind of thing with the detail that Jonathan has attached to it? It's unsettling enough to know that he claims to talk to a boy who's dead, but a boy who's dead because he was abused and beaten?"

Tiffany listened on.

"Has Jonathan ever had any little friends who were abused? Has he ever been exposed to abuse in any fashion?"

"Not at all. He's been raised with nothing but love. Neal even hates to raise his voice to Jonathan. He makes me do all the correcting most of the time."

"Abuse could be a sub-conscious fear," Melissa said. "It could be manifesting itself in the form of another child. He could possibly be more comfortable dealing with it when it's on his mind if he discusses it with another boy his age."

Tiffany brought up the bathroom and the day she found Jonathan sitting in it.

Melissa frowned and pulled a cigarette from the pack in her desk drawer, lighting it with a silver Zippo that she retrieved from her purse. The only time she ever smoked in her office was late in the day, once she knew that she had no other patients to see. Taking a long drag on it, she expelled the smoke from her pursed lips and continued speaking.

"When I say that this is very real to Jonathan," she said, matter of factly. "I mean it's very, very *real.* He feels sympathy for this boy, yet a part of him is still afraid. He feels frustration because you don't believe him, so he takes the camera into the bathroom, hoping for a picture."

"It's just all so...strange," Tiffany said.

"Strange behavior, odd beliefs, and hallucinations are all common in-dicators of an advanced stage of psychosis. That's why I started him on the Thorazine at first. Once he leveled out is when I put him on the Ambien. He's been resting at night, hasn't he?"

"Yes."

"And how about sleep walking? Anymore of that?"

"No."

"That night when he ran across the highway has concerned me a lot too, Tiff."

"In what way?"

A pause, then a reply:

"I've seen children sleepwalk before, but usually that's what sleep-walking people do – they *walk.* Neal told me that Jonathan was running as hard as he could. I just think it's pretty unusual."

"We asked him why he did it," Tiffany said. "He told us the boy *wanted* him to do it. That he would be safe from harm if he would go there and that he wanted to show Jonathan something."

Melissa took another puff of her cigarette. "That's the same thing he told me. He also told me he had no fear of running in the woods through the dark. The only thing he said he was afraid of was a swing. A swing on an oak tree that stands behind this barn he was trying to reach."

Tiffany remembered that Neal had told her that he had said something about a swing on the night he ran away.

Why in the hell would a swing frighten a child?

Tiffany was still lost in thought when the bell for Willow Drive Elementary recess suddenly rang loudly her ears, snapping her out of her spell of remembered conversations with Melissa. The sound of more than two-dozen laughing and excited children surrounded her as they scrambled for the classroom door she stood in. She and the other mothers stepped out of the way of the approaching herd of youngsters.

Jonathan ran by her, managing a short "Hi, Mom", and was hot on the heels of his fellow 1st graders as they spilled into the playground out back. A large window allowed the other moms to see outside and watch as the class swarmed about the monkey bars, sliding board, swing sets, and seesaw.

Tiffany noticed that Jonathan steered clear of the swings, opting for the seesaw instead.

One of the young women standing there with Tiffany looked at her and smiled.

"Your little boy is simply adorable." she said.

Tiffany thanked her and stood at the window, watching her son as he rose up and down against the morning sky.

His laughter was the best sound in the world.

CHAPTER 8

October arrived and brought with it the falling of the leaves and the change in time. Sumter held its annual "Octoberfest – Southern Style" during the first weekend of the month. Days shortened and the darkness began to creep across the fields around five each day.

With Halloween just around the corner, jack-o-lanterns could be seen silently emitting their flickering grins from front porches all over town.

The costume aisles in the local Wal-Mart and K-Mart stores were picked over quite quickly. Candy aisles were nearly empty as well. The Sumter Item newspaper printed an article on how Halloween was fast becoming the second biggest season for retailers next to Christmas. It also ran the usual safety tips for trick or treating youngsters and an article on how Halloween began and the myths associated with the holiday.

Neal Fowler grabbed a copy as he walked out of the Sumter Post Office. Glancing at the local headline, he tossed it in the passenger seat of his white Dodge Durango, climbed in, and started the engine. It was almost five o'clock and the sun was slowly beginning to disappear, streaking the sky with vibrant purple and orange. Backing out of his parking space, Neal saw that the temperature on the bank sign across the street was fifty-four degrees. No doubt it would be in the thirties or forties by morning. He pulled out onto highway 76 and turned right toward home, leaves blowing across the asphalt in his path as the wind began to pick up a bit.

As he drove, Neal thought about how much Jonathan had improved over the past few months. Melissa Grayson was a class act and had been a huge help. Tiffany and Jonathan both loved her. Starting school and making new friends had been good for him too. It was nice for things to be getting back to normal, or at least, *close* to normal.

Halloween was two nights away and Jonathan was looking forward to it. Neal and Tiffany had planned on taking him to a carnival at his school at around six o'clock. The little guy already had his Spider-Man costume laid out on a chair in the corner of his room. Jonathan had insisted on having it when they saw it hanging in a shop at the Sumter Mall two weeks ago. Tiff had given in and bought it for him, then had to sit on the couch with Neal and watch him as he tried it on. They both had told him that he looked *really cool* in it.

Neal felt a great sense of relief. His son was fine — a normal healthy six-year old kid.

He had no idea that in about forty-eight hours, he would be as far from normal as you could get.

Or that people were about to die.

As Neal Fowler made his way home beneath the fading sunlight, Melissa Grayson was sitting alone in her office and preparing to call it a day. She had already seen her last child for the afternoon and had removed her shoes, let her hair down, and lit a cigarette. The silence was a welcome sound to her.

In her lap was the file she had started on Jonathan Fowler. She was so glad that she had been able to get through to him.

Sometimes, he reminded her of little Cody from her childhood.

To Melissa, he was a delightful and adorable little boy, all wavy brown hair, gorgeous eyes, and a spray of freckles across his nose. For a six year old, he was very smart. He was very quiet. She would have known he kept to himself a good bit, even if Neal and Tiffany hadn't told her.

His mental state and unexplainable trip into the field at night were more of a concern to her than she cared to admit. Something about it got under her skin and refused to crawl back out. It wasn't professional to admit such and she still regretted telling Tiffany that it bothered her during their visit a few days ago.

She had just never seen a child go to *such* great lengths sleepwalking.

The swing still confused her as well - the swing, which for some reason had horrified Jonathan.

Thankfully, he was resting much better these days. Neal and Tiffany had happily reported that they had heard nothing out of him about a child's voice for the past couple of months. Whatever or whoever this "child" was that spoke to him, it had apparently gone silent. Jonathan would have told her if the voice had returned. She felt that he trusted her enough to tell her, possibly even before he told Neal and Tiffany.

Whether or not the voice was a part of his psychosis, the result of a rampant imagination, or the actual manifestation of some type of spiritual entity - she knew something really had been disturbing the boy - she just had no earthly idea *what*. To Jonathan, this ghost-child was a real, living, breathing person — one that seemed to be able to influence him with ease. Regardless of what it was, Melissa thought it must be pretty damn persuasive.

Melissa Grayson was entirely too old to believe in such things as ghosts or spirits.

So why was this bothering her so?

Was it because of the day when she was seventeen years old and riding on the homecoming float through downtown Augusta? Was it because her father had been standing there in the crowd smiling and waving at her, beaming with all the pride and love he could?

How could that have been? He had blown his brains out ten years ago. But there he was, standing right there on the corner.

Then, he was suddenly gone.

Melissa took a long draw on her cigarette and removed her glasses, laying them on the table in front of her. She had never spoken of the homecoming incident to anyone, not even her mother. She had been afraid to. Afraid because she had once heard that if you saw the spirit of a loved one and spoke of it, you would never get to see them again.

Still, it was a day she would never forget.

The sun was slowly vanishing beyond the tops of the trees that she could see from her office window. A grinning jack-o-lantern illuminated the glass of the pawnshop across the parking lot from her office.

Halloween was almost here and she realized that she hadn't bought the first bag of candy. There would be some disappointed trick-or-treaters at her door in a couple of days if she didn't pick some up.

She had laid Jonathan's open file on her desk in front of her. She reached out and closed it, hoping to herself that the little guy had fun on Halloween night.

Outing her cigarette, she slipped her stocking feet back into her shoes, grabbed her glasses and purse, and headed out the door. She would stop by the grocery store on the way home and pick up some candy while it was on her mind.

Maybe she would pick up a bottle of wine or two. She felt like she could use a drink.

CHAPTER 9
Friday - October 31st, 2004

Spider-Man bounded down the stairs, plastic pumpkin bucket in hand. He raced across the foyer and into the living room where Neal and Tiffany sat.

"Here I am!" he exclaimed with glee as he made his entrance.

Neal looked at him in mock surprise.

"Honey, look. It's Spider-Man!"

Tiffany gave her best surprised look.

"Ooooh, it *is*. Hello, Spider-Man!"

Spider-Man stood there. Then he reached out with a small hand and lifted the paper mask up to where it rested atop his head.

"It's me, Jonathan." he said, smiling at his parents.

"Well, well. You sure had *us* fooled, little man," Neal said, standing and grabbing his leather jacket from the back of the chair. "So you ready to go rack up some candy?"

Jonathan nodded his head so hard the mask slipped back down over his face and he became Spider-Man once again.

"Let's head em' up and move em' out." Neal laughed. He turned and looked at Tiffany. She had already pulled her light jacket on over her turtleneck sweater and was grabbing the keys to the Durango. They had dressed for comfort tonight, both in jeans and hiking boots.

Jonathan looked up at his father as they walked to the door.

"What time does the carnival start?" he asked.

Tiffany came up behind him, a small windbreaker jacket in her hands, kneeling down to put it on him. She glanced at her watch as she put his arms into the sleeves.

"In about fifteen minutes. That gives us just enough time to get there before all the fun starts."

Jonathan peered back at her through the eyeholes of the red mask and said, "Spider-Man never wears a jacket."

She continued getting it on him.

"Well, no, but he wears long johns up under his costume so that he doesn't get cold at night. You just can't *see* them." she said, winking at Neal as he smiled down at them.

"Oh." said Jonathan, apparently satisfied with the fib.

"Don't worry, you can take it off when we get back inside," Neal said, grabbing his own leather coat from the rack by the front door. "We can't have a superhero that can't show off his costume. Sound cool, little man?"

Jonathan said "Yep, sounds cool."

"Okay, so let's get this show on the road," Tiffany said. "Carnival's waiting on you."

Neal opened the front door and Jonathan rushed out onto the porch, scrambling down the steps and running to the Durango. The sun was almost gone as Neal and Tiffany got him settled in the back seat. Within moments, they were heading into town on Highway 76.

They didn't notice that Jonathan's gaze never left the field across the road from the house. When they were far enough away that it was out of sight, he turned his attention back toward the road and sat in silence until they reached the carnival.

Jonathan watched the world rushing by through the eyeholes in his mask. In the morning, he knew he had to go see Doctor Melly. He thought about Doctor Melly and all the questions she had been asking him; questions about his dreams and about the child-thing that spoke to him in the darkness.

She had *really* been happy when he told her that the voice no longer came to him at night. She told him that it meant that he was *"making progress"*.

Jonathan didn't know what *"making progress"* meant.

His parents' seemed to be a lot happier since they got the news that the nightly visitor had stayed away. They didn't mind him getting into the bed with them when he had scary dreams, but they didn't like the voice.

No one did.

He wondered why.

Jonathan smiled beneath the mask and silently thought of how proud he was that he could keep a secret.

He didn't like the medicine that Doctor Melly and his mother had been giving him. It made him feel funny. Some nights, he would spit it out after his mother had left the room. He also decided that if no one liked the voice and everyone wanted to scold him about it, he just wouldn't tell anyone if he ever heard it again.

Besides, he had promised it that he would tell no one about any more of their conversations.

Not even Doctor Melly.

It was his secret and he intended to keep it.

Jonathan had been talking to the child-thing in his bedroom every night for the past two months — but something had changed in the last few days.

It seemed that the voice had lost its funny accent…and had deepened somehow.

The carnival was just starting when the Fowlers reached the school grounds. Neal carefully guided the Durango through the parking lot, taking extra care to look out for little ghouls and goblins that might be outside. The outside of the school entrance was draped in black and orange paper and a teacher dressed as a witch stood by the door, a basket of candy over her arm and a roll of tickets in her hand.

"My Goodness, Jonathan." said Tiffany, looking at the witch as she unbuckled her seatbelt. "Who is *that?*"

Jonathan peered through the glass as Tiffany reached back to release his belt too. He saw the witch at the doorway.

"That's Miss Kemp," he said. "I'm not scared of her. She's only scary when she yells at me in class."

Neal looked across his shoulder at Jonathan.

"I see," he said. "And what, pray tell, would you be doing in class to make her yell at you, little man?"

Jonathan turned his attention to Neal.

"Nothin'. She's just real mean is all. She likes to yell," he said from behind the mask. "She doesn't spank me or anything. She just has a really, really loud voice sometimes."

Neal chuckled. "Okay, Spidey, whatever you say. Guess I'll have to take your word, seeing as how you're a hero and all."

He stepped out and waited for Tiffany and Jonathan to get out. Tiffany removed the boy's jacket, as promised, and tossed it across the seat. She handed him his jack-o-lantern bucket and shut the door.

"All set, Mr. Fowler," she said, her hands on Jonathan's small shoulders. "I think I know a little boy who can't wait to get inside."

They headed for the building, the shadows they cast in the glow of the parking lot lamps stretching out ahead of them.

The candy bucket by the front door was overflowing at five thirty. By six thirty, Melissa Grayson had given out all but a few pieces, which rattled around in the bottom.

There had been a steady parade of headlights throughout the last hour as parents slowly drove up and down the neighborhood streets, dropping off dozens of little ghouls. Now, the parade had all but vanished. Apparently, the trick or treaters had started early and finished early this year.

She figured it was time to turn out the porch light and call it another Halloween.

Melissa stepped out on her front porch in her sweat pants and Clemson University T-shirt. She leaned over and blew out the jack-o-lantern that sat in the rocking chair right beside the door. She wrapped her arms around herself as a breeze touched her bare arms. The night air was chilly - probably around the low fifties. Not as cold as some nights over the past few weeks, but not warm either. Good weather for all the little ones who walked the streets tonight. Hopefully, half of the children in Sumter wouldn't have colds tomorrow.

Melissa's two-bedroom house was on Sumter's west side in a neighborhood called Guildford Acres. The Elementary School was right around the corner from her. She could see the lights in the parking lot from her front door. The carnival was no doubt in full swing by now. If she listened closely, she could hear the laughter of children carried on the cool, night air.

"Happy Halloween." she said lightly to herself.

She turned and stepped back inside, flipping the front porch light off and locking the front door.

The television was running a monster marathon on the American Movie Classics channel. Melissa settled back into her favorite chair in front of it, kicked off the bedroom slippers she was wearing and lit a cigarette. Maybe she could catch "Night of the Living Dead" at nine if she was still awake.

Her living room was small, as was the rest of the house. It was decorated with cherry furniture, area rugs, and bright red and gold curtains. An elegant look that she opted for due to the fact that every once in a while, she saw a child at home instead of the office. She wanted to have a relaxed yet professional looking environment to place them in.

A half finished glass of wine sat on the round top table at the side of her chair. She took a sip from it and thought of Jonathan, hoping that he was having a good time. She remembered that she had an appointment to see him at eleven in the morning. He would most likely be ready to fill her in on all the candy he got and games he played at the school.

She cruised through all the channels as she sat and finished her wine, the smoke from her cigarette dancing in the light of an antique lamp that her grandmother had given her.

Not a damn thing on to watch.

"Night of the Living Dead" was two hours away and AMC was currently showing "The Thing with Two Heads", a film that Melissa was certain she could do without. If she must watch a scary movie, it would be a good one, not hokey as hell.

She muted the television and picked up the weeks worth of unread *Sumter Item* newspapers on the floor next to her chair.

"All right, Doctor," she said aloud to herself. "Let's see what you've missed in the world for the past week."

She started with last Thursday's issue.

The lottery still hadn't been hit. The President was going to speak in Charleston. Downtown Sumter was being renovated. Clemson was playing Tennessee Saturday. Temps in the high fifties to low sixties. No one she knew died or was arrested.

So much for exciting news. She went on to Friday's issue.

A Bishopville man was facing two charges of animal cruelty. The local school district was under fire for missing funds. A ridiculous picture of the newspaper staff dressed in various Halloween costumes. Safety tips for kids. A run down of all the local haunted houses, hayrides, and carnivals. An article on the history of Halloween called: *The Origin of All Saints Eve.*

That seemed interesting. It definitely had to be less depressing than the real news.

She took another sip of wine and started reading.

CHAPTER 10

Jonathan was surrounded by children. Clowns, pirates, ghosts, fairies, and numerous other little characters filled the hallway of Willow Drive Elementary. The sounds of them laughing echoed throughout the building.

Parents and teachers watched as their children and students went from door to door down the long corridor of the main part of the building, collecting candy from other teachers and volunteered junior high students. Some rooms were decorated in a particular theme. The first grade room was patterned after The Wizard of Oz and had a door attended by a friendly scarecrow.

His candy bucket already nearly full, Jonathan walked up to the scarecrow. He knew the scarecrow was Mr. Tanner, the schools assistant principal.

"Well, hellooooooo there, Spider-Man." the scarecrow said, leaning down to look at Jonathan. "Welcome to Oz. Would you like to see the Wizard?"

Jonathan held out his bucket.

"Trick-or-treat." he said.

The scarecrow laughed and dropped a handful of candy into Spider-Man's bucket.

"There ya go, little buddy," he said. "Happy Halloween."

Jonathan looked at the scarecrow and whispered:

"I know it's you, Mr. Tanner."

The scarecrow faked a surprised look. He whispered back:

"You do? And how do you know that?"

Jonathan pointed downward. He whispered:

"Because you have your black penny loafers on."

With that, he was off to the next classroom for more candy, leaving Mr. Tanner standing there in his scarecrow suit.

Tanner glanced up and saw Neal and Tiffany Fowler across the hall talking with some other parents.

"You got a smart little man there, Mr. and Mrs. Fowler." he said with a smile.

They laughed and nodded in agreement.

"Sometimes he's *too* smart." Tiffany replied.

Jonathan visited two more classrooms. The second grade class was attended by Darth Vader and was decorated with a Star Wars background. The theme from Star Wars blared out of a cassette deck that sat on a corner desk. Darth gave Jonathan some Tootsie Rolls and sent him on his way.

The third grade room was patterned after the Toy Story movie. A tall and lanky junior high student manned the door in Woody the Cowboy attire. He made a good Woody, even in Jonathan's six-year-old mind. Woody was glad to finish filling Jonathan's bucket with gumballs.

Jonathan had plenty of candy. Now he wanted to play games.

He turned and ran to take his nearly overflowing bucket to his parents, not looking where he was going...and ran right into Miss Kemp in her witch costume.

"Jonathan..." was all she could manage before she lost her balance and stumbled on the heels she was wearing. She dropped the basket she was carrying over her arm and caught herself on the hallway wall before she fell. Her hat slipped into a lopsided position on her head and her wig of long jet-black hair moved along with it.

Jonathan stopped and stood there. He said nothing.

The flustered Miss Kemp adjusted her witch attire and gathered her candy from the floor. Jonathan braced himself for what he thought was coming. She liked to yell. She always yelled in class if you mis-behaved. Jonathan didn't like yelling. It made him nervous. It scared him.

He knew she was going to yell now.

"Really, Jonathan," she said, not yelling, but in a very stern voice that was *almost* a yell. "You know you shouldn't be running."

To anyone else within earshot, Miss Kemp's comment would have been delivered in a satisfactory tone to correct a child. She simply just had a loud voice, and she had all her life. She realized that some of her students got a little jumpy when she raised it, as she often had to do. She didn't mean to do it, and she watched herself sometimes to make sure she wasn't too loud.

It bothered Jonathan anyway.

To him, it was the scariest sound he'd ever heard.

Neal and Tiffany were suddenly there. Neal attended to Miss Kemp and asked her if she was okay. Tiffany took Jonathan by his hand and looked down at him.

"Honey, you need to be careful," she said. "You almost made Miss Kemp fall."

Jonathan hung his head. Perhaps the Miss Kemp Witch would yell at his parents. She didn't. Instead, she said:

"Oh, it's no problem. He's just excited. It's hard to not be when you're his age and all this is going on. I just don't want any of the kids to hurt themselves or anyone else."

Neal apologized to her and Tiffany did as well.

"Jonathan," she said, squeezing his hand lightly. "Do you have something to say to Miss Kemp?"

He managed a mumbled "I'm sorry."

Miss Kemp smiled and said, "It's all right, sweetheart. C'mon down and see me in the Haunted House room in a little while."

The Haunted House room was the sixth grade classroom. It was dark in there and filled with crazily flashing lights, scary sounds, and people in masks that hid everywhere. From where he stood, Jonathan could hear other kids running out of the Haunted Room talking about how spooky it was.

Jonathan didn't think he wanted to go in there.

"Sure thing," Neal said. "We'll bring him down after he plays a few games."

"It's not too scary is it?" Tiffany asked.

"No, no." said Miss Kemp. "Believe me, we bear in mind that we have some really small kids coming through. He'll love it."

Jonathan didn't think he would love it.

Especially if *she* was in there.

Miss Kemp whispered to Tiffany:

"It's just a dark room with a strobe light and a cassette of scary sounds playing. There's a couple of students in masks and me in the corner stirring a cauldron full of dry ice. The dry ice makes it foggy. Nothing too scary."

"Oh, well, that's not that bad after all," Tiffany said. "I think Spider-Man can handle that."

"Sure he can." said Miss Kemp. "You folks enjoy yourselves. I'll be looking for you, Jonathan."

She smiled at him one last time and was gone down the hall, her black cape dancing out behind her

The wineglass was empty and the ashtray was full.

Melissa was asleep, her glasses lying on the newspaper that was still spread out across her lap. The television was muted, yet the Monster Marathon went on and on in silence, the light from the screen creating a strobe effect on the living room walls and ceiling.

It was seven thirty - early for her to be dozing, but not unusual. The day had been very long and the wine had been very good. She knew that when she felt sleep creeping upon her that she would most likely be awake again by around ten o'clock. She would catch the local newscast, watch about half of the Letterman Show, and then go to bed. That was usually her routine.

Her last thoughts before she drifted off had been of how the article on Halloween had been really interesting. One specific part in particular had really caught her attention.

She was also thinking about seeing Jonathan in the morning and what they might talk about.

She didn't know that their appointment would be coming much sooner than she was expecting.

The teachers lounge had been converted into the carnival game room. Jonathan played ring toss, bobbed for apples, pinned the tail on the donkey, and got his fortune told by a young girl dressed up as a gypsy. Jonathan thought she might be a girl from the seventh or eighth grade, but he didn't know her.

He won two candy bars, an orange and black pinwheel, and a big rubber bat that flopped about on a piece of elastic string as if it were flying.

Now, he had to go to the Haunted House room.

Miss Kemp would be waiting.

Jonathan knew that once she got him inside, she would yell at him. Yell at him like she did in class - like she did to all the other kids too.

Neal and Tiffany were waiting on him right outside the game room.

He met them at the doorway and lifted his Spider-Man mask up away from his face. He held out the rubber bat and the pinwheel out for them to see.

"Look what I got." he said.

Tiffany said, "I see, I see. You did really good, honey."

He looked to his father for his approval, holding the pinwheel up and blowing on it, making the orange and black foil top go around and around.

"That's my little Spider-Man." Neal said, walking up and playfully flipping the mask back down over the boy's face.

"So, you ready to tackle the Haunted House now?" Neal asked. "If you want, I'll walk through with you."

Jonathan stood there and thought about what his father had just said to him.

If you want, I'll walk through with you.

He looked at Tiffany.

"Or, your mom can go with you." Neal said, seeing that Jonathan had turned his gaze toward her.

Your mom can go with you.

Jonathan didn't see any of the other kids coming out of the room down the hall with their parents in tow. They were all by themselves. Some were running and laughing, others looked a little scared, but none were crying.

He saw little Zachary Welch, dressed as the Blue Power Ranger, come walking out with no grown ups at his side. He appeared unharmed.

Aimee Jacobs, dressed as Snow White, came out in one piece. No parents with her either.

It couldn't be *that* bad in there.

He'd look like a baby if he made his parents accompany him. The other kids would pick on him.

Scaredy cat. Scaredy cat. Jonathan's a Scaredy cat.

He could hear it now in the back of his mind - the taunts of all his friends on the playground.

Jonathan's a yellow belly, got a backbone made of jelly. Saw a ghost and peed his pants, scared so bad it made him dance.

He didn't want that to happen.

"No, it's okay. I'm not scared," he said. "I can go by myself."

Neal and Tiffany looked at each other in surprise, then back at Jonathan. They were both surprised by his announcement.

"Are you sure?" Tiffany asked. "We don't mind."

The tiny Spider-Man face turned her way.

"I'm not *that* chicken," he said. "I wanna go by myself."

Neal could tell that it meant a lot to the little guy to do this alone. It was evident in the tone of his voice. He also knew that he didn't want to look like he was afraid with all of his classmates around. He himself had been the same way. He went through the House of Mirrors at the local fair for the first time all by himself at the age of seven. He wanted to prove to himself, and to his father, that he could do it. It scared the shit out of him, but he made it and he was damn proud of himself.

He looked over at Tiffany and nodded to her.

"It's fine, babe. We can let him go by himself. He's a big boy now. No need in us tagging along."

She knew the game Neal was playing and went along with it.

"Oh, absolutely. We'll just wait outside." she said.

Jonathan knew he couldn't turn back now. He had to go through with it. He turned and looked down the hall to where the Haunted House room was.

Children were gathered outside the door, peeking in. From inside, the flickering strobe cast madly dancing light patterns on the hallway wall. The sounds of moaning ghosts and rattling chains came from the room. Black cats hissed and wolves howled.

Jonathan knew that those sounds were coming from a tape player somewhere, but they were still creepy.

As they began walking toward the room, Tiffany told Jonathan she would hold his prizes while he went in. He gave her his rubber bat, but he wanted to hold on to his pinwheel.

"You think the ghosts will care if I take my pinwheel in there?" he asked.

She stuffed the bat in her pocket and rested her hand on his back as they walked.

"No, sweetie. I don't think they'll mind at all."

He held the toy out in front of him and turned to face the door. A sign hung from above it that had ENTER AT YOUR OWN RISK written on it.

"Go get 'em, little man." he heard his father say from behind him.

"Don't forget that your dad and I are right out here." his mother added.

Jonathan took a deep breath, stood up straight, clutched the pinwheel to his chest, and stepped inside.

It was dark at first.

Then, he was almost blinded by the brilliant flashing of a strobe light — and it was dark again.

From the dark far corner of the room, he could hear the rattling of chains and moans of ghosts coming from the tape player. He jumped a little at the sound.

He was two feet inside the door when the strobe came on again. Apparently it was coming on every minute or so and flashing for about ten seconds, then going back out.

The room had been set up with what looked like black curtains hanging from a piece of twine that went around three walls. There was about three feet of space from the curtains back to the wall. A path was taped on the classroom floor with tape that glowed in the black light bulb that dangled from the ceiling. The object was to follow the path around the room and hope nothing came out from behind the curtain and grabbed you.

Jonathan knew that there were bigger kids wearing masks and waiting back there.

But he was a *big boy*. He wasn't going to be a chicken.

A group of three kids were inside with him and they were already almost at the end of the curtains. He could hear them giggling in the darkness but it was hard to see them. He could only make out shapes. When the strobe kicked in, they appeared to be moving in a jerky motion, like an old black and white movie that he saw one time on television.

Jonathan quit focusing on the other children and kept his eyes on the curtain that was on his right side. Still clutching the black, hard plastic straw that was the handle of his pinwheel, he slowly put one foot in front of another and began walking, making sure to follow the glowing path of tape.

A skeleton made of cardboard jumped out from behind the curtain and began to wiggle in mid-air directly in front of him. It did give Jonathan enough of a scare that he jumped just a little, but he could see the broomstick handle and fishing line that the skeleton was attached to.

"Didn't get me." he said aloud so that the snickering kids that were operating the paper ghoul could hear.

The skeleton was jerked back behind the curtain.

Jonathan walked on, a bit more confidant now having survived the attack of the cardboard creature. He had only gone about three steps when the strobe began to flicker crazily again. He could see a boy in a werewolf mask peeking at him out of the curtain ahead. As he walked closer, the werewolf-boy reached out for him and howled. His hands were adorned with fake black plastic claws that barely brushed Jonathan's Spider-Man suit.

Jonathan thought it was creepy, but he still wasn't really scared. The werewolf-boy had on jeans and sneakers. The only scary thing about him was the mask, and even it wasn't that bad.

Jonathan had seen *much* meaner looking werewolves on TV.

Still holding his pinwheel tightly, he walked on.

At the next opening in the curtain, he heard a voice say "Come in, little boy."

Jonathan stepped through the opening

He found himself in a small space that was about three feet by five feet. The teacher's desk was here, except it was covered by a tablecloth with thousands of little pumpkin pictures on it. Sitting behind the desk was a girl with her face painted a pale white. She was wearing plastic vampire teeth in her mouth and had trickles of fake blood running from the corners of her lips. On her head was a long, black wig, streaked with strands of grey. The hair flowed down across her shoulders and lay across the sleeves of her tattered red gown. Jonathan thought that the pale-but-pretty face behind the make-up was very familiar. It looked just like Wendy Crenshaw from the fifth grade.

A small lamp with a very dim light bulb illuminated four bowls on the desk before her. Each bowl had something dark and glistening in it.

"Feel them," said the Wendy-Vampire, pointing to the bowls. "It's human guts."

Jonathan walked up and looked at the bowls. The first one sat next to a folded card that had EYEBALLS written on it. He reached out and poked them with his finger.

They felt like eyeballs, but Jonathan knew they were really grapes floating in juice.

The next bowl contained INTESTINES that were really rubber fishing worms.

The third contained A HUMAN HEART that felt very much like a rubber glove filled with water.

The final bowl held SEVERED FINGERS, which Jonathan immediately knew were just hot dog wieners.

"I'm not scared," he proudly announced to the ashen-faced keeper of the bowls. "Is that you, Wendy?"

The girl raised a finger to her lips and said "Sssssssshhhhhh. I don't want anybody to know, Jonathan. Go on and have fun."

He smiled at her and darted back out to the tape path, wondering what lay in wait for him next.

Suddenly, the group of kids from the other side of the room erupted into screams and laughter all at once. In a flurry of motion, they nearly ran over each other getting through the door and back into the well-lit hallway. Once they were there, Jonathan could hear their giggles and their whispers of *That was cool* and *Let's go through it again.* He concluded that there must be something really spooky behind the last curtain next to the door, since that was where all of the noise had come from.

Turning onto the second wall of the room, Jonathan was greeted by a boy in a Jason mask that walked out dangling a fake severed head. It might have been scary if the boy was bigger, but he was only about an inch or so taller than Jonathan.

"You're not Jason." he said, scooting on by the masked youngster and being greeted by another who wore an old man mask and was holding a rubber snake.

"Wanna hold my pet?" the Old Man-Boy asked, passing the lifeless lump of rubber back and forth from left hand to right and back again.

"Isn't real." Jonathan stated, pointing to it with his pinwheel as if it was a magic wand and he was going to make the snake vanish.

The kid stepped aside, muttering "Aw, Man."

Obviously, he hadn't had much luck scaring anyone tonight with his rubber "pet".

The remainder of the trip around the room wasn't too bad at all. A big, fake, fuzzy spider dropped down on a piece of fishing line, a boy dressed as Freddy Krueger invited Jonathan to come in and take a nap, and a coffin lid flipped open with a fake mummy inside it. Jonathan dealt with them all, proud of himself because he had only jumped a couple of times. The spider had gotten him pretty good because it had landed on his head, but he knew it wasn't real. The mummy was pretty neat too, but it just lay there in the casket. It might have scared him more if it had gotten up and moved.

He knew his mom and dad would be pleased.

He had made it through like a *big boy* should.

A brave boy - a brave, big boy - a really brave, big boy.

That's what he knew his parents would call him. He was proud of himself and eager to get back to them so he could tell them of all the mortal dangers he had faced. He was coming up on the last curtain near the doorway out. This is the spot where the other kids ran out in a fit of screams and laughter just a minute ago.

Jonathan figured that whoever was waiting to scare him here must be doing a good job of it.

He stepped forward and stopped at the opening where the curtains met, bracing himself for someone peeking out in yet another mask.

No one did.

Instead, a hand with *very* real looking black pointed fingernails slowly reached out from behind the dark fabric. It came out to about its elbow and grasped at the air as if it were trying to strangle an invisible foe. The skin was pale and the arm was draped in a ragged, dark fabric that hung nearly to the floor.

Then, it extended its index finger at Jonathan, turned it palm up, and began to curl the finger back and forth. Jonathan knew what that meant.

Come here.

He watched as the arm and hand began to withdraw back into the curtain just as slowly as it had come out. Before it vanished from view, it stopped and grasped the edge of the opening, drawing the curtains back. A ghostly fog rolled out into the room. Jonathan looked down and saw it surrounding his ankles. It swirled about and crept along the floor, making the room look like a graveyard he once saw in a scary movie. The only thing missing were the tombstones.

"Welcome, little boy."

Jonathan's attention immediately went from the fog back to what lurked behind the curtain. It was a woman speaking to him.

"Come in, Jonathan."

Whoever it was knew his name.

He slowly took a step forward and bent over to peek through the fog to see who waited for him. His eyes grew wide behind the Spider-Man mask when they fell upon the voices owner.

He had forgotten about Miss Kemp - the witch.

She stood behind a black cauldron, stirring it with a twisted branch and causing more and more of the white mist to pour out of it. A red light bulb hanging behind the curtain cast the small area she stood in with an evil looking reddish glow. As she stirred, the Miss Kemp-Witch laughed a chilling laugh and looked straight at Jonathan. He stood transfixed as she spoke again.

"Now, I know a good little boy like you wants some candy." she said, stirring with one hand and pointing at the basket of candy that sat on the floor next to her.

Jonathan remained rooted to the spot. He knew it was only Miss Kemp in a costume, just as he had known that the other "monsters" he had encountered were just other kids.

But this time...he felt himself being frightened. He wished that the child-thing from his room were here with him now. Then he would not be so scared.

The Miss Kemp-Witch leaned over and curled her fingers about the handle of the candy filled basket, lifting it and holding it out toward Jonathan.

"Come, little one," she said. "Come get some candy."

Jonathan felt his stomach tightening up into a solid ball of pure fear. He hadn't felt as though he was going to wet himself in months, yet he thought that he could do so now at any moment.

He would be laughed at if he did that; scolded by his mother and father; yelled at by the Miss Kemp Witch.

The rest of the room and the other children in it seemed to vanish. Jonathan felt that he and the black robed figure before him were the only two people there.

"What's the matter, little boy?" the witch asked. "Are you

scaaaaarrred?" She sat the candy basket back on the floor, realizing he wasn't going to take any.

Jonathan *was* scared. He was more scared than he felt he had ever been in his life. Maybe it was just Miss Kemp that made him feel that way. He was nervous around her even when she dressed as a normal teacher and walked the halls during the day. Her attire tonight and the darkened room with its flashing lights and Halloween sounds magnified that feeling to monstrous proportions. Jonathan stood there, not moving a muscle, his pinwheel still clutched tightly to his chest. Behind the openings in his mask, his eyes were wide and unblinking.

That's when the voice came to him.

"I am here, Jonathan. I am right here."

Relief washed over him, but he still stood rooted to the spot.

"Jonathan?" the Miss Kemp Witch said. "Jonathan, are you okay?"

He remained still, his little hands now holding the pinwheel by the top, squeezing it so hard that they crushed the orange and black foil propeller. His nails dug into his palms.

The Miss Kemp Witch spoke to him again. "Jonathan, answer me. What's wrong?"

The voice came again.

"You don't have to answer her, Jonathan. You don't have to do anything except what I need you to."

Jonathan said nothing. He felt hot, just like he did when his mother told him he had a fever.

Miss Kemp didn't know what had happened to the child. Surely he couldn't be *that* frightened of her. After all, he had just seen her talking to his parents in the hall a little while ago. He knew it was just her in a costume, yet now, he stood there as if in a trance; a statue in a Spider-Man outfit.

She quit stirring the smoking cauldron and began to step toward the child. As she approached, he still remained rooted to the spot. His eyes, still wide and glassy, followed her as she came. He seemed to be squeezing his little pinwheel so tight that his hands were trembling.

She leaned over him and put one hand on his shoulder.

"Jonathan, are you going to answer me?" she asked. "What's the *matter?*"

He said absolutely nothing, waiting for the voice to speak to him again. He thought that maybe the child-thing was trying to come through mysterious door he had spoken about. That meant that they would see each other at last.

Miss Kemp reached out and lifted the mask from his head. His face was pale and glistening with a light sheen of sweat; his hair was soaked from it; his lips trembled.

"Jonathan!" she said loudly and firmly, intending for him to hear her over the loud sounds coming from the tape player in the far corner. "Jonathan, you answer me *now!*"

The voice spoke once more.

"She's yelling at you, Jonathan."

He thought the child-things voice was somehow. . .different. The accent was gone, just as it had been the last few nights.

Miss Kemp shook him slightly by his shoulder, still trying to snap him out of it. He was staring her squarely in the face with his piercing blue eyes. It was at that moment that she saw his expression begin to change. The look of fear was replaced by one of rage. His eyes turned cold and dark.

The voice came once more

"Jonathan. . ."

Miss Kemp had him by both shoulders now. He could see her mouth moving, but heard only the words in his head.

"She's yelling. . ."

The strobe light made the witch appear as if she were an animated figure; a yelling animated figure.

". . .at you."

Jonathan kept looking at her as she reached out and began to lightly pat him on his cheek, attempting to bring him out of the daze.

"We just can't have that yelling, can we, Jonathan?"

He was still trying to decide what else was different about the voice. It didn't sound like the voice of the child-thing. It sounded like. . .someone else.

"No, we just can't have that yelling. . .not without making the bitch pay."

Jonathan realized he wasn't afraid anymore - he was angry.

"The time is now, boy."

Then things happened very fast.

Jonathan's hand abruptly thrust upward, plunging the hard plastic tube that was the pinwheel handle deep into the witches left eye with a sickening squishing sound.

She began to scream, rearing back with blood pouring from the eye and across her make-up covered cheek.

Jonathan stepped back and stared as the Miss Kemp Witch fell to the floor, grasping at her ruptured eye, blood now beginning to shoot from between her fingers in tiny jets. It covered her hands and black fingernails. Her tattered robe and cape flailed all about her as she writhed in pain. The witches hat and wig fell from her head.

Jonathan dropped the pinwheel with its bloody stalk. He stood there and watched.

She screamed and screamed, much louder than she had *ever* yelled in class.

CHAPTER 11

When the screams started coming from the Haunted House Room, Neal and Tiffany along with several other adults within earshot assumed it was part of the act inside.

Then, screaming and crying children began to pour from the darkened room, nearly trampling each other.

Neal had been at the water fountain down near the men's restroom and Tiffany was talking with Mr. Tanner, the assistant principal dressed as a scarecrow. Tanner jerked his head in the direction of the commotion, noticing that the running children were ones that had been working inside the Haunted House. The little Freddy Krueger and Wolf man were babbling incoherently, ripping their masks from their heads as they scrambled away. Wendy Crenshaw sat against the hallway wall, her knees tucked up tight to her chest. She was crying, tears cutting paths through her vampire make-up. The boy in the old man mask ran past her, slipping and falling to his knees on the hard floor and crying out in pain. Other children were running madly away from the room as well, seeking out their parents and clinging tightly to them or running straight out the front door of the school into the cold October night.

"Holy Christ!" exclaimed Tanner. "What's *happening?*"

Tiffany was already searching the fleeing youngsters for her son.

He was not among them.

Tanner broke into a run with Tiffany falling in behind him, his black penny loafers click-clacking on the hallway floor and straw falling from his costume. "Calm down, kids! Calm down!" he yelled as he went.

Neal and a tall man with a mustache that Tiffany recognized as Guy Welch, little Zachary Welch's father, had already reached the doorway to the room. Their silhouettes were outlined by the flashing strobe light from the darkness within as they stood there.

"Where's Jonathan?" Tiffany shouted to Neal as she reached the door with Tanner. "Damn it, Neal, where *is* he?"

Neal held his hand out and motioned for her to stop before coming any further. "He's right here, hon," he said, still looking into the room. "He's fine and he's right here."

"Oh, shit!" Guy said aloud as he ran past Neal into the room. "Somebody call an ambulance!"

The sounds of a woman screaming horribly were coming from the direction of Neal's stare. It was a *real* person, not a Halloween tape. Tanner ran into the room behind Guy. Tiffany could hear him stammering "Jesus, Jesus, Jesus!" over and over. Neal was slowly stepping forward, and Tiffany could hear him asking "Jonathan? What happened here?"

She could stand it no longer. Pushing her way through the rest of the onlooking parents, she found herself looking into the flickering strobe light. The screaming was directly to her left and she immediately cast her eyes in that direction.

"Oh, God." was all she could say, seeing what had sent the children running in fear.

Cradled in Guy Welch's arms was Miss Kemp, blood covering her face and hands. There were puddles of it on the floor all around her. Her witch's hat lay soaking in it. Guy had pulled the chambray shirt he was wearing from his back and was sitting there holding her with only his tank T-shirt on, the shirt wadded up and pressed tightly to Miss Kemp's left eye. The two of them were bathed in the glow of the red bulb that hung behind the still smoking black cauldron.

Tanner had pulled off his scarecrow hat and was headed back out the door, nearly knocking Tiffany down as he went by. "I've got the ambulance covered!" he yelled to no one in particular as he went. "Someone grab some damp towels for Guy from the bathroom! Don't just stand there, for God's sake, do something!"

Tiffany could hear footsteps in the hall and knew that some of the other adults had left the gawking mob and ran to do as Tanner had asked. Then, her attention turned to the center of the room when she heard Neal saying "Jonathan?"

Then she saw her son...just standing there in the flashing light, his hair wet with sweat.

His mask was lying on the floor next to the pinwheel he had won earlier.

The pinwheel had something on the handle. It was red.
Blood.

"No, no, no, no, no, Neal. Please tell me he didn't..." she began, her voice shaking.

"...do it?" Neal finished for her, still looking at Jonathan. "I'm not sure. Something happened. Accident or intentional is anybody's guess. Maybe we can get Jonathan to tell us."

Tiffany looked at her son. He seemed oblivious to everything that was happening around him. Something about him was...not quite the same. The look on his face was not that of a six-year-old boy, but of something else. It was a look that frightened her...because she knew it wasn't *right*.

"Jonathan," she said, keeping her tone as calm as she could. "Come here to us."

Neal squatted down, joining in with Tiffany. "Yeah, son, come on over here. We aren't going to spank you. We just want to make sure you aren't hurt."

The boy regarded them with a stare that was brutal, not moving from where he stood.

"Please, honey." Tiffany asked. "Please talk to daddy and me. Please?"

Jonathan didn't move; didn't blink.

Neal began to hear voices behind him in the hall - a mixture of comments and cries from the turmoil that was unfolding.

Mr. Tanner called 911! Somebody's hurt! Get some help! Contact her husband! There's blood everywhere! The Fowler boy did it! My son said she lost her eye! Keep the children back! Get the lights turned on so we can see! Are the police coming? Is she going to die?

Neal could hear all of the jabbering voices delivering an intermingling sea of statements, questions, and observations, but he only absorbed one.

The Fowler boy did it!

Standing from his squatting position, Neal reached out and put a hand on Tiffany's shoulder, trying to keep her from rushing to the boy. He could tell she wanted to.

"Jonathan?" he asked slowly and quietly. "Did you hurt Miss Kemp?"

Tiffany looked at Neal, her eyes now streaming tears, then back to her son.

The boy just looked at them as if they disgusted him.

Neal repeated himself. "Jonathan, I'm going to ask you one more time. Did...you.... hurt...Miss Kemp?"

Jonathan looked to the doorway at the other watching parents, then back to Neal and Tiffany. He seemed to be...studying them.

His mouth opened and he spoke. His voice was still child-like, but now seemed to have a depth and a seriousness about it that was anything but natural.

"She has paid! Paid, as most of you worthless souls will by morning! You should all be so lucky as to still have your breath as the bitch does when I have collected what is owed me!"

Tiffany felt her legs go weak. She nearly fell to the floor and would have if Neal had not caught her. As he held onto her, he looked back at what he thought was his son until it had spoken.

Jonathan smiled an evil smile that was smug and assured of its confidence. As he slowly backed away he spoke again, not just to Neal and Tiffany, but to the whole crowd.

"Pity the little ones who suffered and the ones who caused the suffering," he said. "The bringers of pain shall feel such torment as they have delivered, and be judged by a greater power than we!"

With that, the small figure turned and ran, scrambling atop the air conditioning unit beneath the window at the far side of the room.

"No!" Neal shouted, still holding his wife on her feet.

The child, still keeping his eyes on the crowd, struck the window with the back of his small fist. Though Neal could hardly believe it, the sound of shattering glass filled the air, mixing with the horror tape that still blared from the tape player and Miss Kemp's screaming.

Good God, how could he be strong enough to...

The small blue and red clad figure leaped from the window and vanished from view, his laughter echoing behind him.

Little Wendy Crenshaw wanted to go home.

She sat with tears still in her eyes, huddled against the hallway wall. Her palms were smeared with the pale vampire make-up she had rubbed from her cheeks. There were so many people crowding in the door of the Haunted House room that she could not see what was going on inside.

Her parents had agreed to let her ride to the carnival tonight with their neighbors, Mr. Welch and Zachary. She wished now that *they* had brought her themselves.

Mr. Welch was busy taking care of Miss Kemp, who was bleeding really badly, and Zachary was standing down near the office with some more adults.

She was ten years old and Zachary was only six. He had left the room before everything had happened. Wendy thought he was lucky that he didn't see what she had. The darkness and flashing light in the room had made it hard even for *her* to see what had transpired. Miss Kemp's screams had startled her, causing her to leave her post at the bowls of bogus human remains. When she peered out from behind the curtain that hung in front of her area, she saw Miss Kemp on the floor, holding her face and bleeding.

Jonathan Fowler was standing there too, just watching. That had seemed weird to Wendy. It was only after she had fled the room with the other children that she learned that it was Jonathan who had stuck something sharp into the teacher's eye. She couldn't imagine why he would do such a thing. At any rate, she knew he was going to be in big trouble now.

She suddenly felt hot and clammy. Standing up, she began to walk toward the exit doors at the end of the hall closest to her, un-noticed by anyone in all the chaos. She stepped out of the doors into the cool night air, leaving the dozens of frantic voices and the sound of Miss Kemp's screams behind her.

The air felt good on her skin. As she stood there beneath a covered walkway that connected the main building with the cafeteria, she heard glass breaking around the corner, back in the direction of the Haunted House room. She hurried to the front corner of the building to see what it was.

In the glow of the lamps that lined the circular drive in front of the school, she saw a small figure in red and blue running toward Broad Street. He was there one second, gone the next.

It had to be Jonathan. He was wearing a Spider-Man costume and it was red and blue.

She thought she could hear him laughing, and then he was gone, disappearing around the corner.

Inside, she could still hear the screaming. In the distance, the sounds of an ambulance siren rose into the night. They were coming here; coming to get Miss Kemp; the witch who had a blood filled hole where her eye used to be.

Wendy still felt hot. The air was cool, so she knew it had to be her. Maybe she was getting a fever, like her mom told her she would if she didn't wear her jacket tonight. She turned to walk back inside...

...and heard a child call her name.

"Wendy."

Abruptly, she spun to see who had said her name.

No one was there. Only the empty concrete walk that went to the cafeteria stretched out in front of her, the night surrounding it on both sides. She tuned back to the door, only to hear it again.

"Wendy. . .talk to me."

The little girl spun around again, her vampire wig of long, straight, jet-black hair swirling around with her body.

Still, no one was there.

"Who are you?" she yelled out to the faceless voice.

There was no reply for a moment...then:

"I'm Jonathan's friend, Wendy. I need you to help me. I need you to listen to me."

Then, as she stood there trying to spot who was speaking to her, Wendy felt as if she was going to faint. Her heart began to beat with such force that she could feel it in her ears. Her body shook, and she could feel her knees giving out on her as blackness rushed in.

"I won't hurt you, Wendy. I just need you right now. Please believe me."

Just before she blacked out, she was thinking about how the voice that had just spoken to her sounded unlike anyone who lived around here. It reminded her of the people who lived in that country where they talked really funny - the place where Mary Poppins was from.

She thought it might be England.

PART II

TRICK OR TREAT

CHAPTER 12

The houses, each with flickering jack-o-lanterns in their windows or on their porches, all looked the same to Jonathan. He ran as fast as his small legs would carry him, urged on by something he had no control over. His body was hot and he felt dizzy, just like he did when his dad would swing him around and around in the backyard.

Words had come from his mouth back at the school — words that he did not understand. How had that happened? He could recall his mouth moving and saying the things he did as all the grown ups stood there watching, but he felt like the voice *made* him speak. It was as if they had been whispered into Jonathan's ear and he merely repeated what he was told. The entire incident, though it happened less than ten minutes ago, seemed like a dream to him.

He knew he had hurt Miss Kemp. The voice had told him it was what he should do, just as it drove him to run now. It had told him that she was *"yelling"* at him and that *"We just can't have that yelling."*

The child-thing had never told him that it wanted him to hurt anyone.

Maybe it was angry for some reason. That could be why the voice sounded so different.

But what if it wanted him to hurt more people?

Jonathan stopped in his tracks. He turned to his left and observed a large, lighted sign across the street at the entrance to a small development. It said Guildford Acres. Beyond the sign he saw several homes and sidewalks bathed in the light of street lamps. As he studied the familiar setting, he recalled coming here. He recalled riding through the neighborhood with his parents, but not why they had done so.

Suddenly he remembered.

They had wanted to show him where Doctor Melly lived.

After the ambulance left, the Sumter police kept Neal and Tiffany Fowler detained in the school office for a half an hour, grilling them on

Jonathan and what may have sparked his behavior. They asked about his therapy, his nightmares, his sleepwalking, and even if he had been abused. Tiffany was infuriated that they would even *ask* such as question, but she kept her cool. Anything to get them the hell out of there so they could go and look for their son.

Three officers in separate cars had already been sent in the direction in which Jonathan had headed, hoping to catch him before he got too far. The boy had moved so quickly when he leaped from the classroom window that he was gone before anyone inside could see exactly which way he was headed. One patrol car headed for Broad Street while the other went in the opposite direction, traveling the neighborhood streets behind the school. The third headed down Lafayette Drive. The officers figured that the boy could have only gotten so far, especially in the dark. Being that it was already late enough for the town's trick-or-treaters to be off the streets, spotting a lone little fellow in a Spider-Man suit *seemed* like it would be easy.

It was almost nine o'clock when Neal and Tiffany were allowed to go and assist in the search for their son. Pulling their jackets on as they ran for the Durango, they both said nothing; they didn't have to, for they both knew what the other was thinking.

They had to find their son before he hurt someone else.

Five minutes later, they were going down Broad Street to get to Highway 76. Maybe Jonathan was heading for home, and if he was, the route he would take would be straight down 76 out of town limits. It was all the six-year-old boy knew in Sumter, other than Doctor Melly's office and the school.

Then again, there was that old tobacco barn over in Weatherford's field.

Neal tried not to think about that as he drove. It was hard to do, but he had to be strong for Jonathan and Tiffany. He could see her from the corner of his eye, scanning the surrounding neighborhood streets and sidewalks, silently frantic as she prayed for a glimpse of her son. Reaching out a hand, he gently patted her on her blue jean clad thigh.

"We'll find him, hon," he said to her. "We'll find him, so don't worry."

She kept her face to the glass when she spoke, not giving up her search.

"We have to, Neal. We have to before he comes in contact with anyone else. God only knows what could happen."

Neal drove on, the houses decorated with their scarecrows, black cats, and ghosts slowly passing by his window.

"The voice," he said. "The little boy or whatever in the hell he's been talking to at night…it's been a while since he's mentioned hearing it, right?"

"Yes," replied Tiffany. "But I guess he could have been keeping the truth from us if he was still afraid we would punish him or yell at him — but we were so sure we had gotten past all this."

Ahead, a large plastic pumpkin with a light bulb inside sat grinning at the corner where Broad turned into Warren Street. Neal hung a right, headed for Main Street and Highway 76.

"I'm afraid this thing runs deeper than any of us feared it would," said Neal. "We aren't just dealing with a child who has nightmares. There's something much bigger at work here. "

Tiffany listened, knowing in her heart that he was right.

"Tiffany," he went on. "That was *not* our son speaking back there. It had his voice, but not his words."

She was silent for a moment. Neal could tell she was thinking. "But, they weren't a *child's* words, Neal. He claims to have heard a *child*," she said. "A child who couldn't play and who was beaten. For the love of God, if there *was* a spirit or ghost of such a child in our house, why would he torture Jonathan so? Why would he make him so skittish around us that we can't even correct him verbally without turning him into a fit of nerves?"

Neal saw the junction to 76 coming up a few blocks away. He clicked on the high beams as he spoke. "Maybe this…child…or whatever it is…is trying to convince Jonathan that the same wrongs inflicted upon itself by its parents or whoever…will also be inflicted upon Jonathan…. by *us*. Maybe it's *warning* him, so that it doesn't have to see another child harmed."

"Warning him? About us?" she replied. "Bullshit, Neal. Jonathan knows we would never, ever hurt him."

"Does he? Maybe he used to," said Neal, "but this thing apparently has a strong enough will of its own to change his mind. Strong enough to make him say whatever in the hell that was about the "bringers of pain and torment" just before he went out the window."

Tiffany felt like she was going crazy. She managed to find a faint hint of a smile as she glanced over at Neal, tears forming in her eyes.

"You know what's funny?" she asked, sniffing as she spoke and wiping her nose with the back of her hand. "Neither one of us have ever believed in ghosts. Don't you think it's kind of ironic to be having this conversation?"

Neal looked over at her, reaching out and wiping a tear from her cheek. "Yeah, I guess it is, honey. I guess it is. I'm still not saying I believe in them now, but I sure as hell know one thing. This is more than sleepwalking and bad dreams."

The Durango rolled out onto 76 and Neal floored it, heading east toward the town limits. The night rushed past outside the windows, cloaking the fields in darkness and harboring the hushed bidding of an evil long dead - an evil that traveled on the night breeze through the streets of Sumter…seeking the ears of children.

CHAPTER 13

Guy Welch was three blocks from his home on Cuslidge Drive. Just two more stop signs and he would be pulling the van into the driveway. He was exhausted. It had been one helluva Halloween night. He could see his reflection in the rear view mirror and realized he looked like shit. His thin hair and his mustache were sticky with blood from Miss Kemp. He had tried to wash it all off in the school restroom but he couldn't get it all. The bloodstains all over his chambray shirt and T-shirt had started drying, turning the fabric slightly stiff in places. He didn't like the way it felt on his body.

His son Zachary, the Blue Power Ranger, was in the passenger seat. The little guy had nodded off, the excitement and then terror of what had happened at the carnival catching up to him. The accident in the Haunted House room had been awful; then there was Jonathan Fowler's little display, which was the damnedest thing Guy had ever seen. If all of that hadn't been *enough*, his neighbors little girl Wendy, who had ridden to the carnival with Zachary and himself, was found by Mr. Tanner laying outside on the breezeway. It appeared that the fifth grader had passed out, no doubt from the shock of what was happening. She had bumped her head when she fell, opening up a small cut just above her right eye. Tanner had been able to revive her, and then he took her down to the office and cleaned up her injury. The police had Neal and Tiffany Fowler locked up in Tanner's office, questioning them about their son. Guy felt sorry for them. Really sorry.

After the paramedics had taken Miss Kemp and Guy had done all he could to help, he took Zachary with him down to the office to get Wendy. When the little girl walked out, she seemed dazed. Her eyes seemed fixed on a point that was a million miles away. A cloth band-aid was above her right eye. The long black wig and crimson gown she wore made her small face seem as pale as bone. Guy knew she had been wearing vampire make-up, but he still wondered how much of her color *was* make-up and how much was actually her skin.

When Guy spoke to her, she wouldn't respond. She wouldn't respond to anybody.

"She's really shaken, Guy." Tanner had said. "You need to get her home to her family."

Guy had taken Wendy's hand in his and led the little girl out to the van, asking her if she was okay at least a half a dozen times on the way. She never answered him. Zachary had crawled up into the passenger seat, pulling his Power Ranger mask off and dropping it to the floorboard. Guy put Wendy in the back and buckled her up. Then he got in, leaned over to buckle Zachary in, and they were on their way. Zachary had turned around twice to ask Wendy why she was being so quiet but Guy had quickly told him not to bother her. When Zachary asked him why, he had told him that Wendy didn't feel very good. The little boy seemed satisfied enough with that and turned his attention back to the road, counting the jack-o-lanterns in the passing windows. Soon, he was asleep.

He dreamed of voices.

The first thing Melissa Grayson saw when she was startled awake was a lumbering zombie on the flickering television screen in front of her. It staggered through a graveyard in silence, the word *MUTE* illuminated in the upper corner of the picture. It was pursuing a blond woman who had her mouth open in a soundless scream. It was ten after nine and "Night of the Living Dead" was on the AMC monster marathon.

Melissa sat up in the chair and picked her glasses up from atop the newspaper in her lap. Slipping them on, she looked toward her front porch and realized what had jolted her awake.

Someone was knocking on the door.

The first thought to run through her mind was trick-or-treaters. It was Halloween after all. But it was after nine and the streets were empty of children. No one in this community had ever kept their kids out past seven thirty or eight at the very latest on Halloween, at least not in the twelve years that she had lived here.

The knocking came again…harder.

"Shit." she said aloud to herself under her breath.

Rising from the chair and letting the newspaper fall to the floor, she stretched and then grabbed a cigarette from the pack resting on the chair side table. Lighting it, she walked toward the door in her bare feet.

Probably teenagers who are entirely too old to be trick-or-treating she thought as she peered through the peephole in her door.

She saw no one.

Damn kids messing around.

Grabbing the doorknob, she pulled the door open to step out onto the porch and see if she could catch the pranksters as they ran away...and stopped.

Standing before her was Jonathan Fowler, who was too short for her to have seen through the peephole. He wore a Spider-Man suit, yet had no mask to cover his face or the strange expression upon it. His breathing was heavy, as if he had been running. One of his tennis shoes was un-laced and his hair was plastered to his head and soaked in sweat. On his face and hands, Melissa saw crimson stains and splotches.

She realized it was blood.

"Jesus. Jonathan, what happened to you? Where are your mom and dad?" she asked, kneeling in front of him and reaching out to put both hands on his shoulders, one hand still holding her cigarette.

He looked at her and smiled, his eyes glaring into hers.

"Jonathan? What's wrong? Can you answer me? Whose blood is this on you? Is it yours?"

The child lifted both of his hands to where Melissa's rested on his small shoulders, placing his on top of hers. His smile began to fade, and a look that disturbed her washed across his face. His eyes had narrowed to slits. When the words came from him, they were in a tone of sarcasm that Melissa might have expected from an adult, but not a six-year-old boy.

"You just know eeeeeeverything, don't you, Doctor Melly?"

She opened her mouth to respond...but Jonathan would not let her, interrupting her before she could.

"Of course you do, Doctor Melly. You're just a regular fucking fortune teller, aren't you?"

Melissa could only stare in stunned silence, talking to herself inside her head.

It's not Jonathan. It's this...thing.... that he hears at night...this boy he talks to. It has to be.

"Boy?" Jonathan said, raising his eyebrows in anticipation of her response. "Oh, much, much more than a boy, Doctor Melly. So much more that even an educated bitch like you wouldn't believe it. So much more that I picked that thought right out of your worthless head. How many heads have *you* picked over the years, Doctor Melly? How many *minds* have you tried to get into?"

Melissa tried to remove her hands from his shoulders and stand. When she attempted to pull away, the boy's hands tightened around her fingers, holding her at his eye level. The strength of the grip was *not* that of a child. It felt like her fingers were about to break. Her burning cigarette fell from her hand and landed on the porch.

"Let go!" she exclaimed, pulling with all her might.

Jonathan squeezed her hands even tighter, and she cried out in pain. "Jonathan, please, no!"

He looked up at her. "Aren't you glad I came?" he said. "After all, we had an appointment in the morning, did we not? I'm just a little early, Doctor Melly. You know, *I* think from now on, I'll refer to you as Doctor Bitch. Would you like that, dear Doctor?"

Melissa jerked one hand free and staggered to her right, nearly losing her step...and put her bare foot down directly on the burning stump of the cigarette she had just dropped. She yelled out and before she could pull her foot away, Jonathan's tennis shoe clad foot moved with amazing speed and stomped down across her instep, grinding the ball of her foot down onto the hot ember beneath. He began to laugh; an evil cackle, void of any pity.

"Smoking isn't good for you, Doctor Bitch," he said. "But, you already knew that didn't you, you mind scrambling, fortune telling, know it all whore!"

"Let...me...GO!" Melissa screamed.

With a sudden jerk she pulled her burnt foot away, the cigarette still hanging to the charred skin underneath, and kicked out with it, striking Jonathan in the stomach. The boy's grip fell away. He tumbled backward and lost his balance on the top porch step, almost falling. As he was flailing to correct himself, Melissa ran for the glass storm door behind her. She pulled it open with such a hard yank that she felt she would rip it from its hinges. Then, she was behind the glass, watching the *thing* that looked like Jonathan Fowler as it stood there, ranting on.

"All will pay! You will pay for my death. The miserable boy will pay too! The reward of his last breath, so rich would it have been to fall on my ears! Because of all of you, I was not allowed that pleasure! *You* will pay, as will *all* I lay my hands upon this night!"

Melissa turned and ran for the telephone, the child's demonic cackle filling her ears as she went.

When Guy switched off the van's engine in the driveway, little Zachary opened his eyes wide. Wendy sat in the back, nothing more than a dark and unmoving shadow in the rear view mirror.

"Home at last, my little trick-or-treaters," Guy said, unsnapping his seat belt. "Bet you can't wait to get inside and eat some of that candy, huh?"

Zachary sat there, looking toward the steps to the house. He looked down at his own seatbelt, then over at Guy.

"Hold on, pal, I'll get it for you." offered Guy, reaching over to free the boy.

From the back seat came the sound of Wendy's voice, uttering a single word.

"Don't."

Guy stopped in mid-motion and looked back at her. She had not said a word all the way here. "Hon, are you feeling better? Zachary and I have been worried about you." he said, reaching for Zachary's seat belt again.

"Don't release him!" Wendy exclaimed.

Guy didn't know what was wrong with her. Maybe the knock on the head had been worse than he thought.

"Wendy, calm down," he said. "I'm sure Zachary doesn't want to sit strapped in the car all night long. I'll have you home in just a second."

He grabbed Zachary's seat belt and went to unlock it.

"I CANNOT LET YOU!" screamed the girl, reaching across the seat with blinding speed. She grasped Guy by the back of his hair and pulled him backward, slamming his head into the headrest and holding him there. He found himself staring up at the van roof as the child held him.

It didn't take him long to realize that her grip was too strong for him to break. She had busted the lock on her seatbelt with ease.

Wendy stared down at his face as she kept him pinned down, her vampire wig hanging down and brushing across his cheeks. She turned and looked at Zachary, then back to Guy.

"Wendy..." he stammered. "Wendy, what are you doing?"

She looked him in his eyes with an intensity he had never experienced before. Her eyes were glassy and her skin hot.

"He's not as he seems, Mr. Welch," she said. "He's not Zachary. Father has taken him now."

Guy tried to pull himself up, but to no avail. She may as well have his head locked in a vise. "Wendy, you aren't thinking straight," he said. "Let me go and I'll walk you on over to your house so you can rest."

She did not release him.

"Wendy!" he exclaimed. "I'm not kidding here! You're scaring Zachary! You let go of me right now or..."

"Please, Mr. Welch." she interrupted. "Please just listen to me and then decide what you wish to do."

He couldn't believe this. Jesus, she was acting like a lunatic. Just like Jonathan Fowler had...

Oh, God . Just like Jonathan Fowler had acted...right after he nearly killed someone.

Her pale face continued to hover over him from the darkness of the back seat. The small hand that gripped Guy's hair at the back of his head felt as if it could rip it from his scalp with one pull. From the corner of his eye, he could see Zachary staring at what was happening.

"Let me out, daddy." he said, appearing oblivious to the fact that Wendy held him restrained in his seat.

Guy looked into Wendy's seemingly black eyes. "Please let go of me and let's go inside, okay, Wendy?"

She didn't let him go, turning her attention toward Zachary, who was fumbling with the seat belt now. He returned her gaze, his face void of expression, and then looked back at his father.

"Daddy, I wanna get out!" he exclaimed.

Guy felt Wendy's grip loosen ever so slightly when Zachary cried out. Bracing for the pain, he jerked his head up and forward. Wendy tried to tighten her grip when she felt him move, but to no avail. Guy pulled free, feeling a clump of hair rip from his head in the child's hands. He disregarded what felt like dozens of tiny needles piercing his skin where the hair had been, turning completely around in the driver's seat to face Wendy. His back rested against the steering wheel, he lifted his hands out in front of him to fight the girl away in case she tried to attack him again.

"Enough, Wendy!" he shouted. "Now you sit right there! I'm getting out, and I'm going to get your mom and dad to come get you!"

The pale faced girl sunk back against the seat, glaring at Guy as if he were absolutely nuts. Keeping one eye on her, he reached for Zachary's seat belt buckle. "I'm taking Zachary with me, okay? You sit right here and we'll be riiiight back." he said, managing a calmer tone.

Wendy looked over at the little figure strapped in the Blue Power Ranger costume and then back to Guy. "I wish to save you, Mr. Welch, yet you will not listen," she said." Father will take you, as he will others in this town tonight. What better way into the homes of the doomed ones than under the guise of a young one? Not only did he rule us and make us suffer as we walked the earth, he now chooses to use us against those who ended his years of torment."

Guy could not believe that the words he was hearing were coming from a ten-year-old girl. Her voice was in its normal tone and it *sounded* like Wendy, but something was different.

She had an accent; a thick English accent.

"I cannot fight him, for he is stronger than I ever could be," she went on. "He seeks the souls of children as his host. Children such as your son, Mr. Welch. Your son...and many more unfortunate innocents he will choose to reside in this night. Too many for a lost soul such as myself to deal with."

His heart pounding in his chest, Guy found himself wondering what had happened to this child. To Wendy, the little girl who came over to watch television with his son on Saturdays. Who jumped on the trampoline with him in the backyard. Who had loved Zachary's mother, Connie, as much as she did her own. When Connie died in the accident on Interstate 20 two years ago, Wendy and Zachary really bonded. Hell, Guy had grown to love her too. She was a beautiful little girl.

How could that little girl have become this dark thing that spoke to him now from the backseat?

"DADDY!"

The cry came from Zachary. It startled Guy and he jumped, turning to look at him. As soon as he directed his eyes away from Wendy, she lunged for the door handle and was out of the van and running down the sidewalk, past the light of the streetlamps and into the darkness. Guy could not believe how fast the child had moved.

Just like Jonathan Fowler when he went out that window.

"Wendy," he called out to her, knowing that it would do no good. "Wendy, don't run from me! Come back!"

She had vanished into the cold, dark night.

Zachary was still calling out to him. Guy turned back to the boy and hoped that this whole ordeal hadn't frightened him too badly.

If Connie were still alive, she would have known how to make everything all better. She always did. But she wasn't here...and never would be again.

"I asked you to let me out," the boy said, grasping the buckle in his hands." Looks like you would rather sit there and think about that rotten whore you lived with than to help me."

The words hit Guy like a punch in his gut. "What did you say?" he asked.

"Oh, I'm sorry if the term whore offends you. I'll call her Connie if it makes you feel better." Zachary said.

With a quick jerk, the child violently pulled the buckle apart...without depressing the release button.

He had *ripped* open the steel buckle with his bare hands.

Guy felt like he was losing it for real.

"Poor Connie," the child said, sitting up on his knees and turning to face Guy. "She spread her brains out across a bridge footing at seventy miles per hour and laid there for a little while before she died completely. Did you know that?"

"SHUT UP!" shouted Guy. "DON'T SAY..."

"Oh, I'll say what I please, Guy," the boy broke in. "I know you don't want to hear it. That she didn't die right away. That she suffered."

Guy noticed that the boy was sliding closer to him. Close enough to reach him.

"I suffered and no one cared, Guy. Why do you suppose that is"

Zachary moved closer, walking across the bench seat on his knees. Guy felt as if he was about to pass out. His mouth had gone completely dry. He knew that he needed to turn, open the door and get the hell inside his house, yet he did not want to leave the boy out here. His parental instincts were telling him to sit here and try to snap the boy out of whatever kind of fog he was in. His common sense was telling him that this was not his son. He didn't know *what* or *who* it was, but it wasn't Zachary Welch.

Just like the child with the accent in his back seat moments ago was *not* Wendy Crenshaw.

"Zachary...please..." Guy began, his voice trembling. "Please, let's just go inside. Stop this craziness and let's go and watch some television. I'll let you sit on the floor and eat all the candy you want."

The little boy cocked his head to the side and grinned. "Well, that's awfully nice of you to offer, Mr. Welch, but I'll eat all the candy I damn well please whether you tell me I can or not. As a matter of fact, I can do *anything* I want without anyone's permission. I am...whoever I wish to be. Do you understand how fucking nice that is?"

Guy felt his own heart begin to pound within his chest. Zachary inched his way a bit closer, still talking.

"It was sooooo nice to take the Fowler boy before the runt could get to him. The Fowler boy is most special, and tonight he will do much work for me. After I sent him on his way, I sought to be within the little Crenshaw bitch as well. Oh, what a fine hostess she would have been, all milky white skin and innocence. But, the worthless spirit-child had already taken her, hoping to reach you before I could so that he could spoil my fun He came and snatched her right out from under me. I guess turnabout's fair play, eh? He took one of mine because I took one of his. That's why I stepped inside your son, Guy."

Guy didn't know if he believed the words, or if he was just fascinated, frightened, or shocked. He found himself reaching around behind himself for the door handle. He sensed that Zachary was coming closer so he could *do* something.

Like Jonathan Fowler did when he took out Miss Kemp's eye and left her screaming on the floor like a stuck pig.

Guy felt the plastic handle fall within his grasp. He knew he had to get away before the boy reached him. He would simply lock Zachary in the van until this madness passed. Until his son was the same little boy who was holding hands with him only an hour ago.

"The bastard spirit-child has gone for now," Zachary said, getting so close now that Guy could smell the caramel apple on his breath that he had eaten at the carnival earlier tonight. "In death, he mocks me as he did in life. No matter. His soul will never rest while I exist"

Guy slowly began to depress the handle behind his back. Zachary was nearly right on top of him now.

"You," the boy said, pointing a small finger at Guy, "shall be the first collection on my debt."

Before Guy could move, the child hit him across the mouth with a closed fist that felt like it was made of lead. The impact knocked his head backwards into the driver's side window with such force that the glass shattered, raining thousands of tiny shards down his shirt and all over the seat.

"Not bad for a little fellow like me, is it, Guuuyyyy?" Zachary said. "Not too damn bad at all."

Guy managed to lift his head back up and grabbed for the door handle again.

Another fist, this time from the left, struck Guy across the nose. The cartilage within snapped and blood trickled from both nostrils, running across his mustache, down his throat, and blending with the dried blood on his shirt.

"Zachary...don't..." was all Guy could say, holding one hand up to shield his face and another to hold his bleeding nose. He couldn't absorb what was happening to him. He could not, for the love of God, understand *how* the child's blows were so strong. As strong as any full grown man's would be, if not stronger.

"Oooh, don't be concerned, Guuyyyy," the child said, pulling Guy's Swiss army knife from the key chain that dangled from the steering column. "You won't suffer quite as long as your precious whore did."

The little fingers found the corkscrew on the knife case, snapping it upright. "No, not quite as long. *Just* long enough that I get to enjoy it."

The small form moved fast.

As leaves danced on the night wind across his front lawn and out into the lamplight on Cuslidge Street, Guy Welch died right there in his own driveway at the hands of his beloved son.

He never even had a chance to scream.

CHAPTER 14

Jonathan had not come home.

Neal and Tiffany had walked both floors of the house from one end to the other, finding no sign of the boy. The first place they looked had been the bathroom that Tiffany had found him in that Saturday afternoon months ago - the very room from which this whole nightmare had started. It had been empty, as was the other upstairs bathroom. They checked all the closets and underneath all the beds. Neal even pulled down the attic steps and looked around in the top of the house. No one was there.

They were on the way back to the Durango when the cell phone mounted on the dashboard began to ring.

"Someone's calling the mobile." Tiffany exclaimed. "Oh God, please let it be someone who's found him."

Neal ran to the passenger side door and jerked it open, snatching the phone up from its mount. His nerves were in such a tangle that he nearly forgot the unlock code he had to punch in to answer it. After a few seconds that seemed like an hour had passed, he got it right.

"Hello, who is this?" he said, his breathing hard and his voice shaking.

There was a cough at the other end of the line, and then a familiar voice came across.

"Neal. . .it's Melissa. Melissa Grayson."

Neal glanced back at Tiffany, who was standing there with a questioning look. "It's Melissa." he told her, and then he spoke into the phone.

"Melissa. We've lost Jonathan. Jesus, it's been horrible. Over at the school. . .one of the teachers. . .one of Jonathan's teachers. . ."

"Neal," Melissa broke in, her voice trembling as bad as his. *"He just left here. Not five minutes ago."*

Neal felt a sense of relief wash over him.

"He came to your house?" he asked in surprise.

"Yes. . .but there's something wrong with him, Neal. He. . .isn't Jonathan. He was talking as if. . .as if he was possessed by something."

Neal recalled how the boy had spoken to everyone back at the school, just before he shattered the window and vanished.

"Are you okay, Melissa? Did he hurt you?" Neal asked.

There was a silence. Then:

"It's nothing. Just. . .a burn. But. . .he would have done more if I hadn't gotten away from him."

Tiffany walked up and stood next to Neal, reading the shock in his eyes and giving him a look that said *what is it?*

"Melissa, we'll be there in a few minutes. You sit tight. Did you happen to see which way he went?"

"No. He was on my porch one minute and gone the next."

Neal hung his head and ran a hand back through his hair, uttering a barely audible "Shit."

"Neal. . .I need to talk to you and Tiffany anyway. There's something I want to show you. It doesn't really seem like a logical explanation of what's happening. . .but it's the only thing that seems to. . .fit."

Neal motioned Tiffany to get in the Durango. She stepped up and got in, Neal closing her door behind her and running around the front of the truck with the phone still pressed to his ear.

"On the way right now." he said as he jumped into the driver's seat. He snapped the phone back into its holder, started the engine, and backed out onto 76.

"Are you gonna tell me what the hell is going on?" Tiffany asked.

Neal floored it, heading back into town.

"Of course I am," he said, never taking his eyes from the road ahead. "Just as soon as I figure it out myself."

It was cold and Jonathan wished he had his jacket.

He felt as if he kept going to sleep and waking up. The last thing he clearly remembered was walking up to Doctor Melly's house and knocking on the door. He had felt lightheaded and very hot, just like he had earlier right before he hurt Miss Kemp in the Haunted House.

The next thing he knew, he was blocks away, walking behind a service station.

He hoped he hadn't hurt Doctor Melly like he had hurt Miss Kemp. The child-thing surely wouldn't have wanted him to do that. The teacher whose eye he had put out scared him and yelled at him. The child-thing didn't like it and it made Jonathan hurt her. But Doctor Melly was nice.

She never yelled or made Jonathan feel frightened. It didn't seem like the child-thing would make Jonathan hurt her. At least he could remember bits and pieces about what happened at the school. Whatever happened on Doctor Melly's front porch was completely gone. It was as if the child-thing's presence had been *stronger*, consuming more of Jonathan than it had before.

He now stood beneath the buzzing light of a Shell Gas sign near the outskirts of town. Cars were passing by on the highway, no one even slowing down to notice him. No big deal to see a child with a Spider-Man suit on roaming around on Halloween night. The bloodstains were only visible when you got close.

Jonathan knew that his house was not far. He could tell because he had just walked past the Coca-Cola plant. Soon, he would be at the bridge where Highway 378 crossed 76, and his house was about one mile on the other side. Maybe his parents would be there. Perhaps they could help him. If he reached them, they could protect him and keep the child-thing's voice from making him do anything bad again.

As he stood there, he realized he had to pee. He thought about doing it over by the hedges behind the Shell Station, but he feared someone might see him. His father had allowed him to pee outside one time when they were in the mountains, but that was because there was no bathroom nearby. There *had* to be one around here somewhere.

He turned and faced the station. On the right side of the building there were two doors marked with the little man and woman symbols. Trying not to wet himself as he went, he began walking toward them. He remembered that most gas stations kept their bathroom keys inside and that you had to go inside and ask for them; at least, all of the ones he and his parents had ever stopped at did. Through the large window at the front of the building, he could see a large man sitting on a stool behind a cash register. That man would have the keys.

A grey Jeep Cherokee filled with teenagers had pulled up to the pumps as Jonathan approached. The driver was a tall and slim boy of around eighteen. He wore a Grim Reaper costume, his hood pulled back to reveal his slightly spiked red hair. Riding with him were two blonde girls dressed as Playboy bunnies and another guy who was apparently supposed to be Hugh Hefner, dressed in silk pajamas, slippers, and a red smoking jacket. Being only a child, Jonathan didn't know who Hugh Hefner was *or* what a Playboy bunny was. He just thought the man was wearing his pajamas for a costume and that the girls had dressed up like big rabbits with panty hose that looked like nets. They were all laughing and drinking out of silver and red cans. As the Grim Reaper pumped the gas, the man in his pajamas and the two rabbits went into the service station. Jonathan thought they were all walking funny and were really loud. He noticed that the man in his pajamas kept putting his hands on both of the big rabbits' behinds as they walked.

Jonathan couldn't stand it anymore. He had to go to the bathroom badly. He walked in right behind them and stood there on the newly mopped floor by a rack of potato chips.

Just a second or two after he stepped inside, a white Durango streaked by on 76 into town, its hazard lights blinking. It turned right at the traffic light on the corner one block west of the station, disappearing down Calhoun Street.

CHAPTER 15

Faye Crenshaw knew that Guy should have brought her daughter home at least an hour ago. She stood looking out her kitchen window at the Welch house next door. Guy's van had been sitting in the driveway for a while now. Usually, he would have Wendy back home by nine whenever she visited with Zachary, but tonight was the carnival at school and she didn't want to ruin the kids' fun. Maybe Guy had taken them both inside and they were sitting on the living room floor eating candy and talking about all the games they had played or goodies that they got. She hoped that Guy wasn't letting them watch any scary movies. Earlier, Faye had been flipping channels and found nothing but zombies, vampires, wolf men, and a dozen other celluloid beasties, all designed to keep little kids up at night. She would have a hard enough time getting Wendy to sleep tonight without her being brainwashed by the TV.

Her husband, Lewis, lay on the sofa in the living room. He had been asleep for an hour now. He was *always* asleep. As dependable as clockwork, he would come in around six every night, eat supper, watch the news, and be totally dead to the world by nine. Usually, she would put Wendy to bed and tuck her in herself. Lewis did it every once in a blue moon, but he usually left it to Faye. From the way he was snoring, tonight would be one of those nights.

Faye picked up the cordless from the kitchen table and called Guy's number. She stood there against the counter, the phone to her ear, and peered out the window. The lights next door in the family room and the kitchen were not on. Zachary's bedroom was dark as well. That seemed odd. If Guy and the kids weren't in one of those rooms, where were they?

She let the phone ring at least ten times. Long enough to realize no one was going to answer.

Something wasn't right.

"Lewis," she said aloud, laying the phone back on the table. "I'm going over to Guy's to get Wendy. Be back in a minute."

Lewis said nothing. He just snored, as usual.

Walking over to the coat rack by her kitchen door, Faye grabbed a light sweater and slipped it on. Making sure that the button on the back of the knob wasn't depressed so that she wouldn't lock herself out of the house, she stepped out onto the small porch. It was on the side of the house and it faced Guy's driveway. Standing there, she wrapped her arms around herself against the chill. The crisp night air caressed her about the ears and across her cheeks.

No sound came from Guy's house. No light had come on yet. No television flickered across the sheer curtains that adorned the windows.

"Weird. Really weird." Faye said to herself, walking down the stairs, across the drive, and onto the strip of dead grass that separated their yard from Guy's.

The van was right in front of her on the far side of Guy's driveway. There was a double carport on his house but he only used one of the stalls now. Connie had always used the other one. Since she had been gone, Faye had never seen Guy park on her side even once. She and Lewis never let on to him that they had noticed it, but they had.

Faye's blonde hair wrapped around her face, tossed by the breeze. She pulled it away as she walked closer, noticing that there was *something* leaking from beneath the van. Something that Faye guessed must have been motor oil. It glistened in the light from the streetlamps and had run down the sloped driveway all the way to the sidewalk. It looked like the lines of a road map etched in black against the concrete.

It seemed like she would have noticed an odor. Stopping at the van's rear door, she *did* smell something.

The scent of burnt motor oil would have been instantly recognizable to her, largely due to her father working on engines the whole time she was growing up over in Bishopville. What she smelled now was not the familiar odor from her childhood. It was a coppery scent. A strong and distinctive coppery scent.

She looked down at the glistening dark lines that had run from beneath the van, noticing now that they were not black as she originally thought.

They were red.

Her heart felt like it suddenly dropped into the pit of her stomach.

It was blood. A *lot* of it.

Slowly stepping over the crimson streams at her feet, she found herself on the driver's side of the van. The first thing she noticed was that something covered the concrete right beside the driver's door. It was sparkling in the dim light like a thousand tiny diamonds. Upon studying it, she saw that it was glass - the type of glass that they put in automobiles so that it would shatter into tiny pieces in an accident, thus not being able to cut someone to ribbons. The driver's door still appeared shut, but the rear passenger seat door behind it stood wide open. Its window was still intact. The driver's window was not visible through the tinted glass of the rear door.

"Good God, what happened here?" Faye said lightly to herself as she stepped around the rear door to see the front of the van.

She stopped in her tracks and felt her breath leave her.

Guy Welch was in the front seat. He was in a reclining position, his feet stretched out across the center console and his back against the driver's door. The back of his neck rested right on top of the line of jagged glass that stood in the bottom of the window frame, the head hanging back out of the van at an impossible angle. His throat had been ripped open from ear to ear, leaving a yawning hole that looked like a second mouth beneath his chin. Blood had run backwards down his upside down face, dripping onto the driveway where it ran downhill to the street. His eyes were still open wide...just like he was staring at something.

"The little bitch you came for is gone," said the voice of a child from behind her. "She ran away before she pissed her pants."

Turning around, she saw Zachary sitting on the front porch steps. He was covered with Guy's blood. A small, red cased knife was in his hands, and he turned it over and over again, studying it as he spoke to Faye without looking at her.

"Of course, I'll catch up to her soon. Then, she'll die alongside the bastard-runt within her."

She could do nothing but stare at the boy. He stood up and faced her, his eyes as black as night and the knife still in one hand.

"So are you just going to stand there, woman? Do you not want to cry out? To ask me what's wrong?" he asked.

Faye *wanted* to speak. She wanted to ask where Wendy was. She wanted to ask why her next-door neighbor was hanging out of his van window with his head nearly severed. She wanted to ask all of these things, but she could not. She began to back up, looking back over her shoulder to judge the distance between herself and her kitchen door. If she could get to Lewis in time she would be okay. The two of them could go and find Wendy. Zachary...or whatever the thing that *looked* like Zachary in front of her was...said that she ran away. If that were true, they would find her. They would find her and bring her home.

"Thinking about trying to make a run for the house, Faye?" the child asked, stepping closer to her. "Think you can make it before I catch you?"

She kept backing up. The back of the van was right beside her now. The grass that separated the two yards was twelve feet behind her.

"Let's race, Faye," Zachary said. "There's always the chance you might make it. Then you and your husband could go look for that little bitch as you wish."

She was almost to the grass now - just a couple of steps more. The boy was coming across the driveway, stepping through his father's blood and leaving crimson footprints as he came.

"First one to the porch gets to keep breathing," he said. "Whaddya say, Faaaayye?"

Turning on the ball of her right foot so abruptly that she thought she had twisted her ankle, Faye broke into a run for the light that glowed through her kitchen window. Her heart was hammering against the inside of her chest. She knew not to look back. Not to look back into the face of whatever hellish demon lived with the first grader from next door. A scream came from within her that made her feel as if her lungs were about to burst.

Not five feet away from the porch steps, the scream was abruptly silenced.

Inside, Lewis Crenshaw slept on.

CHAPTER 16

Neal and Tiffany had to ring the doorbell three times at Melissa Grayson's house before she let them in.

"Thank God the both of you are here," she said as she opened the door. "Did you see him anywhere on the streets on your way over?"

Neal shook his head. "No. Not a sign of him. There are at least three police cruisers out there looking for him now."

Melissa looked past Neal, out through the glass storm door and into the dark neighborhood.

"We have to find him soon," she said." Before someone else does. If you could have seen him, you would understand what I'm talking about. Come in, come in."

As soon as they stepped inside, she immediately locked the door behind them. Neal and Tiffany saw that her living room floor was littered with a sea of newspapers and handwritten notebook pages. Melissa sat down among them and began to dig through an old shoebox that was filled with yellowed news clippings. They both noticed that her hands were trembling slightly and that her face was pale.

Like she's seen a ghost thought Neal.

"He's already hurt someone, Melissa," said Tiffany. "It was at the school carnival. He injured one of his teacher's eyes. She's lost it for sure. He started talking out of his head, and then he smashed a classroom window and ran off."

Melissa stopped her mad search through the clippings and stood up. "Jesus, Tiff. I'm so sorry."

A gauze bandage was wrapped around the front of Melissa's right foot. From underneath it, a red stain had spread out on the surface of the white fabric.

"Is that what he...did?" Tiffany asked, pointing to the bandage.

Melissa looked at her wrapping job. "It's not that bad," she said. "I'll live. The next person he runs into might not be so fortunate. God, if you could have seen him. He looked and sounded like Jonathan, but he was.... something else. Something evil. The thing that he talks to at night...I think it's *inside* him now."

Neal let the words sink in.

Something evil - inside his son.

Taking a seat on the couch, he put his head down into his hands. He looked up at Melissa, his chin resting on his knuckles. "I just told Tiffany that…there was more to all this than what any of us would want to believe," he said. "I'm not a strong believer in the supernatural or things that go bump in the night, but this…this, damn it, is making me consider things I wouldn't normally have given a moment's thought to."

"He hasn't heard noises or voices in months," said Tiffany, sitting down next to Neal. "He's been a perfectly normal kid."

Melissa reached down and picked up a newspaper from the top of the stack she was reading earlier. She opened it and began to flip through it.

"Maybe he just wasn't *telling* us," she said. "He's had nothing but lecture after lecture since it all began. Perhaps he decided that if we didn't know about it, we couldn't correct or punish him for it."

Neal thought about it. He knew Jonathan could keep a secret if it meant being scolded. Tiffany did too.

"I told you both that I had something to show you. It might be reaching…but nothing else makes any sense."

She was still flipping pages of the *Sumter Item*, finally coming to the page she was searching for. She folded down the half of the page she was interested in, grabbed her glasses from the table next to her and put them on.

"The *Item* ran a Halloween issue this week," she said. "There is an article here about the origin and history associated with All Saints Eve, All Hallows Eve, Samhainn, or whatever name suits your religion or belief. After I read it and let it sink in, I realized that it's not that far of a reach to relate it to what's happening right now. When I say right now, I mean *tonight.*"

Neal and Tiffany said nothing. They sat there listening as Melissa began to read the article out loud.

"The ancient Celt's, Pagans, and Druid priests of old world Scotland, Ireland, and England believed that this night was the one night when the veil between the world of the dead and the world of the living was at its thinnest. Some called tonight a Celebration of the Dead or a Festival of Fire. The Celt's knew it as the Eve of the Celtic New Year."

Melissa scanned down the article a few paragraphs and kept reading.

"Common rituals for the Eve of All Saints were bonfires, originally known as bone-

fires, set with piles of bones from slaughtered cattle. These protective fires were kept burning in the fields through the night. Villagers offered up the best of their Autumn harvest to ward off the return of lost souls and swarms of wandering spirits, seeking to return to the places and homes where they had once lived. The voices of the dead filled the air above the burning fields, thriving on the fear of man and seeking out those who were weak of heart or not powerful enough to resist."

Neal reached for Tiffany's hand. He took it within his own and squeezed it reassuringly. "So what you're saying, "asked Neal, "is that you think this dead boy has *come back* tonight?"

She looked up from the paper.

"From what history tells us, if there truly is a time when the souls of the deceased wish to walk the earth, it's tonight. You know, I remember studying this in school but I always dismissed it as folklore or parables passed down through the ages. If there's even the smallest bit of truth to what I've read or what I learned from my history books, then I think it offers a damn good start at explaining all of this."

"Voices of the dead," Neal said, quoting what he had just heard. "Thriving on fear and seeking out those too weak to resist. Is this what's happening to Jonathan?"

"He's filled with fear, Neal," she said. "You know that, especially after all those weeks of night terrors. Who could be weaker...more susceptible...than a five year old boy, alone in his bed and scared of the dark? If this person or *thing* that he's been in contact with has been waiting to cross over into our world, then tonight just might be show time."

Tiffany was putting it together. "Feeding on his fear," she said. "He was *terrified* of Miss Kemp at the school. He said she yelled at him. Before he went into that room, he was fine. Then, he got scared. That's when we heard her scream...and he...changed."

Neal listened on as Melissa replied to his wife.

"Exactly," she said. "Maybe this *child*, or whatever it is, wants to extract some sort of vengeance for being treated badly. If it preys on fear or uses it to communicate with Jonathan, maybe it was biding its time until just the right moment. Don't you see? It might have been waiting for him to be so consumed and vulnerable with fright that it could literally use him as a doorway — a doorway into the world of the living."

"Melissa, do you hear yourself?" Neal asked. "I know that there's something out of our control pulling the strings here, but *dead* people coming back to life?"

"I know you probably think I've lost it," she replied. "I'm supposed to be the damn doctor here and I sound like I need one. Neal, I really wish I had something more logical to go on...but I don't. All I know is that this whole ordeal has been simmering for months now and I'm afraid that tonight it reached its boiling point."

The comment brought silence from all three of them. Then, Melissa began to dig through the shoebox filled with papers again. She pulled one out and laid it on the table beside her atop a pile of others she had placed there before Neal and Tiffany had arrived.

"A few years back," she said as she continued digging, "I was commissioned by the city to assist in writing a historical retrospective of Sumter County. I'm sure you both have heard about it. It was quite a bit of work, but I did turn over a lot of facts about this area that a lot of residents probably don't even know. Most of them are in these clippings in this box. The microfilm at the library goes back to the late eighteen hundreds. During my research, I printed off enough old newspapers to wallpaper a house."

Neal and Tiffany looked on. Melissa pulled one yellowed clipping from the box and reached out to hand it to them. Taking it in his hand, Neal saw that it was the front page of what was then called the *Sumter Daily Press.* The date on the paper was April 30th, 1913. In the center of the page was a poor quality black and white photograph of several children, both boys and girls of what appeared to be ages six through their teens. They were all sitting on the porch steps of what looked like an old farmhouse. Some had blonde hair and some had dark. They were dressed neatly in white shirts and black pants or skirts. None of them were smiling.

"You see the headline for that day?" Melissa asked.

Neal put the article in between himself and Tiffany so that she could read along with him. The black print above the photo said:

Immigrant Children find home with Local Farmer.

"The child that has been speaking to your son is most likely one of the children in that photo."

Neal and Tiffany looked up, their eyes telling Melissa that they wanted to hear more. She grabbed another handful of clippings from the floor and shoved them in the box.

"We can talk about the rest while Neal drives," she said. "Jonathan is out there somewhere. We need to find him fast."

CHAPTER 17

The sound of a child crying just outside his kitchen door woke Lewis Crenshaw from his sleep. He thought he was dreaming at first and lay there with his eyes still shut as the sound went on and on. Then, his eyes popped open and he sat up on the couch, realizing that what he was hearing was not inside his head.

It was right outside his kitchen door.

"Faye!" he called out, rubbing his eyes and slipping his feet into his loafers that lay on the floor beside him. "Faye, c'mere!"

She did not come, nor did she answer.

"Shit." Lewis muttered to himself. She must have gone upstairs and lain down to watch television in the bedroom.

He stood and walked into the kitchen, yawning as he went. He had come in straight from work and hadn't even changed into his lounging pants and T-shirt. He still had on his slacks and button down dress shirt from the day, both wrinkled as hell from rolling around on the couch.

Pulling back the curtains on the kitchen door window, he peered out onto the leaf-strewn lawn. He saw nothing. The crying was coming from the left of the small porch just outside of his view. Reaching over to the switch by the doorframe, he flipped on the porch light.

Sitting on his knees in the dead grass with his back to Lewis was little Zachary from next door. He still had on his Blue Power Ranger costume, all but the mask. It looked like he had bloodstains covering him from head to toe.

Lewis opened the door and stepped onto the porch. "Zachary?" he said. "What's wrong little guy? You hurt?"

Then he noticed that Zachary was kneeling *over* something that lay on the ground in front of him. Something that wasn't moving. It was face down on the lawn and covered in blood. The wind picked up a clump of what looked like blonde hair and made it dance about.

It was Faye.

"Sweet Jesus!" he exclaimed, rushing down the stairs. "Faye! Faye!"

He reached her lifeless form and fell onto his knees beside Zachary, rolling her over onto her back. Her eyes were open wide and her lips slightly parted. A thin trickle of blood ran from the corner of her mouth.

Beside him, Zachary cried harder and harder.

The red handle of a Swiss army knife protruded from the right side of her throat, the blade embedded to the hilt. The grass beneath her head was dark with blood.

"No, no, Lord, no." was all that Lewis could manage to say. He put one hand out, intending to pull the blade from his dead wife's throat, but pulled back. He couldn't bring himself to do it. He turned to Zachary and grabbed the boy by his shoulders, turning him so they were face to face. Wiping the tears from the child's blood streaked face, he looked into the boy's eyes.

"Zachary. Who did this? Did they hurt you too?" he asked, his voice trembling horribly. "Are you cut anywhere? Where's Wendy and your dad?"

The child was crying so hard that he was having trouble speaking. The words came out in a jumble that Lewis could hardly understand.

"Don't…make me…swing…I didn't want to…made me…do it."

Lewis ran his hand across the boy's hair and pulled him tightly to him. "Calm down, calm down. It's okay," he told him, wishing he had someone to hold *him* and do the same. "Please, Zachary. Take a deep breath. I need you to tell me if you saw who did this and *where* your dad and Wendy are."

Zachary wiped his running nose with a bloodstained sleeve and tried to halt the tears streaming from his eyes. He attempted to speak again.

"I…I…didn't want…"

Lewis held onto him, not wanting to look down at Faye's body; the body that had been alive when he had lain down on the couch earlier; that had slept next to him every night for the past eight years.

"Zachary," he asked again. "WHO…. did this?"

The child screamed out "I'm sorry! Please, don't make me swing! He made me…I didn't want to hurt her! He made me! He made me kill her and daddy both!"

Lewis felt numb. This wasn't happening. It wasn't.

"Z…Zachary," he stammered. "What did you say?"

The boy hung his head down, tears still flowing. "I killed my daddy! I killed him because he made me! He was going to make me swing! Please don't let him find me again! I don't wanna hurt no one no more, Mr. Cren-shaw!"

Lewis didn't know what the child was talking about. Had he gone mad? Looking up, he glanced over his shoulder at Guy's van that sat in the driveway next door. From where he was kneeling, he could make out the blood on the ground and the shattered safety glass. There was no sign of his daughter anywhere.

Good God, what if she's dead too?

"Where is Wendy?" Lewis demanded of the child. "Tell me, Zachary! Please! Where is she?"

Zachary raised his small blood covered hand and pointed down Cuslidge Street. "She ran off...that way."

Lewis looked down the dimly lit street and then back to the boy. "Is she okay?" he asked, his eyes pleading for Zachary to say *yes.*

"She has the...boy who talks funny with her," the child said. "She's safe...with him...as long as Father doesn't.... find her."

Lewis had no idea what the boy was talking about.

"Who is Father, Zachary?" he asked, lightly shaking him. "What in God's name is going on here?"

Zachary's tears had still not ceased. He looked Lewis straight in the eyes and said "He was inside of me and he...made me hurt.....Mrs. Crenshaw. He...made.... Jonathan hurt that lady at the...carn...carni-val. He wanted me to hurt...daddy. He would have done...bad things if I...didn't."

"Where is this *Father* now Zachary?" Lewis demanded. "Can you tell me? Is he near?"

"No." replied the boy. "He's gone to hurt more people. To make them pay for what they did to him. He can be in any place he wants and in more than one place....at a time. He's been in Jonathan...me...and he wants Wendy and the funny talking boy."

Lewis was still struggling trying to process this incomprehensible flow of information as hard as he could, but he was totally lost. He couldn't make any sense of it.

"Zachary," he said. "What does this *Father* want with Wendy and the *boy* you say is with her?"

Zachary wiped his nose again with his sleeve and told Lewis the an-swer that he really didn't want to hear.

"He wants to kill them. The boy mostly, but if he's with Wendy when Father finds him…he'll kill her too."

CHAPTER 18

As Neal turned onto Broad Street and headed for the center of town, Melissa leaned forward from the back seat and held the worn article up under the Durango's dome light. Tiffany turned to look at it. It was the clipping with the photograph of the children that she had shown them back at the house.

"This is something else I wanted to show you." she said. "You see this guy in the back?"

The big man stood on the porch behind the group of un-smiling children, off in the corner where he was just about out of the shot. Tall and large-chested with incredibly muscular arms, he looked to be in his late forties or early fifties. He wore a pair of dark pants with suspenders holding them up across his white and neatly pressed shirt. A gray and full beard adorned his stern face, and his equally graying hair lay slicked across his forehead, vanishing beneath the wide brim of a dark hat. His eyes were no more than dark slits, as if he had been looking into the sun when the photo was taken. In his right hand he held something that looked almost like a coil of rope. It was hard to make out.

"Who was he?" asked Tiffany, looking up over her shoulder into Melissa's eyes.

Melissa dug through the box again, speaking as she did so. "He was a prosperous land owner in Sumter, heavily involved in the church and a model citizen for the community. He took in this group of children who were here from overseas."

Neal was trying to scan the streets for his son, drive, and comprehend what he was hearing all at once. "From overseas?" he asked. "How did that come to be?"

"They were homeless." replied Melissa. "Some were orphans, some were street kids or runaways - a little of everything. They had stowed away on a ship out of England heading to Charleston Harbor. The ship docked on the Ashley River to unload its cargo and the kids tried to slip off the docks without being noticed. Of course, the Harbor Master discovered them before they could get anywhere. The original plan was to have them sent off to Beaufort. There used to be a large school for runaway and homeless children there. The man you see here in the photo was there the day the ship came in. He had been at the docks picking up some farm equipment that he had ordered. He offered the Harbor Master a healthy sum if he would forget about Beaufort and allow them to return to his farm here in Sumter. Well, the offer was accepted and the children, not knowing any better, were happy to go with him. They thought they had found a home."

Tiffany hadn't quite formed a connection in her mind yet. "You told us before we left the house," she said, "that one of these children may be who Jonathan is talking to at night. What significance does this man make?"

Melissa pulled another clipping from the box and handed it to Tiffany. "Take a look and you'll see." she said.

This article was also on the front page, but dated November 14th, 1914. The photo at the center was that of many men in suits. They were surrounding an old barn with shovels in their hands. What appeared to be white sheets were spread on the ground all around them. An inset photo at the bottom featured the same chiseled and bearded face of the man who stood in the background of the other photo Melissa had shown them. The man who had adopted the children. When Tiffany saw the headline, she began to understand where Melissa was headed with her story.

Farmer Charged with 7 Counts of Murder

"He made the community think he was doing a noble deed by giving these kids a home." said Melissa. " But what he did was basically use them as slaves. He molested them, beat them, and raped them. Made them work until they were half-dead. He had a wife who tried to intervene, but he made life hell for her and eventually she just let him do what he wished."

"What happened to him?" asked Neal.

Melissa was digging in the box again. "Well, the whole situation ended badly. After his wife died of tuberculosis, he began to molest the children even worse. There was one child managed to get away from the farm. He slipped away while the other children were working and headed for town. Once he was there, he told people what had been happening to his adopted brothers and sisters. From what I've read, he tried to convince a deputy to return with him. The deputy thought the boy was pulling some sort of prank and dismissed it as just that. Feeling like he had failed and that the old man would harm the others once he realized that he was missing, the boy returned to the farm and continued working. The deputy, having a little bit of time to think about the story, changed his mind and decided to investigate the boy's claim after all. Sadly, it was a day too late."

Tiffany and Neal were clearly involved in the tale unfolding before them. They listened anxiously in silence.

"According to the reported history, the old man somehow found out that very same night that one of the children had exposed him. None would come forward and confess, so he began to kill them one by one. When the authorities showed up the following morning, they were all dead."

"My God." said Tiffany.

"It was awful – a dark spot on the reputation of a quaint Southern town," Melissa said. "People wouldn't speak of it for years afterward."

"These children," Neal asked. "They would have had the English accent Jonathan told us about, right?"

"Yes, any one of them would certainly have the accent." Melissa replied. "The only thing that worries me is…the way Jonathan spoke to me on the porch. He didn't speak with an accent. He almost didn't even sound like a child. He was filled with rage, hatred, and sarcasm. He said he was *much more* than just a boy and that he wanted to make me *pay* like the others."

Neal turned his eyes away from the road a second and glanced back at Melissa. "Pay?" he said. "Hell, that's what he told us back at the school right before he smashed through the window. He said something about all of us having to pay - something about *pity the little ones who suffered* and *the bringers of pain being judged.*"

Melissa's eyes widened at Neal's statement. She looked back at the clipping in her hand and shuffled through them.

"He said *that?*" she asked as she looked. "He used those words exactly?"

"Well, maybe not exactly, but pretty close." said Tiffany.

Melissa was intently studying a clipping.

"Jesus," she said aloud. "I didn't want to think…"

She went silent, still reading.

"What?" asked Neal. "Didn't want to think what?"

"It has to be," said Melissa, as if she were speaking to herself. "No child would…say those things."

Neal slowed the Durango to a stop in the middle of Broad Street. He turned around and faced Melissa, a look on his face that pleaded for an answer. Tiffany had the same look.

"Melissa," he said. "Would you please tell us what you're talking about, for God's sake?"

Looking up from the papers in her hands, Melissa stared out the rear windows into the darkness. Then, she turned her attention back to Neal and Tiffany.

"The field that Jonathan ran to that night," she said. "Who owned the property?"

Neal thought for a minute, then he remembered.

"Weatherford - Stuart Weatherford. He owns several acres back there - the old barn and house up on the hill above it. I think his uncle owned it all originally and Stuart inherited it. He's got to be in his eighties now. He moved up to Charlotte so the place is kind of run down. I don't know if there's anyone else in the family that even cares about the property."

Melissa looked Neal straight in the eye.

"The tobacco barn," she said. "That's where Jonathan was heading, right?"

"Yes. Why?" he responded.

She held up the clipping of the bodies draped in sheets spread out on the ground around an old barn.

"Look familiar?" she asked.

Neal grabbed the paper from her hand and stared at it. He felt his breath stop for just a second.

It was Weatherford's barn - the barn that Jonathan was trying to reach. The same oak tree, though somewhat smaller, stood out behind it, the rope swing hanging from its limbs.

"Shit, that's the place," he said. "There's the tree and the swing right there. It's the same damn place."

Melissa pointed out the picture of the bearded man on the page.

"His name was Darius Weatherford. He was sentenced to death in the electric chair for his crime. Half of the community showed up to watch him fry. The day he was executed, the local constable read a speech aloud to all of the townspeople in attendance. It's printed here in this article."

Tiffany and Neal both scanned down to the last couple of paragraphs on the clipping. There, they found a quote that made their blood run cold:

Pity the little ones who suffered and the ones who caused the suffering. The bringers of pain shall feel such torment as they have delivered, and be judged by a greater power than we.

Neal looked up at Melissa while Tiffany kept reading the paragraph over and over in stunned silence.

"Those are...exactly the same words that Jonathan spoke back at the carnival."

Melissa nodded. "I figured as much when you tried to repeat them to me a moment ago," she said. "Weatherford's eulogy. The last thing he ever heard."

"So you think that instead of a frightened child's spirit, this...man... is what has...taken our son?" asked Tiffany. "That he's using his body to...hurt people?"

"To *kill* people, if we don't find him." replied Melissa. "He may have killed already for all we know. Weatherford left this world hating the people who stopped him. When Jonathan said everyone would *pay*, he may have been talking about Weatherford's retribution."

Neal hit the steering wheel with his closed fist and hung is head, having nothing to say. He felt powerless. He asked another question, his mind filled with them - too many to comprehend.

"The *accent* that Jonathan said this child had. Do you think it was Weatherford all along coming to Jonathan pretending to be a child? One of the immigrant children he killed?"

"Either that," said Melissa, "or one of the children *did* try to reach Jonathan before Weatherford did. They found the bodies of seven children. According to the records, Weatherford adopted *eight*. Count them in the photo and you'll see. One wasn't accounted for."

"Any ideas on that?" asked Neal.

"I don't quite understand that part of the puzzle yet," said Melissa. "Or some of the things he spoke about on my porch earlier."

"So this Darius character hitched a ride? You're saying he piggy-backed here through this dead boy...like a fucking computer virus?"

Melissa slowly nodded her head. "Well, that's not the exact analogy I would have used, but yes. Exactly like that."

"The swing at the barn." said Tiffany. "What about the swing?"

"That's a mystery too. I can't significantly attach it to anything yet. At any rate, I have a feeling that come morning, were going to have answers to *all* of our questions, but they might not be very pleasant ones if we haven't found Jonathan."

Neal turned around, shifted into drive, and swung the Durango into a U-turn. He floored it and headed east, back the way they had just come.

Tiffany and Melissa both knew where they were going - Weatherford's tobacco barn.

CHAPTER 19

The big man behind the Shell station counter wore an Atlanta Braves baseball cap and had a bushy mustache. The name *Tom* was stitched on his shirt pocket. Tom had given the bathroom keys to the guy in the Hugh Hefner costume and the two girls dressed as bunnies. Laughing and hanging onto each other, they all staggered out the side door and around the corner to do their business.

Once they were gone, Tom saw Jonathan standing there next to the snack stand in his blood stained Spider-Man costume.

"Well, hello, young man," he said to the child. "Where did you come from?"

Jonathan still had to go. He hoped that the people with the keys would hurry up. The big man talking to him from behind the counter seemed nice, but Jonathan was scared to talk to him. What if the child-thing wanted him to hurt the man? He didn't want to hurt anyone anymore. Not after what he had done at school and at Doctor Melly's house.

"Cat got your tongue, buddy?" asked Tom. "You look a mess. Where are your folks?"

Jonathan just stood there, his legs crossed tightly so that he wouldn't wet his pants and embarrass himself.

The big man stood up, the wooden stool beneath him creaking in relief as he did so. He stepped up to the counter and leaned across it on his elbows to get a better look at Jonathan.

"Is that blood I see on you, kid? You hurt?" he asked. "You need me to call somebody for you?"

Jonathan figured that the man named Tom would not yell at him or hurt him. Surely the child-thing wouldn't wish for him to hurt such a nice man. Feeling like he was about to wet himself any second, he decided to speak.

"I...got to pee bad." he said.

Tom laughed lightly and nodded toward the side exit. "Oh, well, the bathrooms are right outside that door to the left," he said. "I just let some other folks go use them, but if you can hold on just a minute, I'm sure they'll be right out."

Jonathan's face was twisted up in an expression that Tom knew meant he *wasn't* going to be able to wait. He now had both of his small hands holding himself between the legs, trying to hold back the inevitable.

"You...ain't gonna make it, are you?" asked Tom.

Jonathan shook his head. "No sir." he replied.

Tom came from around the counter and opened the side door, motioning for Jonathan to step outside.

"C'mere and I'll show you where I go when the bathrooms are full." he said.

Jonathan didn't question him. He had to go so bad that he didn't care anymore. Hands still over his crotch, he ran in short steps out the door and onto the concrete sidewalk that surrounded the Shell station. He stopped and looked up into Tom's face questioningly, waiting for the big man to tell him where to go next.

"Walk right down to the corner of the building there, buddy," said Tom, pointing toward the dimly lit area at the end of the sidewalk. "Just step over behind that dumpster and do what you have to do, okay?"

Jonathan looked at the dumpster and then back to Tom.

"I was gonna do it in the bushes, but...I only do it outside when my daddy tells me I can." he said.

Tom laughed a little, his gut jiggling. "Well, if your dad asks, you tell him that old Tom from the East Side Shell told you it was okay to pee outside when it was an emergency, okay?"

Jonathan nodded in agreement and took off for the dumpster. He didn't need any more convincing.

"When you finish, we'll call your folks!" Tom called after him as he went.

Tom could hear the drunken teenage girls through the women's room door as they laughed and giggled. Hugh Hefner was just as bad as they were. Damn kids weren't even old enough to be drinking. As long as they did their business, paid for their gas, and left without trying to buy any alcohol, he could deal with it. He turned and saw that the kid in the Grim Reaper outfit had finished pumping gas and was headed toward the building. With one more glance at the dumpster to make sure the little boy was okay, he stepped back inside and resumed his position on the wooden stool behind the counter.

The Grim Reaper came in the door digging beneath his black shroud for the money in his jean pockets. He walked up to the counter and laid down a twenty and three ones.

"Twenty dollars worth at pump four and a pack of Camel Lights, please sir." he said.

Tom looked at the young man with his spiked hair and pimply face. "You eighteen?" he asked.

The Grim Reaper seemed annoyed by the question. He reached back beneath his shroud and pulled out his wallet, flipping it open and lifting it up so Tom could see his license.

"Last Tuesday, big fella." said the kid, a smart-ass tone developing in his voice.

Tom nodded and reached above his head to grab the smokes. He slid them across the counter and took the money. He could tell that the Grim Reaper had been tipping the old bottle just like Hugh Hefner and his bunnies out back. The smell was the first thing to give it away, not to mention the fact that none of them were could walk very straight.

"Happy Halloween." said the kid, turning and walking out the side door toward the restrooms.

Tom thought about telling him to drive carefully, but decided not to even open his mouth. The sooner they were all back in the Jeep and on down the road, the better.

He was thinking about filling up the soft drink cooler when he heard laughter erupt from around the corner of the building. At first, it was just one voice. Then, others, both male and female joined in. It had to be the Grim Reaper and his buddies.

"What the hell?" Tom said aloud to himself. He stepped over to the side exit and walked out onto the sidewalk leading to the restrooms.

Jonathan was standing in the pale light by the dumpster. He looked like he was about to cry. Hugh Hefner and his bunnies had come out of the bathrooms and caught him right in the middle of relieving himself. Of course, they couldn't mind their own business. Being half lit, they decided to taunt the little fellow. The Grim Reaper had walked up on them and joined in on the fun. Tom could barely see the boy, for the teenagers had crowded around him so they could antagonize him better.

"Boy, what a little pecker you got there, Spider-Man." laughed Hugh Hefner. "Maybe Santa Claus will bring you a real dick this Christmas."

The Grim Reaper couldn't resist either. "Didn't your mommy tell you not to pull your wee-wee out in front of people?" he asked.

Jonathan said nothing. He was trembling slightly, wishing he could just disappear.

He could feel himself starting to get hot and clammy again, just like he had been earlier.

"Oooh, his is almost bigger than yours." laughed one of the bunnies, slapping Hugh Hefner on the back of his red velvet smoking jacket. Hefner told her to kiss his ass.

The Grim Reaper went on. "So you like whipping your little wiener out in public, do you, Spider-Man? Well, I think the girls here would like to see it again. Whaddya say, my sexy bunnies?"

The girls laughed, so drunk they were holding each other up. "Yeaaah, baby, let's see it again." they both said.

Tom had heard enough. He could see the boy was about to burst into tears. The poor kid was shaking from his head to his toes.

"That's enough, guys!" he said loudly. "Leave him be. I think you need to get your asses back in your vehicle and take it somewhere else."

The Grim Reaper looked at Tom and smirked. "Well, I'm so sorry if I scared the little wimp with the eenie-teenie weenie." he said.

"Put a sock in it and hit the road." Tom demanded, walking toward the group.

"C'mon, Russ. Fuck this. Let's go." said Hugh Hefner, grabbing his bunnies by the arms and turning to head back toward the front of the station. One of them nearly tripped over her own feet when she tried to walk. The other one had a case of the giggles.

The Grim Reaper shook his head. "Pansy asses," he said, reluctantly falling in behind them. "All scared of the Pillsbury Dough Boy, I guess."

He brushed past Tom, bumping shoulders with him. Tom let it slide. He knew he was big enough to flatten the punk if he wanted, but there was no need to. The little kid in the costume was scared shitless and no doubt ashamed as hell now. He wanted to make sure he was okay and hopefully find his parents.

"Fuckin' kill joy!" he heard from behind him. He turned and saw the Grim Reaper standing beside the Jeep with his middle finger extended. Hugh and his bunnies were crawling in the passenger doors.

"Go park your big ass back on that stool and eat another doughnut!" the Reaper shouted, starting to laugh and lighting a cigarette.

Ignoring the remark, Tom turned back around to check on the child

standing behind the dumpster. He felt kind of bad now about even sug-
gesting that the boy pee outside, now that this had happened.

The boy was gone.

He had *just* been standing there. Now, there was nothing but dead
grass and the wet spot on the side of the dumpster where he had urinated.

Where in the hell did he go?

While Tom was standing there puzzled, the Grim Reaper turned to
open the door to get in the Jeep. He reached up and grabbed the steering
wheel and lifted one leg up to step in. Then, he heard a small voice come
from behind the door that stood open right in front of him.

"So you disguise yourself as Death himself in hopes that he will pass
you over tonight?"

The Reaper was turning in the direction of the voice when he heard
one of the bunnies cry out "Russ, it's the kid!"

Standing up on the side rail and looking down, the Reaper saw the
little boy in the Spider-Man costume. The only thing in between the two
of them was the door itself. The kid had walked right up behind him and
he hadn't even heard him. He had to have come from around the front of
the Jeep, but, how in the hell could he have made it from the dumpster to
here so *fast?*

"Trying to scare me with your big talk, little boy?" the Reaper
laughed, taking a drag on his cigarette and looking back at his buddies.
"The boy with the world's tiniest pecker is trying to scare me, guys."

He turned back around to further taunt the child and caught a quick
glimpse of a small tennis shoe clad foot thrusting forward. There was a
fraction of a second where he heard the impact of the child's kick in the
center of the door that separated them…then, the cold metal of the door
frame struck him in the face. It made impact with tremendous force, split-
ting his skull open from chin to forehead. His cigarette flew from his
mouth and landed on the gray concrete. The door swung back open from
the impact so violently that it nearly ripped from its hinges. The Reaper
fell face down on the edge of the green concrete island that the gas pumps
rested on, a crimson pool spreading out around his head.

Hugh Hefner and the bunnies began to scream.

Tom reached the front of the station just in time to see the Grim
Reaper hit the ground, his black shroud billowing about as he fell and
settling down upon his unmoving body. At first, he didn't know what had
happened. Then, he saw the blood and he heard the screams.

"Shit." he muttered to himself, picking up his pace and heading for the Jeep.

Hugh Hefner crawled across the center console and out of the driver's door so fast that he stumbled, falling on top of his friend. He caught himself with his hands on the concrete and felt the stickiness of blood spread across his palms.

"Russ? Russ? Oh, holy livin' shit, Russ!" he was crying, attempting to see if the Reaper was breathing. Behind him in the Jeep, the bunnies screamed on.

Tom had reached the other side of the vehicle and he pulled open the door, motioning for the girls to get out. They were panicking and he didn't need that. Things looked like they were about to be bad enough without two frantic young girls yelling their heads off.

"Get inside, now," he demanded. "There's a phone by the door. Call an ambulance. I'll see to your friend until they get here."

The girls leaped out onto the concrete, looking back at Tom over their shoulders as they ran into the station. One of them pointed toward the front of the Jeep and stopped, her eyes wide with fright.

"It was the fuckin' kid!" she shouted. "He did it!"

Tom shot her a look that made her turn and go inside with the other girl. He hurriedly made it around the back of the Jeep to see what the situation was with the injured boy.

What he found stopped him cold.

Jonathan stood there motionless by the front left tire, surveying what was going on in front of him. The Grim Reaper was dead. It looked like someone had split his face open with a shovel. Blood was running down the concrete island he rested on and across the pavement.

Jesus, a little kid couldn't have done that! Tom thought.

Bent over the body was the guy in the smoking jacket. He was sobbing violently. He had one hand rested on his dead friend's shroud and the other on the gas pump right beside him.

"Russ, man, don't die on me. Shit, man, you can't do this, you just can't." he was saying.

Tom took a step toward them. "Son - he's gone. All we can do is call someone now." he said.

The teenager didn't respond - he only sobbed more, not taking his hand from his dead friend's back. Jonathan still stood like a statue not three feet away from him.

"You.... wanna tell me what...happened?" asked Tom.

The kid looked up and wiped his eyes. He looked into Tom's eyes and then back to Jonathan. His expression turned from one of sadness to one of anger. He pointed his finger at the child in the costume and yelled aloud.

"He did it! Miserable little fucker! He...kicked the door into his fucking head!"

Tom was kneeling beside the panicking Hugh Hefner before he could complete his accusation. He gently put an arm around his red velveteen shoulder and spoke calmly, keeping one eye on Jonathan the whole time.

"Okay, okay, let's chill for a moment, okay?" he said, trying to comfort the kid. "Son.... there's no way a little fellow like that could have done this, at least not without an ax."

"But he DID!" shot back the sobbing young man. "Jesus, we all saw it. He kicked the door.... and Russ was halfway inside.... the Jeep. He fucking killed him, man!"

Tom didn't know what to say. The Reaper had indeed been hit by the door, or *something*, hard enough to bust his head open like a melon. For the life of him, he just didn't see how the child could have generated power like that, even if he *had* kicked the door closed on him.

Glancing at the blood that was spreading out across the concrete from the Reaper's head, Tom saw the still burning Camel cigarette lying on the concrete. It was burnt about halfway down and was resting about two inches away from the growing pool of red.

It was just about to be snuffed out by the warm blood when a small hand reached down and plucked it from the ground.

"Damn shame to waste." said Jonathan as he raised the cigarette to his lips and inhaled deeply.

Tom stood up and looked at the child. The sobbing young man crawled back away from his dead friend. He staggered to his feet and began to back up, his eyes never leaving Jonathan.

"See? There's something...not right with that kid! Something's not right!" he shouted.

Tom took a step toward the little boy and reached out to him with an open hand. He had never seen a child act quite like this; much less smoke a cigarette without having a coughing fit.

"Okay, little fella," he said gently. "I don't know your name, but if you'll come with me, I'll call your folks and we can find out what happened here."

The child smiled at him, his eyes narrowing to nothing more than slits. He took another puff on the cigarette and spoke.

"My name will be known come morning. Rest assured, it will be known by *all* here in this festering pile of shit you call a town."

Tom couldn't believe what he was hearing. He stepped a little closer to the boy.

"Please, come with me, okay? I won't hurt you." he said.

Jonathan began to laugh. "Hurt me? No, I don't believe you will, Tom. As a matter of fact, I think *I'll* do all the hurting tonight if it's alright with you."

Tom knew now that something *was* wrong with the boy. The girls and the kid dressed like Hefner hadn't been lying. Now, the only thing he had to figure out was what the hell to do with him.

"Oh, you don't know what to do now do you, Tom?" said Jonathan. "Not that often a six year old kills someone in your parking lot and lights up afterward, is it?"

Tom glanced over at the station and saw the girls on the phone. He prayed that the ambulance and police would get here quickly. Something was happening here that he didn't understand, nor did he want to.

Jonathan reached out with his right hand and pulled the gas nozzle from the pump.

"Don't do that!" exclaimed Tom. "Please, kid, just put it back."

Jonathan stepped up and flipped the lever to start the pump. It whirred into life, the counters all flipping to zero. The *begin fueling* light blinked on.

"Don't do what?" he asked, pointing the nozzle at the Grim Reaper's sprawled body. "It's All Saint's Eve, Tom. What better night for a bonfire? If the wind sees fit to do my bidding, perhaps I can rejoice in burning the flesh from *everyone's* worthless bones before this night is done."

He depressed the trigger and gasoline spewed forth from the nozzle, soaking the Reaper's body and mixing with the blood on the ground. It ran beneath the Jeep and toward the station itself. It flowed toward the street and swirled around Tom's shoes. The kid in the smoking jacket turned and ran as fast as he could down Highway 76 Street toward town.

"Don't!" shouted Tom, stepping forward and grabbing the gas nozzle in his large hand, pulling up on it forcefully in an attempt to snatch it from the child's grip.

But the child held on.

"I had it first, Tom." said Jonathan, jerking the nozzle back with such force that it ripped the skin from inside Tom's fingers. Before the big man could try anything else, Jonathan had slid his hands down to the black hose that fed into the back of the steel nozzle and swung it in a wide arc around his head. The tip of the nozzle struck Tom across the forehead, sending his cap flying and ripping through skin. Blood ran down into his eyes. The blow had made him dizzy - terribly dizzy.

"You will pay, Tom," said the child. "The little bitch who walks these streets somewhere tonight will pay too when I find her, but for now, you will do."

Tom fell back against the Jeep and tried to wipe the blood from his eyes so he could see. The smell of gasoline filled his nose. He tried to step forward and slipped on the wet concrete, falling down hard next to the Reaper. When his eyes cleared, he found himself staring into the dead kid's split-open face. He looked up at Jonathan one last time.

"You are among many who will die, Tom," said the child, taking one last drag on the Reaper's Camel, its orange tip glowing bright. "It's only just beginning now."

He flipped the burning cigarette from his fingers.

As Tom lay there and watched the white stump with its smoldering tip flip end over end toward the gas-covered ground, he wished to himself that he hadn't traded first shift for second tonight.

Then, amidst the screams of the bunnies and the evil laughter of a little boy, he burned.

CHAPTER 20

Across town on Marshall Street, little Aimee Jacobs walked into her sleeping parents' bedroom and blew their heads off with a shotgun. Her father had always kept it locked in the cabinet in the foyer, but Aimee simply had smashed the glass and removed it. It hadn't hurt one bit. She returned the shotgun to the cabinet, went back to her room, and got back in bed.

Over in Cypress Oaks, Ron Styles found his son Chandler standing in the family garage with the portable welder turned on and the welding gun in his hand. When Ron attempted to take the welding gun away from him, the boy plunged the welding rod through his left ear where it penetrated his eardrum and plunged into his brain. Chandler laughed when he squeezed the trigger on the welder and heard the buzzing sound coming from the inside of his father's head. The smell and the big mess it made was the only part he didn't care for.

On Liberty Street downtown, Perry Giordano was locking the door of his Pizza shop while his twin daughters, Teresa and Ellen, watched from the front seat of his truck. He had cranked it so the heat could circulate, loaded the girls up, and stepped back over to the door to lock up. When Perry turned around to return to the vehicle, he found that the girls were behind the wheel. The last thing he saw before he died was the grill of the white Chevy coming at him and his daughters' eyes glaring at him from above. Then, there was nothing but a crushing impact and the sound of glass and his own bones breaking.

Half a mile away on the Broad Street Extension, nineteen-year-old Wal-Mart Employee of the Month Stan Harrelson was hard at work collecting stray shopping carts from the parking lot. Suddenly he found himself surrounded by a small group of children. There were two little boys around seven or eight years old, and three girls who appeared to be between six and ten. When Stan asked them where their mommies and daddies were, they all began to laugh — then they swarmed over him and beat him to death right there next to the plastic patio furniture and gas grills.

Near the west side of town on Bultman Drive, Shelly Walker was having a Halloween pajama party for her little girl, Scarlett, and three of her second grade classmates. The girls sat in front of the fireplace roasting marshmallows while Shelly read them some ghost stories. When bedtime finally came, they were told to take their two pronged forks they had been using for the marshmallows and put them in the sink. Instead, they opted to put them into Shelly, over and over and over again. Once that was done, they all went to sleep.

Two blocks over on Folsom Street, eight-year-old Trey Comerford was watching television in the den when his mother, Diana, came in and told him it was time to take a bath. When he protested, she told him he would get a *"beating"* if he didn't get up and go *"right now"*. Reluctantly, the boy got up from his chair and walked over to the fireplace. There, he removed the poker from the fireplace tool set. With one swing, he cracked his mother's skull open. She fell to the floor and didn't move again. Trey sat back down in front of the television and continued watching his program, keeping the poker by his side in case his father showed up.

Sumter Fire and Rescue arrived at the Shell station on the edge of town within five minutes of receiving a hysterical call about a child who was killing people. They arrived along with the police, but found no child anywhere nearby. What they *did* find were two flaming piles of flesh that used to be eighteen-year-old Russell Watford and big Tom Selznick. There was enough of the kid's face left to tell it had been split wide open by something. The fire was luckily put out just before it ignited the pumps, and the horrified girls were taken home to their parents. The only evidence that could be found to verify their story was on the ground leading from the pumps to the wooded area behind the station.

Dozens of small, bloody tennis shoe prints.

CHAPTER 21

As they neared the outskirts of town, Tiffany pointed toward the sky. Above the darkened outline of the houses in the distance were intermittent flashes of blue and red lights.

"Look, Neal, look."

"I see it." said Neal, turning right at the intersection of Calhoun and Broad.

Tiffany knew that something awful had happened up ahead. Something that, more likely than not, had involved her little boy.

Remembering a short cut from Broad over to 76, Neal whipped the Durango down a dimly lit side street that was lined on both sides with seemingly abandoned homes and businesses. It was one of the oldest and most rundown sections of town.

Melissa was peering across the seat, trying to get a glimpse of what was happening in the distance. She, like Tiffany, immediately associated the trouble with Jonathan. The child was capable of doing anything right now. She thought about how impossibly strong his grip had been on her porch. If he had gotten his hands around her throat he could have…

"Neal, stop the truck! Stop it now!" shouted Tiffany.

The sudden cry and squeal of rubber on the pavement snapped Melissa out of her thoughts and back to the matters at hand. The Durango slid to a stop, turning slightly sideways before completely doing so.

Tiffany was pointing toward a vacant lot on the right side of the road. A sign from Re-Max Real Estate stood at the front of the lot, proclaiming *Commercial Property for Sale*. The square piece of land was covered with dead weeds that stood about knee high. A chain link fence separated it from the two metal buildings on either side of it which also had *For Lease* signs in their windows.

"What is it?" said Neal, looking out at the lot. He couldn't see anything.

"The headlights!" exclaimed Tiffany. "Swing the headlights over toward the center of that lot!"

Neal backed the truck up a couple of feet and turned the wheel to the right, angling his high beams to illuminate the middle portion of the weed-strewn patch of ground.

"There." said Tiffany, pointing to where the beams fell across something that Neal and Melissa hadn't noticed at first.

A little girl in a ragged crimson gown stood motionless in the middle of the darkened lot. Her face was painted a ghostly pale and what appeared to be a long, black wig danced gently in the night breeze. Her eyes were focused straight ahead.

"Shit." said Neal, not taking his eyes from her. "Is that the little Crenshaw girl? The one who lives next to Guy?"

Tiffany nodded her head. "It's her. I saw her at the carnival earlier. Her name is Wendy. She left with Guy and Zachary, remember?"

Tiffany opened the door to step out onto the pavement. Melissa's hand came across the seat and gripped her shoulder lightly. Neal had reached across as well and caught her by grabbing onto the elastic band around the bottom of her jacket.

"Tiffany, she might be...like Jonathan."

Melissa looked through the streaked up windshield at the girl standing in the tall weeds. "He's right, Tiffany. Look at her face. There's no expression there. No fear. No anger. It's blank, just like your son's was when I opened the door to him earlier. Jesus, I seriously doubt that any little girl trick-or-treaters would be out here on the highway just standing in a dark lot."

Tiffany saw what Melissa meant about Wendy's face. This was certainly not the same laughing and happy child they had seen a few hours before. She was like a statue, just standing there and watching.

Melissa removed her hand from Tiffany's shoulder. "Let me try to speak to her," she said, looking to Neal and Tiffany both for their approval. "I won't get close to her, I swear. Just let me try to see if she's okay."

"How in the hell are you planning to do that?" asked Neal, looking at Melissa as if she had lost her mind. "After what...Jonathan *did* to you back at your house? You said yourself he was as strong as any adult was. And what about Guy and Zachary? If she was with them, then *where* the hell are they? I know Guy wouldn't have just dumped her out here and left her."

Melissa was calm. " Neal, take it easy. Like I said, I won't get within her reach. I'll stand right here on the side rail of the truck."

"No, Melissa." said Tiffany as she turned around and tried to keep her from getting out. "It's not a good idea. We can tell the police down the road that she's here and they can come and get her."

Melissa took her eyes away from the girl long enough to look them both in the eyes. "I *know* it may be a bad idea, okay? You forget, I'm a doctor. Jonathan has been *possessed* by someone. That point is very clear. This girl has got to be connected in some way, shape, or form to what's happening to him. All I want to do is initiate a response from her - just enough to see if she's being controlled by the same murderous son-of-a-bitch that I'm afraid has gotten inside your son. If she seems to be effected in the same way he is, we can get the hell out of here, I promise. Once we know, then we won't have to feel guilty about just leaving her out here alone in the dark."

Neal had turned and was watching the small form out there in the dead weeds. Melissa could tell he still didn't like the idea. Tiffany had gone silent, leaving the final word to her husband. She released her grip on Melissa's arm.

Neal turned around and asked, "What if she's baiting you? What if she lures you to her and then...does something to hurt or kill you."

Melissa depressed the door handle and the rear passenger door popped open. "She won't get the chance, Neal. Besides, if she rushes us, you'll just have to run her over with the truck here. Deal?"

Neal shook his head in disbelief that he was even having such a discussion at all. "Go, then," he said, "but watch yourself. If she makes a move this way, you get your ass back inside and close the door."

Melissa gave a quick nod to the both of them and then put her right foot out onto the Durango's side rail. Gripping the top of the truck with her right hand, she hoisted herself out and up into a standing position. The cold night air swirled about her, an unpleasant contrast to the truck's warm interior. The chilly breeze lifted her hair and blew it across her eyes. She quickly brushed it away and looked out at the child in the empty lot.

Wendy Crenshaw's red gown billowed all around her, riding on the same cold wind that had tossed Melissa's hair. Her eyes were still fixed on some point straight ahead and her hands hung limply at her sides. Her face was nothing more than a small white oval amidst the dark, flowing hair of her wig.

"Wendy?" called Melissa, watching to see if the girl's attention would turn to her at the sound of her name. "Is your name Wendy?"

The girl kept looking forward, not moving at all.

Melissa tried again. "Please, honey, can you talk to me? If your name is Wendy, at least nod your head."

The girl did nothing. She didn't even blink.

"Wendy, I'm looking for a friend of mine. He goes to school with you. His mommy and daddy are in the truck here with me and they want me to help them find him. His name is Jonathan."

The girl's head turned toward Melissa at the sound of Jonathan's name. Her eyes, though still blank, widened a bit from the slit like position they were in just seconds before.

Melissa nearly lost her grip on the truck and fell when the head turned in her direction.

Careful what you ask for, sweetheart. You may get it.

It was what she had often heard from her father. There was no better example of a phrase being proven right than what was happening now. She tried to shuffle through the dozens of questions in her mind that she had for the child. She was just about to ask one, and then Wendy beat her to it.

"He is with Father," the small voice said, thick with an English accent. "Father has taken use of him for retribution and to kill those who would defy him."

Melissa's eyes grew wide with realization and fear. She felt her heart begin to beat rapidly inside her chest. The *accent.* The child was speaking with the *accent* that Jonathan had described, yet it now confirmed her worse fear. The voice that Jonathan had spoken with on the porch earlier was definitely not the one she was hearing now.

"Can you tell me...who you are?" asked Melissa, her voice shaking a little more than she would have liked.

The girl stood there silent for a moment, and then she spoke.

"I am the one who was left behind - the one who carried word to the masses of his cruelty. I am the one who Father despised above all others."

Melissa could hardly believe it. She felt excitement, fear, confusion, and pity all at once.

"What is your name?" Melissa asked.

The girl raised a hand and pointed at herself. "I am Conner. My birth name, I do not remember."

"Your birth name." asked Melissa. "You mean, your *last* name?"

The girl slowly nodded.

"Yes. My birth parents passed on after an accident in Kent. My adopted name was Conner Weatherford from the time I arrived here until my passing."

Melissa asked the question that she really didn't want an answer to.

"Conner Weatherford? Adopted son of Darius?"

Nodding again, the girl replied "Yes."

The eighth child? Could it be?

The girl cocked her head slightly, the way a dog does when its interest is peaked. "I am the eighth, Melissa," she said. "The one whose body was not covered neatly with a white shroud for the newspaper photo that you keep in your little box."

Melissa realized that the girl knew her name. On top of that, she seemed to have known what she was thinking at that exact moment.

"You.... you know my...name," she said. "How do you know my name?"

"I know many things, Melissa," the girl said. "I know you want to know what happened in that tobacco field. That you want to know about me."

Melissa nodded. "Yes, Conner. I do. Jonathan's parents would like to know too."

Neal killed the Durango's engine. He and Tiffany had been able to hear only bits of the conversation so far. When he heard what Melissa had just asked the child, he reached up and flipped the ignition off. Tiffany sat beside him, her window rolled down and her clenched fist up to her mouth as she listened intently. Neal had already rolled his down a bit, but now he opened it even further.

The girl continued her conversation with Melissa.

"You would like to know where Wendy is?" she asked.

Melissa nodded to her. "Yes, I would."

"She is unharmed and still within this body," the girl said. "I need physical form to interact with others. I came to her at the school after the woman was hurt. It was there that I took her as host."

Melissa was trying to piece everything together in her mind and ask questions at the same time. "Conner, did you visit Jonathan at night?"

"Many times." came the reply.

"Can you tell me why?" Melissa asked.

"He was an innocent. He was young, as I am. I needed to show him something. I meant him no harm in any way."

"What did you have to show him?"

"Where my bones are spread across straw and yellowed with age. The place where I left this world. I had called to him on the night he went into the field."

"The field." asked Melissa. "Jesus, is that where you..."

"Died?" the girl said. "Yes. I died there. Father did not include me with the others. He mercifully dispatched my brothers and sisters with his rifle. I was put on the swing."

The swing.

"What is the swing, Conner?" Melissa asked. "Jonathan always talked about it."

"Father put me in the swing when he discovered I had gone into town to seek help. He taught me my final lesson there. He placed me on the seat and bound my hands and feet with twine. Then, he set the swing into motion while he stood alongside it with a wooden tobacco stick. Each time I would swing by him, he struck me brutally. When he grew bored with that, he opted to use his whip instead. He was very good with the whip. It was my special punishment. He knew that I had exposed his cruelty to the townsfolk."

Melissa listened on.

"He untied me and left me to die on the ground beneath the swing, having not an inch of my body left untouched by the stick or whip. Then, he called the others down to the barn one at a time, telling them he had something to show them. Once there, he shot each of them in the head. I lay there on the ground slowly dying and watched him steal the life from every one of them."

Melissa slowly shook her head in disbelief and disgust. "I'm so sorry, Conner," she said. "But, why were you left behind while the others were taken by the authorities?"

"Father had left me there for dead among the corpses of the others. He returned to the house, assured that no one would be coming to see what he had done until at least the next day. I managed to make my way into the barn, pulling my body along like a wounded and dying animal. I crawled into the loft in which I had sought refuge on so many afternoons. It was where I found my peace. It was where I died and where my bones still lay. I was simply overlooked."

Melissa silently hoped to herself that Neal and Tiffany were hearing all of this clearly. She didn't want to break the roll she was on by leaning down and checking on them.

"Conner, I'm still confused," she said. "Jonathan told us about you - about how you were beaten and mistreated. We all thought it was your influence that was making him so skittish and nervous when it came to being punished or corrected."

The girl nodded. "I fear that I am responsible for that. I meant not for it to happen, but he became frightened that the cruelties I suffered would eventually befall him."

Melissa continued on, each question being followed by a response that was putting more and more of the past few months in perspective - like lost pieces of a bizarre puzzle finally falling into place.

"Conner, we all originally assumed that if you had suffered at the hands of an adult, then it was your spirit that wanted to achieve retribution through Jonathan."

"I only wanted his help. Vengeance is not what I sought."

"But he has hurt people tonight, Conner. Judging from what seems to be happening down the road and all the lights, he may have hurt or even *killed* others. Surely you didn't want this."

The pale face turned in the direction of the dancing blue and red lights in the distance, then back to Melissa.

"No, I did not, and I am most regretful for the fact that others have been hurt. It was not meant to be that way. I should never have gotten Jonathan involved. Father has him now and I am sorry to be the cause of it."

Melissa felt Tiffany reach up and gently take hold of the hand she wasn't hanging onto the truck with. It was a reassuring touch that she needed.

"After all these months you say you talked with Jonathan, why did Darius Weatherford, and not you, take him?" asked Melissa.

"I intended to use Jonathan as host with no intention of harming him or anyone else, but Father reached him before I could. His spirit is much stronger than my own. He took him at the school, just before the woman was hurt. I could do nothing, so I took this girl child's form in the hopes that I could stop Father before he could bring any harm to anyone."

Melissa knew that no *child's* spirit would have forced Jonathan to do what he did. "How did Darius get here, Conner?" she asked.

"I meant not to let him back into this world of the living when I came," the girl replied, "but he pursues me in death as relentlessly as he did in life, intent on tormenting me for eternity. He does not wish for me to ever rest and will go to great lengths to see that I do not. Earlier tonight, I attempted to warn the man named Guy Welch that Father had entered his son, Zachary. It was to no avail. He would not listen to me. Guy is now dead, as is the mother of the girl whose body I now inhabit."

Inside the truck, Neal and Tiffany glanced at each other in silent shock. Tiffany put her head down into her hands and closed her eyes tightly, wishing that all of this insanity would just stop. Neal reached across and comfortingly placed his hand on her shoulder, listening in awe as the conversation between Melissa and Wendy continued.

"Father has left Zachary, at least for right now," she said. "But Father can be in many hosts at once. He comes and goes as he wishes. He has been in many other children tonight and will move from one to another at will. Several people have died. Jonathan has now killed as well, and will again if Father wishes."

Tiffany began to sob. Neal pulled her to him and held her close. Melissa stood there and listened in fascination as well as horror.

"If Father crosses paths with me again tonight, he will do his best to harm me," the girl said. "If it means killing this child or any other form I am within, he will."

"Conner - why has Darius singled out Jonathan and focused on him so?"

The girl looked into the distance toward the flashing red and blue lights at the Shell station on the edge of town. "The other children he has used as host tonight have served him well, but Jonathan is his favorite," she said. "He is afraid, weak, and highly open to suggestion. Father will remain within him and continue to grow stronger and stronger by the hour. There may be moments when Father's influence may wane and the boy will briefly realize that something is happening to him - but as the night goes on, Father will totally consume him, body, mind, and soul. Eventually, the boy that was your Jonathan will be gone and only Father will remain."

"How do we stop him?" asked Melissa, afraid of what the answer might be.

The child turned her face back to stare at Melissa. She paused for just a moment, and then spoke. "While Father's spirit is still within it, the host body must be incapacitated or killed. Then, it must be quickly burned to prevent the spirit from escaping and taking another host."

Melissa felt a wave of numbness slowly begin to grip her, creeping down to her very bones. She could hear Tiffany saying *no, no, no, no* to herself from the inside of the vehicle.

"Can we do...anything else?" Melissa asked.

The girl's dark and seemingly lifeless eyes turned away toward the highway out of town, then back to face the headlights that illuminated the lot.

"I must leave now and go to the place of my death," she said. "I will be at the barn in the Weatherford field. Father will come for me there. He is on his way now. The disturbance you are witnessing in the distance is the death and destruction he has left in his wake. He will come for me and then continue his onslaught throughout your town."

Melissa wasn't quite sure what Wendy was telling her and a look of puzzlement spread across her face. The child saw it, and offered one last statement.

"Should you meet me there, *you* can do what I came to Jonathan for in the first place and see that I am put to rest at last with my brothers and sisters. We may prevail if we face Father together. I pray that I see you there."

With that, the small form turned away.

"Wait, don't leave." Melissa shouted. "You can come with us."

As the red gown danced in the wind behind her, the little girl stepped from the light of the Durango's high beams and vanished quickly into the darkness at the back of the lot.

It was as if she had never even been there at all.

CHAPTER 22

Lewis Crenshaw knew if he called the police, they would think he was stark raving mad. He couldn't blame them. He would think someone was mad too if they called up with the story he had to tell.

Yes, could you send a car over to 401 Cuslidge Street? My neighbor's son just stabbed my wife in the throat with his dead dad's pocketknife and tells me that he's doing the bidding of someone he calls "Father". Oh, and my daughter, who I believe is also possessed, is missing.

He turned up the shot glass he had filled with bourbon and felt it burn as he drank it down. The warm sensation soothed him, but only a little.

Now what the hell was he going to do?

Zachary was still outside on the lawn, kneeling next to Faye's body and crying. The child's story was impossible to believe. With a trembling hand, he poured another shot and downed it, knowing that it wasn't helping a damned thing. He didn't care. Thirty minutes ago, he had been taking a nap and all was well with the world. Now, his wife was dead and his child was somewhere out in the dark roaming about alone and frightened. This just couldn't be happening.

Standing up from the table where he had been sitting with his bottle, Lewis tried to figure out how to handle the situation. It wouldn't be long before someone driving by saw Faye's body sprawled face down in the yard. If they missed that, they would be bound to see Guy's blood soaked driveway and what was left of him hanging out of the van window.

Whether they believed him or not, he realized he *had* to call the police. He just wouldn't tell them the part about anybody being possessed.

But then, what would they do to Zachary? Send him away to a home? A mental hospital?

Who gives a shit?

Lewis snatched the wall mount phone from its cradle and dialed the sheriff's office. He was pacing across the kitchen floor like a wild animal, the phone held tight against his ear. As he walked, he figured he would step over to the window and take a peek out to make sure the boy was still outside. The police would no doubt want to talk to him when they arrived. He reached out and pulled the curtain back, leaning down to look through the glass.

Faye's body was still spread out on the ground and now partially covered with dead leaves. Some of them were stuck to the dried blood in her hair that was blowing about her neck. Zachary was still there, but he was standing now instead of kneeling.

Right beside him was another child.

"Shit." said Lewis under his breath, hanging the phone back up. "What the fuck is happening here?"

A tall boy of about ten stood on the lawn next to Zachary. He had dark hair and was wearing a pair of sweat pants and a T-shirt. The kid was barefooted. He looked like he had just crawled out of bed.

Lewis took two big steps over to the kitchen door and yanked it open, stepping onto the porch. The two boys and his wife's dead body were only a few yards away.

"Excuse me, son, but you need to go home, okay?" he said, directing his voice toward the tall boy. "You don't need to be here right now."

The boy did not turn around. Zachary didn't either.

Lewis stood his ground on the porch and again spoke to the silent child.

"Look, son, I don't want to have to call your parents, so please just go back home."

The boy still didn't move.

Lewis was getting frustrated. His nerves were already shot and he was not in the mood to deal with another whacked out kid like Zachary tonight.

"Hey!" he shouted. "You hear me, boy? I said go home!"

There were another few seconds of silence, and then Zachary's voice floated back to Lewis on the cool night air.

"What if he doesn't *want* to go home, Lewiiisssssss?"

The sound of the child saying his name was like that of a snake hissing. Zachary had not sounded this way a few minutes before. He had been bawling like any other little kid his age would have been.

"Zachary?" was all Lewis could manage to say.

The small boy in the Power Ranger outfit turned around to face him, the taller boy following his actions and doing the same.

Lewis saw instantly that something wasn't right.

Zachary's eyes were as dark as the night. A grin was spread across his face that gave Lewis chills. The tall boy's expression was the same. Lewis recognized him as the son of Ronald Grooms, who owned a small electrical shop in town. He had seen the kid around town with Ronald on occasion, but never looking quite like this. Lewis knew that Ronald lived on the other side of Sumter. What the hell was his son doing walking around at night, all the way over *here* in his sleeping clothes?

Lewis began to back up on the porch, away from the two kids. Neither one moved, blinked, or showed any emotion. They just stood there...grinning as if they both knew some horrible secret.

"C'mon, Lewwiiiiisssssss." hissed Zachary. "C'mon out and play with us awhile."

Lewis had one thought in his mind that repeated itself over and over as he backed away.

Get away from them, Lewis. Get away from them, Lewis.

"Yes, Lewwiissssss. Can't you see how much fun your neighbor and your little Faye bitch had with us?"

This time, the voice came from the mouth of the tall boy.

"Sorry we woke you, Lewwiiissss..." began Zachary.

"...but you can go back to sleep in a just a few minutes," finished the tall boy, "for a long, long time."

They began to walk toward the porch.

Lewis turned around and pulled the door behind him open, then slamming and locking it behind him as he ran back into the kitchen. He glanced through the window in the door and saw that the boys were already coming up the steps.

Then he looked beyond his yard into the street.

"Oh, Jesus, no." he said to himself, his eyes growing wide.

Bathed in the light of the streetlamps, the silhouetted forms of at least a dozen children were slowly making their way down the sidewalks and through the yards on Cuslidge Street. Both boys and girls, they all walked at the same pace. As they got closer to the house, Lewis could see that they all had the same look about them that Zachary and the Grooms boy had.

"No, no, no!" shouted Lewis, turning and scrambling through the kitchen. He ran through the den and into the small room off the foyer that he had turned into his home office. Pulling open his top desk drawer, he dug madly through the sea of papers and found his Smith & Wesson. He pulled it from the drawer and snapped it open to check the chambers.

Empty.

He began to dig through the drawer again for the box of bullets he usually kept with the gun. As he searched, he heard the back door glass being smashed in. Then he heard footsteps on the kitchen floor.

"Shit, shit, shit!" he said to himself, pulling out another drawer. There were no bullets there either. Then he remembered. He had kept the gun and the ammo in his nightstand drawer upstairs for years. About a month ago, he had moved it downstairs to his desk drawer so he could lock it up. He had moved the gun, but he must have left the box of bullets *upstairs*. He had to get to that nightstand. He slammed the drawer closed and spun on his heels to run for the stairs.

Zachary and the tall Grooms boy were standing right in his office doorway, blocking the way out.

"Going somewhere?" asked Zachary.

"Perhaps to get your bullets, Leewwwiiiissss?" said the Grooms boy. "Is *that* were you're going?"

Lewis didn't know what to do. He could try to run through them. They were just a couple of kids. Surely he could overpower them easily enough. Then he thought about Guy and Faye, wondering why they weren't able to save *themselves*. Then, he thought of Wendy.

"Where...is my daughter?" he asked

"The little bitch who ran away?" asked Zachary. "The miserable runt rides inside her tonight, but I will deal with them very soon. You need not worry about her."

"What's happening?" screamed Lewis aloud. "Would somebody, for God's sake, tell me what the hell is happening?"

Zachary stepped forward. He looked up into Lewis's face. "You're about to die," he said. "*That's* what's happening, Lewiiissssssss. It's not that hard to figure out. It's a big party, all in your honor. Just take a look at all your guests outside."

Lewis looked out the window to his left and into the front yard. The sidewalk was lined with the forms of children. They stood motionless - waiting.

"No!" Lewis screamed, rushing toward the two boys and pushing out with his arms to knock them from his way. He felt the impact with their bodies and anticipated them falling to the hardwood floor where they would lay dazed while he made it upstairs to the bullets. Instead, he was met with a resistance that felt as if he had hit two full-grown men. He was shoved backwards with such force that he flew across his desk. The Smith & Wesson fell from his grasp and spun across the floor. Papers and pens went everywhere. The green domed banker's lamp shattered. Lewis landed hard on the floor against the wall on the other side of the desk, his leg bending under him at an impossible angle and snapping in two with an audible *pop.*

Zachary motioned to the Grooms boy to pick up the revolver from the floor. The tall child bent over and snatched the gun up. The both of them stepped around the desk to stand over Lewis, never losing the demonic looks that they had when he first saw them in the yard.

"Please...I'm hurt." managed Lewis, holding one hand up as if to fend the boys off. "My...leg is broken."

Zachary hoisted himself up and sat on top of the desk.

"Well, we can't have that, Lewwiiisssss," he said. "You know, they shoot horses that break a limb."

"But, we have no bullets." said the tall boy, holding the gun up and pulling the trigger repeatedly, the *click, click, click,* of the rotating drum filling Lewis's ears. "Looks like a pistol whipping will have to do."

"Yes, it's time to pay, Lewwiiisssss. Time to pay at last," said Zachary. "My friend here will do the honors."

With that, the tall Grooms boy leapt upon Lewis like a wild beast. Zachary sat there on the desk and watched in contentment as the Smith & Wesson rose and fell again and again and again and again and again.

CHAPTER 23

Neal wheeled the Durango into the Shell station parking lot, rolling his window down and coming to a stop next to a police cruiser. It was parked beside the building away from all the chaos out front. An officer was sitting in the car with his radio mike in his hand. While Tiffany and Melissa were watching the two covered bodies being loaded into the ambulance, Neal leaned out of his window and waited for the officer to finish his radio conversation. When he saw the mike being snapped back into its holder, he spoke.

"Sir, could you tell me what happened here?" he asked.

The officer looked at Neal and at his two female passengers as if he were annoyed that they were here. He stood from the seat of his car and walked over to the window of the truck. He was an older man who looked like he had very little patience and a zero tolerance for bullshit.

"I'm not sure if I should tell you anything at all," he said. "What I *can* say is that I think you need to get yourself and these two ladies here on home and behind closed doors as soon as possible."

Neal looked back at Tiffany and Melissa. They were both being silent, letting him handle this. He turned back to the officer and spoke to him again.

"Look, don't treat me like I'm Joe Citizen, okay? I *know* that a child was responsible for whatever happened here."

The officer's stern look turned into one of mild surprise. He stepped a little closer. "Sir, how do you know that?" he asked. "Did you see anything going on before those two poor bastards under the sheets were burned?"

Neal shook his head. "No, none of us did, but I believe it was *our* son that did this. We haven't seen him for over an hour. He took off from the school and we lost him."

The cop looked over his shoulder as the ambulance driver slammed the doors shut on the Grim Reaper and Tom's charred corpses. He turned and looked back at Neal, speaking in a lower tone, as if he were afraid someone might hear him.

"Your boy...he was the one who injured that woman at the carnival tonight?"

"Yes." said Neal. "I'm afraid so. We were told he'd been here by...a friend. Can you verify that? Did *anybody* see him?"

The officer looked to his left down 76 as it stretched out into the darkness heading out of Sumter. Then he turned and looked back toward town. "Some girls who where here claim a little boy did all this," he said. "Said he was in a red and blue costume. Spider-Man, I believe."

Neal sat there and listened on, amazed as the officer's words proved Wendy Crenshaw's statements true.

"Things are happening all over town tonight," he said. "That's why I think this is business best left to us. We've got around eight reported deaths so far. People are saying that children are responsible. They're saying that *kids,* for God's Sake, are killing their own families, neighbors, and friends. Now, with poor old Tom and the teenager who got cooked, it's a grand total of ten. Damnedest thing I've ever seen in my life."

Melissa leaned up across the seat so she could see the officer. "Have any of the children been...picked up or hurt in any way?"

The cop shook his head. "They tell me that a lot of them are in tears and don't know why they did whatever they did. Some of them have vanished. Some of them are in a catatonic state, just sitting there with whomever they killed. Groups of them have been seen walking the streets. Two rookies picked up a nine-year-old walking through the mall parking lot and said he went berserk on them in the back seat. Kid damn near ripped the metal screen between the front and back seat down with his bare hands. Five minutes later, he was as docile as a kitten."

Melissa looked at Neal and Tiffany, then back to the officer. "They don't know what they're doing," she said. "Unless it's a life and death matter, please try not to hurt any of them. Hopefully, this will all be over soon."

The officer crossed his arms and asked, "Well, since you seem to know so much, can you enlighten *me* on what in holy hell is going on?"

Neal lifted his hand up to cut Melissa off before she could speak. "You wouldn't believe it if we told you," he said. "The boy in the Spider-Man suit that you said did this. Did anybody see if he headed toward the highway out of town?"

The cop nodded. "Tracks are all we found, but they vanished about twenty feet into those pines behind the station."

Neal looked toward the trees that the officer was pointing at. Six acres of thick pines began right behind the Shell station. Beyond them was an unplanted field, then a canal ditch, and then their home. Weatherford's field was directly across the street from the house, just behind a patch of trees.

They all knew then, without a doubt, that he was heading for the barn, just like Wendy Crenshaw had said – and just like they had all figured he would do when they left Melissa's house earlier.

"Thank You." said Neal, stepping on the gas. The Durango's back tires spun on the asphalt for a second, then the vehicle whipped out onto 76 and headed for the city limit sign, leaving the officer standing there amidst the scent of melted rubber, gasoline, and burnt flesh.

There was nothing left of Jonathan Fowler.

Darius Weatherford had taken away what little will power that the boy had left and invaded his soul completely. The small costumed form in bloodstained tennis shoes that now stood in the gray dirt at the field's edge looked like Jonathan, but it was not him.

He already knew *they* were coming. That little bitch was on her way too with the bastard spirit-child within her. She would be here soon. Then, he would finish what he had started on the swing years ago. He would make sure that the traitorous child was damned to an eternity of unrest. It was what he deserved for squealing to the miserable sons-of-bitches in town. If the Jonathan child's parents or the bitch doctor tried to intervene, he would just have to kill them first and then deal with the girl, instead of saving them for later. Then, he could return to the darkened streets of Sumter to finish collecting his debt.

Stepping out across the dirt, he began to head for the tobacco barn on the field's far side. He could hear the two large and nearly rotted doors out front creaking in the light wind, the rusted hinges screeching in protest.

Swaying gently from the tree out back was the swing.

A hideous smile stretched out across the small face that used to belong to a little boy known as Jonathan. He picked up his pace, breaking into a run.

He had to get ready for the company he had coming.

CHAPTER 24

The blue Saturn coupe was headed west on Highway 76 at around eighty miles per hour. Behind the wheel was twenty-two year old Brett Parnell, who was late for an engagement with a young lady at Plum's Lounge in the Sumter Holiday Inn. He knew he was driving dangerously fast, but he was way beyond the city limits of his home town, Lynchburg, where the law would bust your ass for even *thinking* about speeding. Besides, there was a hot woman waiting for him and he had all intentions of doing everything within his power to get laid tonight.

He knew he was getting close to Sumter when he began to see the blinking red lights on the radio stations towers that loomed high above the tree line on the edge of town. The lights had always seemed ghostly to Brett - like the masts of a distant ship signaling for home against the lonely, silent canvas of the night sky. Seeing the towers reminded him that he didn't even have his radio *on*. He reached down and flipped the power switch on the in-dash tuner to "on", searching for a good station. As he continuously pressed the scan button, he kept glancing up at the darkened road ahead of him. He knew he was only about a mile from the 378 by-pass.

Finally, he tuned into a station playing something worth a damn. Averting his eyes from the radio, he looked back to the road for a second, then up into the mirror to make sure he looked presentable.

"Looking good, Parnell." he said to himself.

When he looked back down, there was a small girl wearing a red gown standing in the center of the road just ahead.

"Fuck!"

Brett jerked the wheel hard to the right, trying to avoid running over the child. The car swerved madly. The small red clad form was nothing more than a blurred shape seen through a window as the vehicle slid by. Brett realized he had lost control of it the very second he turned the wheel. With the sound of tires screeching on pavement mixed with his own scream ringing in his ears, he desperately struggled to keep the now spinning vehicle on the road. He felt as if he were on a ride at the county fair - the one that spun you around and around until you felt drunk. Only thing is, you went home after that ride. He knew he might not live through this one.

The Saturn slid a distance of about twenty-five yards, spun one last time, and slammed backwards into a ditch by the roadside. The impact rocked Brett forward, his head slamming into the steering wheel. He felt a tremendous sensation of burning pain travel up his spine and culminate in his neck. Then, everything was still again. The only sound he could hear was that of his own heart beating.

So much for getting laid he thought, finding it odd that such a thing would matter to him in the current situation.

He tried to move his head, but when the searing pain would not allow it, he began to realize that he was injured seriously; so seriously that he needed an ambulance. He tried to reach out for the cell phone that had fallen from its holder above the sun visor and landed in the passenger seat. It hurt like hell to extend his arm, but he managed to reach it.

He was about to punch in 911 when he heard the voice of a child. It was to his left and a bit distant.

"I'm sorry." it said.

Brett could not turn his head, but he rolled his eyes in the direction of the voice. What he saw was the little girl he had just nearly died trying to avoid. She stood down the road, no more than a red shape in the dark, facing the wreck.

"I meant not for this to happen," the child said." I cannot help you, for I have a task that must be dealt with this night."

With that, she turned and began to run, heading straight down the center of the darkened highway and then cutting through the tall grass on the right shoulder of the road. Soon, she would vanish into the trees.

"Wait!" he shouted, pain hitting him like a sledgehammer when he strained his neck muscles to do so. "Please, don't leave, kid!"

He thought he could barely hear the faint voice calling back to him from the distance. "There is nothing I can do, for they are stronger than I. Please know that I am sorry, but I must go."

Then, she was gone, leaving Brett wondering what in the hell she had been talking about.

Turning his attention back to the cell phone, Brett tried to punch in 911 again with shaking hands, but the phone slipped out of his grasp and fell to the floorboard. It slid up under the brake pedal and stopped.

"Shit!" exclaimed Brett.

The phone was only two feet away, but it may as well have been a million miles. There was no way he would be able to lean down to retrieve it, not with the injury he had just sustained. He turned his eyes back toward town to see if anyone was coming that could help him.

There was no one.

For the next few minutes, he unsuccessfully tried to make his broken body work. The pain was too much to bear. He was just about to pass out when he thought he saw someone walking down the roadside.

It was more than one person, and they were heading straight toward him.

They were children — at least eight or nine of them, slowly walking down the side of the highway. Though they were nothing more than dark shapes from this distance, Brett could tell they were just kids, spanning the ages of what looked like five to twelve years old. Some were in their nightclothes, some still wore their Halloween costumes, and some were naked. They moved along through the highway grass that lined the sides of 76 as if they were searching for something. The smallest of them, a nude boy of five or six, was out front. He stopped and froze in his tracks, looking straight at the wrecked Saturn.

Then, they all began to run straight for him, the sounds of their bare feet slapping across the asphalt.

Holy Shit! Brett thought.

Grimacing against the pain, he reached his seat belt and released it. With his left hand, he pressed the lever to open the driver's door. It wouldn't open. Maybe it would have if he could have put his full strength against it, but there was no way he could do it without blacking out.

The Saturn was resting backwards in the ditch at about a thirty-degree angle, its headlights pointing into the night sky. The twin beams were given substance by the swirling cloud of dust that had not yet settled around the wreck. Brett lay there, looking up at the stars and wondering what the hell was happening.

Then, he saw a small form pass in front of the car, blocking the lights for just a second.

"Christ." he mumbled, trying to open the door once more in vain. He turned his eyes back toward the front of the car just in time to see two more shadows rush by.

The children he had seen approaching along the roadside had reached him…and he sensed — no, he knew, that there was something horribly *wrong* with them.

"Car trouble?" said a small voice right outside his window.

Brett turned his eyes in the direction to face the nude little boy standing atop the ditch bank and peering down at him. His eyes were strange looking and he had something red all over his bare skin. It looked to Brett like spattered blood.

"Don't worry. My friends and I will help you out, Brett." said the child. "It'll only cost you a little."

Brett was wondering how the kid knew his damn name when another boy appeared. He was holding a small metal pipe in one red stained hand and had on a Bugs Bunny costume. Two girls followed, both in nightshirts. They giggled as they stood there peering at Brett, a heartless sound that was so bone chilling that it almost overpowered the pain he felt in his back and neck.

On the opposite side of the car, the other four children appeared along the edge of the ditch, all straining to bend down and get a better look. It was a girl and three boys, all covered in blood that Brett realized was not their own.

"You little sons of bitches!" shouted Brett. "What the hell is the matter with all of you?"

As the children slowly began to converge on the car, he suddenly understood exactly why the little girl in the red gown had told him she was sorry.

Tiffany saw the lights in the windows of their house as it came into view up ahead. She looked across the road and could see the dense patch of trees that Jonathan had fled into on that awful night many months ago.

"Almost there." she said.

It was then that she noticed two shafts of light shining at an angle against the night sky. It appeared to be coming from the left side of the highway. She could tell by Neal's expression and by Melissa leaning up and peering between the seats that they saw it too.

As they got closer, they saw more.

Children were standing by the roadside ahead — many children. They were all in a large group over by the ditch that the county had dug about a year ago. They appeared to be gathered *around* something.

"Jesus, there's a car in the ditch." Tiffany said, pointing to the front end of the blue Saturn that was visible behind the group.

"I'm not stopping," said Neal. "We have to get to that barn."

As the children broke their bizarre formation and turned to watch the Durango speed past, Neal saw the body they had been surrounding. It looked like it was torn to pieces.

"What is it?" asked Tiffany. "What did you see?"

Neal shook his head. "Nothing that we can do a damn thing about."

About two hundred yards beyond the wreck on the other side of their house, Neal pulled over onto the shoulder and turned to look at Melissa and Tiffany.

"I'm going to take it off road from here," he said. "It'll take us too long on foot. You and Melissa hang on to something. It's gonna get bumpy."

Tiffany reached up and grabbed the handle that was mounted above her window. Melissa sat back in her seat and gripped the armrest on her door tightly, keeping one hand on the back of Tiffany's seat to act as a brace. Neal reached down and shifted the Durango into four-wheel drive.

"Ready?" he asked.

Melissa and Tiffany both nodded.

Neal punched it, heading across the tall grass on the roadside and turning toward the tree line. The truck bounced along the downward slope for about twenty yards, cutting a path through the dead grass. When the ground leveled out, Neal turned to the left to run parallel to the trees, never even touching the brake. He was running at around forty-five, which wouldn't have been considered much on a paved road. But this *wasn't* paved and it was unfamiliar territory to boot. The truck was vibrating as if it were about to fly apart, the tires bouncing across the hard and uneven dirt.

"You okay?" Neal asked, casting a quick glance toward the two women. They both nodded but said nothing, keeping their eyes on the path ahead while they held on tightly.

The trees that were flying past on the right began to grow further and further apart from each other, finally giving way to a field of gray that stretched out for several acres. Neal hit the dirt and turned right, heading away from the highway and following the depth of the wooded area. He could feel the traction of the four-wheel drive kicking in as the truck moved through the loose surface.

"Where is it?" asked Tiffany, not seeing any barn or house ahead.

Neal was reaching a point where the trees began to curve to the right and he steered into the same pattern. "Not far," he said, never taking his eyes from where he was headed. "It's around this curve where the trees stop. I had to chase Jonathan straight through the center of all that thick growth the night he ran away. All I'm doing now is cutting around it."

Melissa was watching along the tree line as she listened to their conversation, straining to see if she could spot a small boy dressed in red and blue somewhere in there. All she saw was darkness.

"You both recall what Conner said back on the lot, don't you?" she asked. "Jonathan. . .may have to. . ."

She trailed off, not finishing her sentence. Neal turned around to look her in her eyes. "What?" he said. "Die? Maybe - maybe not. I'll deal with that problem when we find him."

Tiffany didn't want to hear any of this. She didn't want to think of having to take her son's life or of burning him alive to exorcize a murderous demon. There had to be another way. She just knew there had to be. It wasn't fair. What if the police reached him before they did? They wouldn't *intend* to hurt him, but if the influence of Darius Weatherford drove him to attack them, they would be left with no choice but to unload on him. They would shoot her baby.

She decided silently that she would take his life *herself* before she saw it come to that horrific of an end.

Shit!" Neal suddenly exclaimed. The Durango had started sliding rapidly sideways in the gray dirt, its right rear end heading for a pine tree at the fields edge.

"Hang on!" he cried out, reaching over and holding his right hand protectively across his wife's midsection as if to hold her in the seat while he managed the steering wheel with his left hand. Melissa let out a gasp from the back seat as she saw the trunk of the tree coming straight at her right door. She crawled across to the other side of the seat and held onto the back of Neal's headrest to steady herself. Tiffany closed her eyes and felt her breath stop in anticipation of the crash that she knew was coming.

It never came.

The Durango had not slid quite wide enough to hit the tree dead center. Instead, only the very back corner on the passenger side made contact, shattering the taillight and the glass in the rear double doors. Both women screamed when the impact came, but they stopped as soon as they saw that the contact with the tree had slowed the sliding vehicle just enough so that Neal could get it back under control. He veered shakily out into the field about thirty feet from the edge of the tree line and slowed to a stop, his heart pounding like a jackhammer. The dust cloud that lingered around them floated through the headlights like a ghostly fog.

"Damn, that was close." Neal cursed.

Melissa opened the back door of the truck and swung her feet out, sitting there sideways on the seat with her feet on the side rail.

"You okay?" asked Tiffany from the front seat. Neal had turned around to check on her too.

"Fine, fine," she said, running her hands back through her hair. "I just need to calm down a little."

She reached into her pocket and pulled a cigarette from the pack there, placing it between her lips and lighting it with a jittery hand. She took a long drag from it and looked up at the stars above, trying to slow down her heart rate. She was finally feeling it wind down a little when she heard Neal speak.

"There it is." he said.

She turned and looked in the direction that he and Tiffany were looking, straight ahead of the Durango.

The dust cloud still hung in the air, but as it began to clear, she saw something taking form in the distance. Had it not been for the truck's headlights casting reflections on a pane of broken and filthy window glass, it would have been almost impossible to see in the darkness.

It was Weatherford's barn.

As their eyes slowly brought the shape of the dilapidated structure into focus, they all were as silent as the grave.

Behind it, a huge oak stretched toward the night.

Flipping the cigarette into the gray soil beneath her, Melissa pulled her feet back inside the truck and pulled the door shut behind her.

"Let's do it." she said.

CHAPTER 25

Just moments before Neal Fowler steered his truck into the tall grass alongside the highway, Wendy Crenshaw had emerged from the trees along the southwest side of the field and was already standing in the open doorway of the Weatherford barn.

It would end here. It had to. Far too many innocents had suffered or died this night, as would many more if Father's murderous crusade continued. The voice of the child named Conner within her told her that the first step toward ending the madness would be to try to make a deal with Darius - to satisfy his undying need to torment and bring pain.

A sacrifice would do. A sacrifice of *himself* that Conner knew would surely mean death for the host body of Wendy Crenshaw.

He hadn't wanted that, but there was no other way to barter with Father, short of destroying him.

How ironic that in the beginning all he had wanted to do was show another child where his remains lay so that he could be buried and rest in peace with his brothers in and sisters. Now, he would wind up offering himself to save the lives of others.

Wendy stood there in the darkened doorway, aware of what was happening around her and inside her, but totally unable to control it. She felt like she was on a wild ride at the county fair, strapped into her seat next to a boy she had never seen before named Conner. What was so strange about it was that *Conner* was controlling this ride and the car that they were strapped into was her own body.

She heard something from behind her and turned toward the sound. It came from across the field to her left and was faint at first. Then, it began to get louder and louder.

It sounded like a vehicle.

The headlights of the Durango suddenly came into view from the direction of the highway. They were visible against the backdrop of the pines as nothing more than two bright, bouncing points of light in the distance.

What was left of Wendy in the small body realized that it was help coming. Conner knew that too, but he wished no one else to come to harm this night.

It was then that the voice came.

"So, the bastard spirit-child has come back home to take his medicine at *last.*"

The words had come from behind and above. Wendy spun around and looked upward toward the loft. The square opening above the barn doors was barely visible in the dark, defined only by the rotted remains of straw and hay hanging over its edges and clinging to spider webs in each corner.

Then, Jonathan Fowler was standing there, filling up the blackness of the lofts door.

"The worthless runt-child...finally." said the blood covered figure in the blue and red costume, placing his hands on the top of the small doorway and leaning his body out and over Wendy. "How sweet it will be to kill you...again."

An evil grin stretched across the small, twisted face as it stared down at the girl.

"I've *found* something up here quite interesting, my child," he continued. "Some bones wrapped in rat eaten clothing. It would appear that someone...someone of about your age...crawled up here and waited to die. Do you have any idea whose they may be?"

Wendy said nothing. She stood there, her small pale face turned upward toward the taunting figure that was speaking to her. She said nothing.

"Silence, child?" Jonathan asked, anger building in his voice. "You refuse to answer your Father, do you?"

Raising her hand and pointing at Jonathan with a trembling finger, Wendy spoke back to him in a firm and defiant tone.

"A godless killer and butcher of innocent children, you are, Darius Weatherford."

Jonathan laughed, letting go of the loft doorframe and kneeling down so he could see more her more clearly.

"Your words do not hurt me, nor does your opinion of me matter," he said. "Tonight, I am unstoppable as well as unmerciful. The injustices reaped upon me shall be repaid tenfold before I am through. *Your* end, though too long in coming, will be especially gratifying, my child."

The headlights were getting closer in the darkness. The sound of the truck engine was louder now. Only a few more moments and it would be here.

"Was taking the lives of the others not enough for you?" Wendy demanded, keeping her focus on the boy above her. "Why deny me peace? Have I not endured enough at your hand?"

Jonathan kept the demonic grin on his face. "*You* sold me out," he exclaimed. "*You* led the people against me, you disrespectful piece of shit. I saw the red clay on your shoes that evening from where you had crossed the hills to town, yet you would not confess to running away. Had you done so, then you and your miserable siblings may have lived."

"I was sick of watching my brothers and sisters being beaten, Father," said Wendy. "Just as I was sick of watching you teach your *lessons* on the swing. Don't you recall how we screamed? How we cried? How we slept on out stomachs at night because our backs were too bloody and bruised to lie on?"

Jonathan pointed down at her and ranted on.

"*I* provided for you! *I* put a roof over your head and clothes on your worthless hide! In return for my kindness, you dare to cry to the town about my teachings of right and wrong? You turned them against me and in doing so, brought all of this on yourself!"

"It had to end, as does the killing tonight." Wendy calmly said.

The boy above stared down at her, his chest heaving with anger but still listening.

"We must put to rest what has gone before. I know that you will not stop until you have what you desire most — to extinguish my lingering soul. If it means offering myself and this child to you to end the suffering of others tonight, then so be it."

Jonathan stood from his kneeling position, his grin growing even wider. Burning in his eyes, however, was a look of pure hatred.

"So be it, my young one," he said. "So be it, indeed."

With that, he turned and vanished into the darkness of the loft. In a matter of seconds, Wendy could hear the sound of the old wooden ladder creaking as he began to make his way down, rung after rung.

PART III

CONFRONTATION

CHAPTER 26

Neal slowed the truck to a stop twenty feet from the barn, switching on the high beams so that they fell across the open doorway on the building's south end. The interior of the dilapidated structure was now partially illuminated, but the far wall was still hidden in shadows. A ladder ascended from the dirt floor and vanished into the darkness of the barn loft.

There were no children to be seen. No Jonathan. No Wendy.

"I don't like this one damn bit." said Neal, straining to spot any movement or to hear anything.

Nothing - only emptiness and silence.

"Do you think he's in there?" asked Tiffany, never taking her eyes from the path cut by the headlights. "Maybe he isn't coming here. Maybe he..."

"No, he's here," said Melissa, stopping Tiffany before she could finish. "If Wendy...I mean, if Conner said Jonathan would be here, then he's here. If not, he will be soon."

Neal directed his attention away from the barn and to the barren acres of land that surrounded them. He could see no children lurking anywhere, but that didn't mean they weren't there. It was pitch black in the fields around them, thanks to the moonless night. He could only see so far before the darkness made it impossible.

"Shit." he muttered, reaching beneath the seat and pulling out a plastic case. He lifted it and placed it in his lap, flipping the lid open and clicking on the interior dome light so he could see what he was doing.

"Jesus, Neal, what are you doing?" Tiffany asked, watching as he removed the 9-millimeter Beretta pistol and dropped the clip to check it.

"Not taking any chances," he said, locking the full fifteen round cartridge back into place. "I know that Jonathan is every bit as powerful as a full grown man right now. I can deal with him one on one, but if any of those children we saw up on the highway happen to wander down here, I want to have an equalizer."

Melissa put her hand on Neal's shoulder but said nothing. She didn't know what to say. Tears were forming in Tiffany's eyes as she watched Neal pull back and release the slide on top of the gun, a bullet shifting into the firing chamber with a loud clicking sound.

"You can't...shoot him, Neal," she said, trying her best not to break into a full-fledged cry. "Please tell me...that you won't."

Neal put the gun on the dash in front of him and turned to her and Melissa, reaching out with one hand to wipe the tear from his wife's cheek.

"I have no intention of using this on our son," he said. "I can't make any promises about the others. If Jonathan *does* show up here and I find that I can't deal with him without hurting him, I'll get my ass back in this truck and get us the hell away from here."

Tiffany reached up and pressed Neal's hand to her cheek, nodding gently. "Okay," she said. "Okay."

She kissed his hand and held it tightly. Neal looked at Melissa and knew what she was thinking. Her eyes were looking toward the wooden ladder that ended in the darkness of the loft just beyond the barn door-way.

"I guess I have to go and see if Wendy's...and Conner's story was true," he said. "If I find the remains of a child up there, then we'll know."

Melissa's face was showing the strain of what they had all been through. It was the first time that Neal thought she had ever really looked her age.

"I have no doubts that you'll see exactly what Conner said you would," she said. "If we fail at stopping Weatherford, at least maybe we can bring a child peace."

Neal took another look around the Durango to make sure there was no one crouching in the darkness, waiting for him to step out. There was nothing. He looked back toward the two women as he popped open the glove box, pulling out a small flashlight.

"Okay, this is the deal," he said. "You two stay here and keep your eyes open and the doors locked. I should be able to make it up that ladder and see what I need to see in just a few seconds. As soon as you see me coming back down that ladder, unlock the doors and I'll be right back in here with you. Simple enough? I'm going to leave the truck running so we can get out of here fast if we have to."

Tiffany's expression told him that she didn't want him to go. Melissa's wasn't any better, but she knew that it *had* to be done. It was step one toward whatever chance they would have of stopping the demonic thing that had taken Jonathan.

"Please, for God's sake, be careful. I don't want to lose you, too." said Tiffany, squeezing his hand one more time.

"You won't lose me, baby," he said. "Not tonight."

Melissa tried to manage a smile, not doing a very good job of it. "You watch your ass in there, Neal," she said. "We need somebody to drive us back out of here."

Neal picked the Beretta up from the dashboard and reached for the door handle. "Consider my ass watched." he said.

He opened the door and stepped out onto the dirt beside the truck, gently closing it behind him. Peering back through the glass at Tiffany, he motioned to her to hit the auto-lock button on the armrest of her door. She took her eyes off him just long enough to turn and do as he instructed, all four doors instantly locking with a *click* that seemed much louder to Neal than it really was.

Then, he turned and faced the doorway that yawned open before him, the gun held tightly in his right hand, the small flashlight in the left. He aimed the light at the dark corners inside where the Durango's headlamps didn't reach. There was ample space in those shadowy places where a small child could crouch and wait for him to approach. He hoped not to come across a surprise such as that.

He hadn't expected to be *this* afraid, but he was.

Slowly, he began to step forward. The night now seemed colder than it had been before. He thought that perhaps it was just his mind playing tricks on him, the fear and anxiety taking their toll. As the distance between himself and the truck grew wider, he felt as if he were totally alone, even though he knew Tiffany and Melissa were right behind him.

Nothing out here, Neal. Nothing at all. Only a few more feet and you'll be at the ladder. Just a simple climb up to look around and then back down again. Piece of cake.

The self-assuring thoughts and the gun seemed like they should have made him feel better, but they didn't. As he entered the doorway, he began to understand why. It was because the ultimate reason he was here was to confront evil *incarnate* in the form of his own son. In any other situation, the solution would be simple - he would just unload the fifteen round clip into the son-of-a-bitch. But this was his own flesh and blood - his little boy. There would *have* to be a way other than the Beretta to stop him. Neal began to realize that unless he was physically strong enough to restrain Jonathan himself, he wasn't sure what other way there would be, especially considering the incredible strength that the boy now possessed.

The barn was still filled with the aroma of old tobacco. It hit him as soon as he was inside. As a child, it had been a refreshing scent that reminded him of summer. Tonight, it reminded him of children wrapped in white death shrouds stained with red, Darius Weatherford standing over their lifeless bodies.

The ladder was about eight feet inside the door to Neal's right. He slowly stepped toward it, directing the flashlight beam on the time worn wooden rungs. Upon reaching the base of it, he pointed the light upward toward the loft. He could see nothing but the end of the ladder and the barns cobweb ridden rafters. Placing the bottom of his hiking boot against the bottom rung, he applied pressure to test the wood's sturdiness. Then, he shook the whole ladder with his weight to further make sure it would hold him. Dirt and old straw fell down upon him from above as wood groaned against wood, but the ladder remained steadfast.

Glancing over his shoulder at Tiffany and Melissa one more time, he gave them a nod as if to let them know it looked okay. Then, he slid the gun into his belt, looped the flashlight around his wrist by its carrying strap, and grabbed the side rails, hoisting himself up onto the first rung. He didn't feel it giving any so he stepped up to the next one, taking care not to grab hold of any of the rusted nail heads which protruded from the sides. The wood creaked and moaned with each movement he made.

Okay, hard part's over. No turning back now he thought.

About halfway up, he began climbing a little faster, both his hands on the rungs to pull himself along instead of on the side rails. The adrenaline in his system was beginning to flow and he could feel it. He welcomed it, proceeding hand over hand, rung over rung into the blackness that swallowed the loft above. As it surrounded him, he removed his right hand from the ladder and let the flashlight drop over his wrist into his grip, pointing it up above him.

He was only three rungs from the top.

Not letting go of the light, he hurriedly climbed the remaining rungs with it still held loosely in his grasp. Then, he felt the dirt on the loft's hard wooden floor pressing into his open palms as he used them to lift himself up and onto his knees over the edge. As soon as he was certain he was standing on steady ground, he stood quickly and pulled the Beretta from his belt, sweeping the light across the expanse of the loft.

The floor was littered with trash and clumps of hay and grain, quite deep in some places. Empty oil cans and glass soda bottles were piled in one corner. On the opposite wall were stacks of bags filled with grain. They were all ripped and frayed, their contents spilled out over the wooden floor. The rats had obviously gotten into them over the years and helped spread the grain from one end of the loft to the other. Hanging from the rafters above was a variety of old and rusted chains, ropes and steel pulleys. The night wind that drifted through the loft doors slipped between them, causing them to gently swing back and forth. They clinked together every now and then, making a sound that to Neal could have done without – a sound like wind chimes for the dead.

He stepped toward the open doors of the loft that looked out onto the barnyard. The Durango would be parked where he could see it from there. Stepping across the filth-ridden floor, he brought the light into position so that he could see right beneath the opening. As the beam moved across the wooden surface and the piles of rotted grain and hay, something flashed by that caught Neal's attention. He moved the light back along the path he had just swept it, letting it settle on the space between the doors and the right hand corner of the wall lined with grain bags. An old barrel lay there on its side, sandwiched in between the last stack of grain and the wall. The open end of it faced outward. It was there that Neal saw it, feeling his breath catch in his throat.

Wrapped in a sleeve of white that lay sprawled out of the barrel's mouth were the bones of what used to be a human hand. A small one, like from a child of no more than ten or twelve.

"I'll be damned, she was *right*." Neal whispered aloud as he walked over to the barrel and kneeled down. He pointed the light into its mouth to get a better look at what was inside, not wanting to, but knowing that he had to for Jonathan's sake.

The flashlight beam traveled along a sleeve of white that extended out onto the floor. The sleeve ended at the neck of a collarless shirt. Protruding from the neck opening was a grinning and yellowed skull; it's jaw agape as if in a final scream. Black suspenders held what may have been old dungarees onto the corpse. The pants, as well as the shirt, were so moth and rat eaten that it was hard to tell exactly what type of material they were. The legs were bent almost flat over the body, the muscle and skin that once limited their motion long decomposed. One foot still had a shoe on it; the other was bare bone. The other arm was twisted at an impossible angle underneath the body. Reaching out with the muzzle of the gun, he used it to pull the fabric of the shirt away from the bone. Neal saw that it was broken in two. It was a bad break on the forearm, no doubt the result of a crushing blow by something hard.

The swing. The stick. Father's lesson.

Wendy's words came flooding back to him. He let the fabric back down gently onto the arm and brought the light back up to the skull. He leaned in close and saw what he thought he might. Fractures ran across its surface on both sides. They were hard to see, but they were there.

That bastard thought Neal, suddenly understanding why his son was so deathly afraid of the swing in the oak outside.

Two of the teeth were missing as well. They must have been lost at the same time the arm was broken and the skull fractured.

Just like she said - the crazy son-of-a-bitch beat this child nearly to death on the swing and left him to die. Just like Wendy...like "Conner"...had said.

Neal stood and looked down at the pile of bones dressed in rags that lay at his feet. They were all that was left of a well-meaning child who tried to help himself and others, only to die a slow death up here in the dark for his efforts. There was nothing fair about it - nothing at all.

"I'm sorry, Conner," he said. "I'll make sure you find your peace. Now, please...help me get my son back."

With that, he turned and headed back for the ladder, shining the light down onto the barns ground floor. There was nothing there but the shafts of light from the Durango's high beams and shadow filled corners. He put the gun back inside his belt and turned around at the loft's edge to step down to the top rung. It creaked in protest when he rested his weight on it, but it held fast. He stepped down to the next rung with his other foot, holding the side rails with both hands. The light was once again dangling from his wrist as he went. In a few seconds, he would be on the ground again and then he could get back to the girls to tell them what he had seen.

How they planned on going about handling Jonathan was still beyond him. Wendy, or rather Conner, had told them back on the vacant lot that she would meet them here and that they would face Darius Weatherford together. So far, he had seen no sign of the girl. Perhaps she would be here soon. Conner surely knew that coming here in Wendy's form would be a dangerous risk, especially since Weatherford hated him so much. To at last be put to a proper rest must have been of great importance to the spirit child for it to have taken such a step.

The Durango's horn suddenly split the silence, startling Neal. It emitted three quick blasts, and then went silent.

Shit, something's happening.

Neal was five rungs down now. Eight more and he would be on the ground. He began to climb faster, his heart pounding. The top of the barn's main entrance was rapidly rising upward in his line of vision. On the next rung down, he saw the grill of the Durango sitting just beyond the doorway. He climbed down two more, keeping his eyes on the truck so that he could see if Tiffany and Melissa were okay.

He stopped cold only four feet from the ground.

The truck was empty.

Jesus, where did they. . .?

His thoughts were abruptly halted by a sharp, cracking sound – followed by an intense, stinging pain as something wrapped tightly around his throat. He was pulled backwards with great force, his hands tearing free of the ladder so quickly that he felt long splinters dig into his fingers and palms. The flashlight flew from his wrist. He landed flat on his back on the dirt floor in a cloud of dust, the back of his head hitting the ground hard. The world was spinning slowly and beginning to grow dark around the edges. He realized he was about to lose consciousness. Trying to turn his head to see what had happened to him, he was blinded by the headlamps that were right outside the door. Then, he heard footsteps coming from the darkness in the corner of the barn to his left. He was straining to turn his head in the direction of the sound when he heard the voice.

"Hope you didn't hurt yourself, Neeeaaaallll."

Jonathan Fowler was slowly emerging from the shadowy corner, an aged leather bullwhip clutched in his hand.

"You seek to stop me, do you?" he asked, his small blood smeared cheeks glistening in the lights. "No need. You will pay. The runt-child, he will pay as well. And those whores with you. . .I'll save them for last."

He was right beside Neal now, standing there with the whip coiled in his hand and a hellish grin on his face. Neal looked up through eyes that were about to close and tried to reach out to him.

"J...Jonathan. Please...don't.... it's me..." he managed to say.

The boy looked down at him, his eyes dark as the night. "I know it's you," he said. "The problem here is, *I'm* not your fucking son, Neee-aaaalll."

The child stepped forward and put his tennis shoe clad foot across Neal's throat, right on his trachea. Slowly, he began to apply pressure.

As Neal felt the unbelievable force starting to constrict his breathing, he heard Jonathan begin to laugh.

CHAPTER 27

Tiffany and Melissa had seen Jonathan suddenly appear from around behind the barn, heading for the open doorway with what looked like a black whip in his hand.

Reaching over to the steering wheel, Tiffany had managed to blow the horn three short times in the hopes that it would warn Neal. She knew it would alert Jonathan to their presence, but there was *no* other way to get her husband's attention.

Then, as she anticipated, Jonathan stopped and turned his head in the direction of the truck. She and Melissa, not knowing what else to do, crawled down and crouched on the truck's floorboard. Hardly breathing and motionless, they remained there still.

Nothing happened. No glass shattered. No small hands tried to rip the doors from their hinges. They realized then that Jonathan was more interested in catching Neal inside the barn than he was with bothering them.

Tiffany raised her head long enough to see the child going into the doorway and vanishing out of sight. Then, she ducked back down, feeling herself start to perspire in spite of the cold. Dread of what could possibly happen now consumed her.

Neither she nor Melissa realized that only a second or two later, Neal had made it down the ladder far enough to look outside and see what he *thought* was an empty truck.

"Jesus, he's in the barn with him," Tiffany said aloud softly so that Melissa could hear her from the backseat. "What do we do now?"

Melissa could hear the panic starting to swell in Tiffany's voice. She wasn't much better herself right now. Trying to shift her weight into a less uncomfortable crouching position, she was about to respond to the question she had just been asked when the silence was broken by a loud crack, followed by a dull thud.

It sounded like a body hitting the ground.

"Oh God, no!" she heard Tiffany exclaim.

The both of them scrambled up from their hiding positions, their eyes following the twin headlight beams into the yawning mouth of the barn in front of them.

Neal was sprawled on the barn floor with Jonathan standing over him, whip in hand. It looked like the boy had his foot on Neal's throat and was attempting to crush his windpipe.

Tiffany reached for her door handle in a frantic effort to get out. She could hear her husband starting to choke as she pulled up on the handle, hearing it disengage the door lock.

"Tiffany, no!" shouted Melissa, reaching across the seat and grabbing her by her jacket collar. "Don't get out!"

Tiffany turned and grabbed Melissa's arm, trying to push her away from her. "Let go of me! He'll kill him if we don't do something!"

Melissa kept her grip on the jacket, shaking Tiffany hard and forcing her to look her in the eye.

"He'll kill *you* too, Tiffany," she said. "You're his mother. You're too close to him. You'll play right into his hands and he knows it."

Tiffany's eyes had filled with tears and her breathing had grown rapid. She sounded like she was going to start hyperventilating any second. "We've got to do *something*," she said. "We can't let this happen."

Melissa could see Neal's eyes beginning to bulge in their sockets from where she sat. It would only be a matter of a few more seconds and Jonathan would...no, it wasn't Jonathan...it was *Darius*. Darius Weatherford would kill him.

"Tiffany, move over." said Melissa, tossing her leg up and over the seat. She quickly scrambled across and settled into the front seat behind the steering wheel. The Durango was still idling, and she put one foot on the gas pedal, depressing it to the floor. She placed her palm flat on the center of the steering column, sending the blast of the horn rolling forth from beneath the hood along with the roar of the V8 engine - anything to draw the boy's attention away from Neal. Tiffany realized what Melissa was doing and quickly joined in, pounding on the dashboard in front of her to create a distraction. Maybe he would leave Neal alone and come for them. They could back the truck up, luring him away from the barn. Once he was far enough away, they could leave him in a cloud of dust and go back to get Neal.

Jonathan lifted his head and slowly turned it to face the truck. The smile that was stretched across his face faded and became a burning glare. He kept his foot on Neal's throat, not letting up on the pressure.

"He's not stopping," said Tiffany. "He's still choking him."

Melissa realized that distracting the child was not going to work. He wasn't going to walk away from Neal until he was dead.

"We've got to do something else," she said. "He's not going to come for us until he finishes with Neal."

Before Melissa could grab her this time, Tiffany opened the passenger side door and was out of the truck. She stopped there holding the door ajar and looked at Melissa, her eyes darting back and forth between what was happening in the barn and Melissa's concerned face.

"Melissa, I have to," she said. "I can't just sit here and watch Neal die. Jonathan may be beyond help, but I can't watch this anymore."

Though the fear of what could happen now had crept deep into her soul, Melissa understood that Tiffany was right. She herself was a doctor; an outsider looking into the lives of others and trying to help. As much as she genuinely cared for Jonathan, she had let it slip away from her how much she would risk if he was *her own* flesh and blood; how she would feel if *her* husband was out there.

"Damn it," she said, opening her door and stepping out onto the ground. "Hold on, I'm coming with you."

Tiffany had already started walking toward the barn door while Melissa was getting out of the truck. She didn't notice Melissa open the rear door and grab the short tire iron from its mount under the back seat.

Jonathan kept his dark eyes locked on both women as they approached the barn entrance. He *still* had not removed his foot from Neal's throat. Tiffany saw her own shadow loom across him and onto the barns back wall as she stepped into the path cut by the trucks high beams.

"Jonathan, let him go." she said, the fear in her voice instantly recognizable.

The boy looked straight at her and the grin began to form on his face again. He glanced down at Neal, who was seconds from passing out. Then, he looked back up at Tiffany and Melissa, opening his mouth and speaking with a voice that was void of pity and laced with cruel sarcasm.

"The faithful whore comes to stand up for her husband. A touching effort indeed."

Melissa stood there and let Tiffany do the talking this time. She had taken her turn earlier in the field with Wendy. If Tiffany wanted to handle this, she would let her. Still, she kept the tire iron clutched tightly in her left hand, letting it hang against her upper thigh so that it would be less noticeable.

"Jonathan...I said let him *go!*" Tiffany repeated, louder than before. "You're hurting him."

The boy just shook his head and began to chuckle under his breath. "You've got the wrong kid, mommy dearest. I don't give a rat's ass if I hurt him or not."

Melissa spoke as quietly as she could to Tiffany, never taking her eyes from Jonathan.

"Tiffany, you have to remember – it's not Jonathan. It's his body, but it's not him."

The boy's head immediately snapped in Melissa's direction. "Oh, it's Doctor Bitch," he said, slowly looking her up and down. "Nice to have you with us, Doctor. You know, it's rude to talk about people when you're right in front of them."

Melissa didn't know what to say. She could see Tiffany nervously glancing her way, as if she was asking for support on what in the hell to do next. There was no time to hesitate now or Neal would be dead.

"Darius...let him go now!" she demanded.

The boy seemed startled and his eyes widened slightly. "Why, Doctor Bitch...I'm *impressed*. Finally, someone knows who they're talking to."

Melissa saw from the corner of her eye that Tiffany was trying to step closer to the boy and her fallen husband. She raised her right hand and motioned for Tiffany not to go any further – at least not until she could lure the boy away from Neal.

"I know who you are, Darius." she continued. "I know you've taken this child from his family. God only knows how many others you've gotten to."

"I see." said the boy. "This is extremely interesting, Doctor Bitch. You've got my attention. Go on."

Jonathan removed his foot from Neal's throat at last. Neal madly began to try to breath, taking in great gulps of air and coughing horribly as he crawled away. Melissa watched him as he pulled himself over to the base of the ladder he had just fallen from, resting with his back against it.

Tiffany wanted to run to him, but Jonathan was in between the two of them. She knew that if she tried to make it past him, he would be upon her before she could blink. She moved closer to Melissa, feeling stronger now that Neal was safely away from the boy. Melissa continued speaking.

"Darius Weatherford," she said. "You lived here many years ago. You adopted a group of homeless immigrant children whom you proceeded to abuse and molest."

The boy stood there and listened as she went on.

"A child named Conner took the risk of going into town to alert the authorities about you. His punishment, as well as that of the other seven children, was death."

Jonathan let the whip in his hand come uncoiled, its tip and length rolling out across the ground while he held the handle tightly in his small fingers. "I see you're a history buff, Doctor Bitch," he said. "In light of that, I guess you know what happened to me when the townsfolk came calling."

Melissa nodded, keeping one eye on the whip. "You were made to atone for your sins, Darius. You were locked up and eventually electrocuted. You died in front of a crowd who thought that death by the chair was way too kind a fate for you. I can't say that I blame them."

Jonathan was twirling the whip in the dirt at his feet and he took one step closer to the women.

"You're here tonight to get payback," Melissa said. "Payback that you damn sure don't deserve. Even in death, you prey on the fears of children. You use them to kill, like you've used Jonathan - like you've used all the others."

The whip twirled on, Jonathan's eyes still focused on Melissa. Tiffany stood her ground beside her, keeping watch on Neal who still sat against the ladder, his cough beginning to subside as his air returned.

"Jonathan was *special*, wasn't he, Darius? You just had to have him. The others are nice, but Jonathan's your favorite plaything, isn't he? I can't believe we all have been *so* afraid of a grown man who hides behind a child."

The boy spoke back, raising his voice almost to a shout.

"I've heard enough, bitch. I should have fucking killed you back on your front porch!"

Before Melissa could respond, Tiffany had stepped forward and beat her to it.

"We have Conner with us," she said. "Let my husband and my son go and we'll give him to you."

Melissa knew Tiffany was bluffing him. They didn't even know where Conner.... or Wendy...*was* right now. Even so, it was a good bluff, and if Weatherford hated the boy so, he just might go for it.

Jonathan looked at Tiffany with an expression of mock surprise. "Oh, you have the child, do you?" he asked.

Tiffany shot Melissa a quick glance, and then turned her eyes back to the blood covered child eight feet in front of her. She had started this yarn so she had to keep it going.

"Yes, we do," she said. "She's…I mean, *he's* in a place where you could never find him. We told him we would protect him from you."

Jonathan laughed again. "The worthless runt seeks to have his bones placed at rest, *doesn't* he, whore? He wanted to bring you here so you could help him in his task, just as he did your miserable, weakling son."

"You bastard!" shot back Tiffany. "Just because he chose to crawl off and die in peace somewhere instead of suffering for your pleasure, you choose to torment him. Why not leave him be?"

Jonathan raised his voice again, this time in a full-fledged shout that echoed in the barn's gloomy interior. "Inquisitive slut! It is not your duty to question the likes of *me*! I do it because I wish to and nothing more!"

Melissa joined in with Tiffany now, the conversation obviously getting to Weatherford.

"Conner may have died a child, but he was a thousand times more a man than you ever were, Darius," she said. "He deserves peace. He endured a painful existence in life. There's no need for it to continue for him in death."

The boy pointed a finger at Melissa, taking another step forward. "I *won't* tell you to shut the fuck up again, Doctor Bitch!" he exclaimed. "You both *lie!* Do you think I do not *know?* You can hide nothing from me! The runt is already mine tonight! He has offered himself to me to save the lives of others! You do not have him, nor did you ever!"

Tiffany and Melissa both were silent then. They looked at each other, then back to the boy. Melissa gripped the handle of the tire iron tighter and asked "What do you mean?"

A self-assured tone coating his voice, the boy replied.

"The little Crenshaw bitch arrived before you did. The runt offered himself and the bitch in the hopes that I would spare those whom I would have destroyed."

"Where is she, Darius?" asked Melissa.

Jonathan grinned and nodded his head in the direction of the barn's back yard. He spoke the words that both women knew they were going to hear.

"On the *swing*."

Silence filled the barn following the reply to Melissa's question. She didn't know what else to say. All she could do was stand there and pray that Wendy was still alive.

Neal was moving now. Tiffany saw him. He was reaching beneath his jacket for something. She knew it had to be the gun. Her mind was racing.

Please, Lord, don't let us have to shoot our own son.

Quickly, she spoke to keep the child's focus on her and Melissa.

"And will you honor the deal?" she asked.

Jonathan took another step forward, still twirling the whip in the dirt. "Never been accused of being a man of my word," he laughed. "Wasn't one when I was alive - still no reason to be one now."

Then, things happened fast.

Dirt flew from the barn floor and into Melissa's eyes as the whip lashed out, coiling about her hand left hand and the tire iron. The stinging pain was immediate, making her hand feel like it was on fire. Jonathan had acted so quickly that her eyes saw nothing more than a blur of motion, followed by the sound of the leather cutting through the air. She didn't even have time to react or cry out before he had her. With one mighty pull, he jerked her from her feet. She heard the pop of her shoulder joint as it was dislocated, then she hit the cold ground on her stomach, arms splayed out in front of her. The tire iron was torn from her hand and hurled across the barn into the darkness.

Tiffany hadn't even realized what had happened until Melissa was on the floor. It had just been *too* fast. She saw the tire iron sail into the corner behind Jonathan and barely had time to register what it had been before the whip cracked the air again. She heard Neal scream in pain as the black leather struck his right hand; the hand holding the Beretta. The frayed tip of the whip coiled around the gun. Neal felt a searing pain in his fingers as the gun was pulled from his grasp. He was lifted forward from his resting position against the ladder, but he caught himself with his uninjured hand before he fell face first into the dirt.

Jonathan had disarmed both Melissa and Neal both in less than four seconds. He stood there now with the whip coiled again in his right hand, Neal's gun in the other.

Tiffany was frozen where she stood, scared to move. She knew he could have taken her head off with the whip had he wanted to. The speed at which he had employed it was unbelievable.

"I know what you're thinking, whore mother." said Jonathan, slowly stepping toward her. "You're thinking how proficient a whip master I am. Ah, many summers of practice here in the barn have seasoned me well. As a boy, I could take the wings from a dragonfly in mid-air with it. How blessed I was to find it still hanging right here on the barn wall where I left it all those years ago...still stained with the runt's blood."

Tiffany still didn't dare move. Instead, she spoke.

"How.... do you know what I'm thinking?"

Jonathan let the whip slide down onto the crook of his right elbow and lifted the gun in his other hand, pointing it at Tiffany. "I always know," he said. "I know what all of you think. That's why I anticipate your every move, whore mother. That's why I took Doctor Bitch's and your husbands weapons. That's how I know that right *now*, you're thinking about what to do next. Do you run, or do you help your husband and your mind-fucking friend? Which will it be, whore mother?"

Tiffany looked over at Neal. He was standing, leaning against the ladder. Melissa was still on the ground, having managed to get herself into a sitting position. She was clutching her left shoulder in pain. If Tiffany tried to make a move to reach either one of them, the child would easily have her in a matter of seconds.

Neal spoke then, uttering one simple statement that clearly had an effect.

"Darius. I found Conner's...remains."

The boy turned his head to face Neal, keeping the gun trained on Tiffany. He regarded Neal with a disgusted sneer.

"Neeeaalllll. Don't you know better than to make me mad by now?"

Standing away from the ladder now on his own power, Neal began to step very slowly toward Tiffany, replying to the child's question as he went.

"He'll find his peace, Darius. He'll be put to rest with the others you killed. I'll make sure of it."

The boy smiled and waved the gun slightly about. "You'll do no such thing. I have your gun, Neaallllll. If you piss me off anymore than you already have, I might have to shoot the whore mother here."

Tiffany felt her heartbeat increase until she felt like it would explode. She knew that the boy…that Darius…. would shoot her without hesitation.

"No one in the town of Sumter gives a shit about what Darius Weatherford did nearly a hundred years ago," Neal said. "You were forgotten about, just as you should have been. If anyone around here has any memories at all of what happened here in this field, I'm sure it's of the *children*, not you."

The boy kept the gun on Tiffany, listening. Melissa began to try to stand, joining in with Neal's tirade against Weatherford.

"He's right, Darius," she said. "You're nothing. You never were. The people who have died tonight may have given you some type of satisfaction, but nothing is going to save you from burning in hell when this is over."

Jonathan glared at her. "And *how* is it going to be over, Doctor Bitch? I believe you would have to burn my soul from the flesh to do that, and then, you'd be killing the boy along with me. I'm sure Neeaaalll and the whore mother would disapprove."

Melissa looked over at Neal to see how much closer he'd gotten to Tiffany. She kept speaking, trying to keep the child's focus more on her.

"Conner will help us," she said. "He stopped you before. With our help, he'll stop you again."

The response came back suddenly and in the form of a shout that was high and startling:

"The child is DEAD, as you will ALL soon be!"

Neal stopped, the words conjuring up an image of little Wendy's battered and bruised form twisting in the wind out back, strapped to the swing by her tormentor and bludgeoned almost beyond recognition.

No. It was a lie. Wendy…. and Conner…. weren't dead. He didn't know how he knew it, but he just did. The thought seemed to invade his mind.

"Now *you're* the one lying, Darius," he said. "You haven't finished Conner's final *lesson* yet, and you don't want us to stop you before you do. Isn't that right?"

Melissa didn't know exactly what was happening, but she too began to feel strange. Like Conner was still alive and she was *meant* to know it.

"He's right," she said aloud. "You would have killed her if we hadn't arrived when we did, but we interrupted you."

The child's expression changed. The evil smirk transformed into a curious look of concern. "You know nothing about what I have or haven't done," he said in a low and angry tone. "Neither of you are very wise to presume that I haven't finished what I started."

This time, Tiffany felt it. She *heard* it inside her head - the voice of a young boy, thick with an English accent, calling to her.

I live, Tiffany. I live.

Before she realized what she was doing, her mouth opened and the words came out.

"He lives, Darius. Hanging by a thread, it's true, but he lives. I pray, as he does, that he hangs on long enough to see you die at last."

The barn was suddenly filled with the loud crack of a gunshot. It happened so fast that the shell casing from the Beretta's 9-millimeter slug hadn't even hit the ground yet before Tiffany fell. She went down clutching her stomach, blood already starting to seep through her fingers.

CHAPTER 28

The sharp report of the single gunshot echoed across the barren expanse of Weatherford's field.

Inside the barn, Neal cried out, the desperate sound swirling up into the rotting rafters, through the chains in the loft that danced on the breeze, and out into the cold night.

"NOOOOOOOOO!"

Melissa, standing only a few feet away from where Tiffany had fallen, tried to scream. The sound stuck in her throat. Her eyes were wide with shock.

Neal had just about reached Tiffany when Jonathan had pulled the trigger. The child stood there now, still pointing the gun at her. It was as if he was waiting to see her move so he could put another bullet in her.

"Just like the worthless brats," Jonathan said. "Better seen than heard, right, Neaaaaallll? Knowing when to shut the fuck up *does* have its merits."

Neal went to her, oblivious to the boy's taunting remarks. He kneeled beside her and brushed away the hair that had fallen across her face. She was trying to speak, but appeared to be in shock. Her face was wracked with a grimace of pain, and she was keeping her hands pressed tightly to the spot on her midsection near her right side. There was so much blood that Neal could not determine exactly where the bullet went in. She looked Neal in the eyes as he slipped one hand under her head and rested the other gently on her cheek.

Struggling with the effort, she managed to speak.

"It's not...our son, Neal. Just like...Melissa keeps telling us...it's not...Jonathan anymore."

Neal felt himself being overcome with grief, anger, and fear all at once. Still holding her head, he looked over at Melissa. She stood just a few feet away, still stunned by what she had just seen. Then he turned to Jonathan, who still had the Beretta pointed straight at him and Tiffany.

"I'm sending you back to Hell, Darius." he said.

Jonathan cackled into the darkness of the barn, his breath turning to mist as it came out. "You are a fool, Neal – a fool who will do nothing."

Tiffany took one trembling hand from her wound and placed it across Neal's. Sensing her touch, he immediately looked back down into her tear filled eyes. She opened her mouth and the words came out as a whisper.

"He's still…alive, Neal. Can't you…feel it? Can't you…. hear him?"

The look on his face told her that he *did*, just as all three of them had only a moment ago.

"Don't try to talk anymore, honey," he told her. "You stay as still as you possibly can. The more you move the more blood you lose. Understand?"

She managed a faint nod. Neal gently let her head rest back on the ground. Leaning down, he kissed her forehead and then pressed his cheek to hers.

"Hang on, Tiffany," he said to her softly. "I love you. I won't let you die. I promise on my very soul."

A weak smile came to her face. He kissed her once again and then slowly stood, looking over to Melissa. She was now leaning against the wall just to the inside of the barn doors left side. He knew her shoulder had to be hurting terribly. Neal reached across his chest and grabbed his own left shoulder, raising his eyes questioningly at her. She nodded to let him know she was okay.

To Neal, it seemed like an eternity had passed since the sound of the gunshot. In reality, it had only been a couple of minutes.

The boy, gun still raised and whip still in his other hand, was watching with a look of disgust. He began to twirl the whip in the dirt again.

"Yes, Neeeaaaallll, Doctor Bitch will live," he said. "If only for a few more minutes. The whore mother will bleed herself dry right here on the ground while I deal with you."

Neal had heard enough. He had to do something and do it now. Tiffany would die if he didn't. Jonathan had moved *fast* earlier, so trying to rush him would be a bad idea. Besides, he had the gun aimed right at him. The boy was probably going to unload the rest of the clip into him and Melissa any second now if something didn't happen.

"Melissa," Neal said aloud, keeping his eyes on the boy as he spoke. "Can you drive?"

She kept her attention on Jonathan too, responding to Neal without even turning her head. "I think so."

Neal readied himself to move, already mapping out the path in his head that he was going to take to get out of the gun's range. He slowly began to dig the front of his right hiking boot into the dirt and fine gravel on the ground at his feet. Melissa was closer to the driver's door of the Durango, which still sat idling just outside. If she made a move to get to it, Jonathan would either try to trip her up with the whip, or direct the gun toward her. Either way, his attention would have to leave Neal for at least a second or two.

"I think it's time we went and got Conner, don't you?" Neal asked aloud to Melissa.

She began to slowly inch her way backwards out of the barn, the open door of the truck about fifteen feet behind her. As she moved, she replied "Yes, I think so."

Neal watched as Jonathan's eyes began to dart back and forth between Melissa and him. Weatherford knew they were getting ready to make a break for it. He was just waiting for it to happen.

"You will go nowhere!" the boy exclaimed loudly. "I told you, the bastard child is dead!"

Neal knew that the time was now. With one fast glance down at his injured wife on the ground behind him, he shouted to Melissa "NOW!"

The scenario that was being played out in the barn doorway erupted into a frenzy of sudden motion, beginning with Melissa spinning on her heels and running for the Durango. Neal never took his eyes from Jonathan's, waiting for the exact moment when they began to follow her actions. She was halfway to the truck when they did. The whip lashed out with unbelievable speed, managing to sting her across the back of her calves, but falling too short to entangle her legs and trip her. A fraction of a second later, the boy swung the Beretta toward her.

Neal moved when he saw the barrel of the gun begin to arc toward Melissa.

Kicking forward with all his strength, he sent a spray of sand and gravel raining across Jonathan's face. The sound of another gunshot echoed throughout the barn as the sand filled the child's eyes, nose, and mouth. Neal heard shattering glass as he turned and dove for the left side of the doorway, hitting the ground on his shoulder and rolling out onto the dead grass. He came up in a hard run, his heels digging into the ground in some spots. Behind him, Jonathan began to shout.

"You'll pay with more than just your lives now!" he screamed. "Rich suffering will befall the both of you for daring to defy me!"

Neal didn't bother to look back. He kept running as hard as he could, heading for the back corner of the barn and hoping to God that Melissa wasn't hit. He tried to block the image of Tiffany bleeding and lying back in the doorway, but he could not. Leaving her there was almost unbearable, but this was the only chance they had at beating Weatherford before he killed them all.

Reaching the rear of the building, he heard the Durango's engine being gunned and the sound of its tires spinning on the dirt. He glanced back just long enough to see Melissa backing up and swinging the head-lights his way. Two more gunshots split the night air, followed by more breaking glass and then the distinctive sound of a tire being taken out.

Jonathan was *still* shooting at her from inside the barn.

The headlights began to move toward Neal. He could see her dark silhouette hunched down at the wheel, trying to find where he had run.

Stepping away from the barn wall so she could spot him, he waved her on, keeping one eye on the barn door so he could warn her if Jonathan appeared. She floored it when she saw him, throwing up a cloud of gray dust in her wake. Once the truck was close enough, Neal could see that the window in the driver's door had been shattered and that the side view mir-ror was destroyed. The rear tire on the driver's side had been hit by the last shot Neal had heard. It was already flat and thumping through the dirt.

"We've got to get to the swing!" Neal exclaimed, jumping on the side rail as she pulled alongside him. "Go, go, go! Head for that oak over there!"

Melissa did as she was told and pointed the front of the truck toward the shadow of the gigantic oak that stood in the far right corner of the lot behind the barn. It was about thirty yards from where Neal had been standing when he jumped on. Trying to keep her left shoulder from bang-ing into the driver's door as she sped toward the tree, she glanced up at Neal. She shouted out a question to him, one that she had started consider-ing the second she had turned to run for the truck from the barn.

"Neal. Even if Wendy and Conner aren't dead...what in the hell are we going to do? I don't think we can stop him!"

Neal held tightly to the luggage rack that ran across the top of the truck, wincing as the night wind stung his face. "I have no choice but to put blind faith in the fact that Conner can tell us that," he said, shouting the words so she could hear him over the sound of the engine. "If he can't, then we'll die, Tiffany will die, and God knows who else will."

Neal turned and looked behind them just in time to see a small figure running alongside the barn wall in the darkness. It took the same path Neal had only a moment ago. Then, instead of pursuing them diagonally across the back lot from the barn's rear corner, it rapidly vanished into the shadows along the back wall.

Weatherford was coming.

"Damn it!" Neal exclaimed, "He's on the move, Melissa. There are eleven more rounds in that clip!"

She began to slow the truck to a stop, the menacing limbs of the oak tree twisting out above them and upward into the night sky. The massive trunk was right in front of them, at least seven feet in diameter at its widest point. Turning the truck at a slight angle to the tree, the headlights knifed into the pitch-blackness on its opposite side.

There was something there. It was rocking gently in the breeze. One of the beams of light partially illuminated it.

"Jesus, don't let us be too late." Neal said aloud to himself.

Wendy Crenshaw was hanging there in the swing.

At first, she appeared to be just a dark shape, moving back and forth ever so slowly. Then, Melissa saw the bare foot dangling, its toes scraping the crimson stained dirt.

"Jesus, Neal, look." she said, putting the truck in park.

Neal was already off the side rail and on the grass. "I see, I see," he said. "We gotta move fast. Jonathan's on his way out here. I'll grab her and bring her back to the truck. You sit right there and be ready to haul ass as soon as I get her in, okay?"

"No problem." said Melissa. "Be careful and hurry."

Giving her a quick nod, he turned and ran for the limp form that was draped across the round wooden seat at the end of the rotting rope. Melissa watched him go, keeping her eyes open for any sign of a small red and blue clad form hiding in the dark nearby. In her mind she could picture the boy leaping on Neal and ripping him to shreds right in front of the truck, then finishing off Wendy while she sat there and watched.

Melissa promised herself that *if* that happened, she would have no choice but to run Jonathan down. If she had to, she would burn him *herself* to exorcise Weatherford once and for all. Having spent most of her life helping children, she thought that entertaining the thought of killing one would have been harder. Given the horrors she had witnessed tonight, it wouldn't be very hard to do at all.

Neal reached the swing in a matter of seconds. He dropped to his knees beside it and felt his heart sink when he saw the bruised and bloody child that hung there.

"Sorry I couldn't stop this, Conner," he said to her in a whisper. "I tried. God, we all did."

Wendy's arms were lifted above her head, and her hands bound together at the wrist by rough twine. Neal could see the lines on her skin were it had cut into her, leaving awful looking red indentions in her flesh. Her legs were straddling the rope that extended upward into the oak and bound together from the ankles all the way up to above her knees. Her vampire wig had fallen to the ground beside her and her own brownish blonde hair was tainted with red. Her gown was riddled with long gashes, the skin beneath either bruised, bleeding, or both.

He had used the whip on her, quite brutally.

The child's head hung limply to the side, eyes open and looking at Neal. A small trickle of blood ran from her lips and her pale make-up was smeared with it.

Tears began to flow across her cheeks.

Neal madly began digging through his jean pockets for the small pocketknife he usually kept on him. He kept glancing to the dark yard off to his right and behind him to make sure that Jonathan didn't appear.

"Neal…" she said in a voice so faint he barely heard it.

Looking up at her as he found the blade and pulled it from his pocket, he looked into her eyes and spoke softly.

"Conner…I'm getting you out of here. Just hang on."

He began to saw at the twine around her feet, working his way upward toward her knees.

"Neal…I called to you. I called to all of you…and you heard." she said, the heavy English accent now almost undetectable in the weak tone she used.

Working feverishly on the twine, Neal nodded. "Yes, we did, Conner. We heard you. Hell, we felt you."

The girl turned her face toward the sky and stared up at the stars.

"Voices carry, Neal," she said. "The voices of those of us long dead. Do you believe that now?"

Neal ripped the twine apart at her legs, freeing them. "Yes, I do," he said. "I believe in a lot of things now."

Melissa could see Neal working on the twine as hard as he could. She still didn't see Jonathan anywhere, but she knew he was out there. From wherever he was, he could probably easily dispatch Neal, Wendy, or herself with the gun, but that would be too easy for him. Darius would want to toy with them before striking them down. Maybe he was laying low because they now had Conner. Perhaps they could barter with him. After all, Conner was the ace up the sleeve in this whole horrific card game.

Neal was working on the twine at Wendy's wrists now. As he cut through it, he put one hand beneath her back to keep her from falling backwards from the swing. He knew that she would be too weak to hang onto the rope. As he kept slicing through the numerous strands, he saw something sitting against the trunk of the tree. It was red with what appeared to be yellow letters on its side.

It was a gasoline can.

Jesus, he was going to beat her to death and burn her! he thought to himself.

He remembered what Conner had said back in the vacant lot about what must be done to destroy Weatherford once and for all. The host body had to be killed and then burned to vanquish the spirit forever. It looked like Weatherford's intentions had been to do exactly *that* to Wendy...ridding himself of Conner and finally gaining the satisfaction he never gained all those years ago.

With one more pass of the blade, the twine came apart. The little girl became dead weight, just as Neal had figured, and he gently lowered her backwards until her head rested in the crook of his left arm. He placed his right arm beneath her knees and stood slowly, lifting her from the wooden seat. Her eyes were still open, looking right at him. She spoke to him again in a whisper.

"He is coming for me, Neal. He is coming now."

The words were the last thing Neal wanted to hear, but he knew they were true. He turned and quickly headed for the Durango, trying to keep his eyes peeled for any signs of movement from the surrounding darkness. At any second, he expected to see his son, still in his blood soaked Spider-Man costume, burst forth from the shadows. Perhaps the sound of the whip would rip the night air and he would feel his feet jerked from beneath him, or maybe gunfire would explode from somewhere just out of his line of vision, followed by the searing pain of lead tearing into his body as he ran. His mind was overloaded with thoughts about Tiffany lying in the barn, slowly bleeding to death; about Wendy and Conner and Melissa; about the countless others who would die tonight if Darius made it out of Weatherford's field and back into town.

Nothing happened. After about fifteen steps that felt like fifteen hundred, he found himself passing through the headlights in front of the truck and heading for the passenger door. "Back door!" he exclaimed, his breath coming out in labored gasps. "We need to lay her down!"

Melissa was up and on her knees in an instant, leaning across the console between the two front seats and grasping the handle on the rear passenger door. There was a horrible second when she realized it was locked. She fumbled madly along the armrest to find the switch to unlock it. After what felt like forever, her fingers fell across it. Neal stood back a couple of feet as the door swung open, Wendy's body draped in his arms as if she were a rag doll. Then, he stepped forward, gently laying her down across the back seat.

Melissa thought the child looked terrible. Her gown was filthy and torn, blood seeping through where she had been struck by the whip. She was trembling slightly, no doubt from either the cold or from shock. Her eyes turned to Melissa, looking up at her almost pleadingly.

"Conner?" said Melissa, reaching down and brushing strands of the child's hair from across her face. "Are you still with us?"

The child whispered a faint "Yes - for a little longer."

Neal closed the rear door and then climbed into the passenger seat up front. He locked all the trucks doors once inside, then turned to look across the seat at Wendy. Melissa saw that he was covered with a light sheen of sweat, even though it was in the forties outside.

"Conner, can we stop him?" he asked. "You said earlier we would all face him together and we would have a chance."

The little girl coughed, her expression changing to one of pain as she did so. Melissa knew that she must be broken up inside, most likely her ribs. After the spasm passed, Wendy directed her attention to Neal and spoke. Her voice was so weak that Neal had to lean over to hear her.

"I offered myself to him...in the hopes that he would be satisfied and leave everyone else be."

Neal cast a glance to Melissa then back to the girl. "Conner, we won't let him get to you anymore," he said. "We want to give you what you always wanted. Peace. I found your remains."

The small and tear filled eyes seemed to light up, if only for an instant.

"In the loft?" she whispered. "You went to the loft?"

Neal nodded. "Yes, Conner, I went there," he said." I saw where you left this world and I intend to make sure others know about it too. I promise you that you will rest with the others who died at the hands of that son-of-a-bitch."

Wendy lifted her left arm and extended her small hand to Neal. He reached down and took it in his own. It was dreadfully cold to the touch. He felt the child give his hand a light squeeze.

"Thank you." she whispered.

Her hand fell from Neal's, landing on the seat alongside her body. It must have taken every bit of strength the child had left just to manage the brief contact.

Neal turned around and scanned the darkness around the truck. "We don't need to stay here," he said to Melissa. "We'll be sitting ducks if we do. We need to get back to the barn and get Tiffany."

Melissa shifted the truck into reverse and began to back away from the tree.

"I just hope to God she hasn't already lost too much blood." Melissa said, stopping and shifting into drive. She headed back toward the dark silhouette of the barn, the flat tire causing the truck to violently jolt up and down as it went. Not wanting to cause Wendy any more discomfort, she had to drive slower to cut down on the bouncing motion.

"He was going to burn her, Melissa," said Neal. "There was a gas can by the tree."

He turned around and looked at the child, who had closed her eyes. The rise and fall of the girl's chest assured him that she was still breathing.

"It's the only way." Melissa replied to Neal. "Burning the host body after it's been incapacitated is the only way to destroy the controlling spirit. By incapacitation, I mean that the host body has to be killed or damaged. Conner's physical limitations seem to be the same as Wendy's. In this state, he's inside a useless host. Wendy can't walk. She can't run.

Neither can Conner. Don't you see? He's only capable of doing what her body is capable of."

Neal was watching the darkness as it passed by his window. His breathing was still labored, but it had slowed a little. "Why can't Conner just leave her? he asked. "He has the power to, especially since Weatherford didn't burn her."

The weak voice came from the back seat.

"Neal, listen to me and you will know why."

He quickly turned around in his seat, leaning over to look at Wendy's small face. Her eyes were open again, this time wide and with a seriousness about them that had not been there before.

"This host body I am within has been damaged beyond repair. She will most likely die, yet I will not leave and seek another host. I am too weak now and I am willing to burn if I must. I will do all these things because I am assured that you will lead others to what you have found in the loft – to what I wished for Jonathan to do when I first came to him months ago."

Neal placed his hand across Wendy's and gripped it lightly, just as she had gripped his a few moments ago. "Jonathan," he said. "How can I save him?"

Wendy coughed once more, and then spoke again.

"Father is strong. He needs a host that will give him the physical ability required to carry out his task. In the guise of a child, he can approach anyone without them suspecting him. He has vitality and energy. If his host is rendered useless, he will be forced to seek another. Without...one...he is...powerless."

Conner's words grew fainter and fainter. Neal had to strain to hear the last few. The girl's eyes closed again and the slightest hint of a smile came to her lips. It was the most peaceful expression that Neal had seen on her face since all this had started. Slowly, he removed his hand from hers and turned back around in the front seat to face the darkened barn ahead of them. The truck was rolling through a patch of what felt like extremely soft dirt. He noticed that Melissa had her eyes locked straight ahead.

"Neal." she said.

He waited for her to finish whatever she was about to say. She said nothing, still staring ahead as hard as she could.

"What is it?" he asked, trying to follow her gaze. After a few seconds, she replied.

"I thought I just saw s…"

A gunshot broke the silence.

The windshield shattered in a round webbed pattern just to the right of Melissa's head. Neal knew instantly that it had been a slug from the Beretta. It whizzed between the seats at an angle and burst through the rear side glass on the Durango. Melissa screamed and instinctively stood on the brakes, rocking Neal forward in his seat.

"No, no, no!" he shouted. "Don't stop! Go! Go!"

She floored it this time, the tires spinning in the dirt beneath them. The V8 roared loudly.

The truck didn't move. The wheels did, but the truck didn't.

"Shit!" she exclaimed, throwing it into reverse and trying to back up. The wheels still didn't cooperate, spinning in the soft ground with a heart sinking whining sound. Neal reached for the four-wheel drive shifter to ensure that it was still engaged. It was, but the truck still was digging itself deeper.

The second shot burst through the passenger side window and Neal felt a sudden burning as it grazed the flesh of his right cheek, shattering the driver's window on its way out. He cried out in shock and reached up to feel the blood welling up in the two-inch gash that the bullet left in its wake. Had he not had his head turned down toward the shifter in the floorboard, it would have killed him.

Underneath, the wheels spun on and on in vain.

Neal forgot about his injury, grabbing Melissa and pulling her down into the seat seconds before another shot came through the window. As long as his heart was beating, he intended to get them out of this nightmare. Wendy's still form was still stretched across the rear seat, but from the position he was in, Neal couldn't tell if her eyes were open or not.

The next two shots ripped into metal at the front of the Durango, one of them going straight through the grill and the radiator. A hissing sound erupted from beneath the hood, followed by an outpouring of white steam. The engine began to falter, emitting a labored sound as if it were struggling. Two more shots tore through the trucks grill and into the engine. After about a minute, it slowly died.

"He's gonna shoot this truck to pieces with us in it," Neal said. "It won't be long before he goes for the gas tank."

"Where is he?" Melissa asked, her voice trembling with fear. "Jesus, it's like he's all around us."

Neal kept his hand comfortingly across her shoulder as they crouched there. "If he's moving as fast as he was in the barn, then he probably is."

They stayed low for the next few minutes, waiting for more shots. The only sound that could be heard was the sound of their own breathing, the tick of the engine, and the hiss of rising steam.

Then, they heard Jonathan's laughter from somewhere out there in the dark. After it faded, it was replaced with the sound of his voice.

"Come on out, Neaaalll. Bring that mind fucking Doctor Bitch with you!"

They lay still, not moving, hardly even breathing. The voice came again.

"You have the bastard spirit-child with you. I *know* you do. Give him to me or face the consequences!"

No reply came from within the truck. It sat there, a white and bullet riddled wreck sunk in a patch of soft dirt with white steam rolling from it.

"I'm impatient, Neeaaalllll." Jonathan taunted. "An impatient man with a loaded gun is no one to fuck with, I assure you!"

In the floorboard, Neal took his hand from Melissa's shoulder and grasped both of her hands in his. He looked her in the eye and squeezed them tightly.

"Run for the barn," he said. "Go as fast as you can."

Her eyed opened wide. "Why? What are you doing?" she said, her voice still thick with fright.

"The only thing I can," he snapped back. "Don't ask me any more questions and don't try to talk me out of it. Just run like all hell when I get out, okay?"

She bit her lower lip, tears streaming down her face.

"You have to reach Tiffany. You have to get her some help," he said. "Conner and I will handle Jonathan. It's up to us. If we can't stop it here and now, then it may never be stopped."

Melissa didn't want to release his hands. She closed her eyes tightly.

"For God's sake, Melissa, it's my own son," Neal said. " I have to at least *try* to save him."

After a few more seconds, she nodded her head weakly and let her grip on his hands slowly loosen. She opened her eyes and wiped them dry with her sleeve, trying to regain her composure. Neal reached a hand out and gently grasped her chin, lifting her eyes up to face him.

"You're clear on this, right?" he asked. "You know it's our last chance to save at least one of our *own* lives, don't you?"

She nodded again. "I do," she said. "But I'm scared shitless, Neal."

He tried to smile at her. "Then it looks like we've got ourselves a pretty good little club going on," he said, "because so am I."

"I guess so." she said.

Neal reached around behind himself and felt for the door handle. When he felt it in his grasp, he motioned for Melissa to do the same. She inched her way backwards and grabbed her handle as well.

"When I get out, give me a few seconds to call him to me, and then run," he said. "If you hear shots, keep running. If you hear me scream, keep running. Tiffany is depending on us - on *you*. Understand?"

"Loud and clear," she said. "Neal, I just..."

"What?" he asked.

She lowered her eyes from his. "I just wish I could have helped him more. That it hadn't taken me so long to piece this thing together."

Neal gripped the handle behind him tightly, preparing to depress it and open the passenger door. "You did all you could and more than we could have asked for," he said. "Just do me a favor and tell my wife I love her, okay?"

She gave him the same thumbs up signal that he had given them from the barn ladder earlier, and then tightened her grip on her door handle.

With one quick motion, Neal flung his door open wide and stepped out onto the gray dirt. Melissa watched as he took a few steps away from the truck and was swallowed up by the darkness.

CHAPTER 29

Jonathan emerged from the field directly in front of Neal. He appeared so quickly from the shadows that it was like he had come out of thin air. In his right hand was the Beretta. In his left, was the red gasoline can that had been sitting under the oak tree a few moments ago.

He was right there watching the whole time Neal thought to himself. *He could have killed me any time he wanted to.*

"Yes, Neaaalll, I could have," the boy said from behind a knowing and wicked smile. "But you have something I *want*. I won't be robbed of his glorious death *this* time. Give him to me, *now!*"

Neal didn't move. He cast his eyes over toward the front seat of the Durango, knowing that Melissa was crouching there, waiting to run for the barn.

Jonathan saw his eyes move. The glance to the left had only taken a fraction of a second, but Jonathan saw it.

"Doctor Bitch is still in hiding, I see," he said. "I smell the worthless runt there as well."

"Leave them alone, Darius!" shouted Neal. "I'm the one who you need to be concerned with right now!"

Jonathan laughed to himself. "Really?" he said. "I concern myself with what and with whom I fucking wish, Neeaaalll. Don't you know that?"

Neal saw that the boy did not have his finger on the Beretta's trigger, nor was he pointing it directly at him. He was standing about fifteen feet away, just out of the slowly weakening high beams from the Durango. Closing that distance would take no time at all for Neal, but if Jonathan managed to squeeze off one good shot….

"Thinking of rushing me, Neeaaall?" the boy asked. "I would have expected a *wiser* decision from a man of your intelligence."

Neal felt anger starting to rise within him. He was having a standoff with his own flesh and blood. His wife lay dying less than fifty yards away. His whole world had turned upside down and gone totally out of control.

"Give me back my SON, you son-of-a-bitch!" he shouted. "You've tormented him long enough!"

Jonathan raised the gun and pointed it straight at Neal, his small finger wrapping around the trigger. "I'm not through with him just yet," he said. "But *you*, I've had my fill of."

He squeezed the trigger.

The bullet that Jonathan Fowler had fired would have passed straight through Neal's heart and lungs, emerging from his back through a gaping wound and dropping him to the cold dirt. At the very second he applied pressure to the trigger, Melissa burst from the driver's side of the Durango and ran for the barn.

Jonathan jerked his body in her direction involuntarily when he sensed her movement, causing the shot to barely pass by Neal's left arm. Neal felt it across his jacket sleeve as it went, then saw Jonathan fire two more shots blindly into the field at Melissa.

The second one hit her.

Neal heard her cry out, and then she went down. As he watched her fall, his mind was filled with but one powerful and consuming thought.

Jesus, please, no more. No more. No more. No more. No more. No more.

"NO MORE!" he screamed aloud, breaking into a run straight for Jonathan. His body had sprung into motion almost even before he realized what he was doing. He had seen enough tonight. It had to end.

Jonathan brought the barrel of the gun around quickly, but not quick enough to squeeze off a shot before Neal tackled him. The shot went skyward as Neal wrapped his arms around Jonathan and drove him backward into the gray dirt. The gas can fell from his hand, hitting the ground with a dull thump and rolling over on its side. Neal and Jonathan both landed in a cloud of dust. Jonathan was still holding onto the gun. Neal immediately grabbed the boy's wrist and began to slam it repeatedly into the ground, hoping to make him release the weapon. With the other hand, he held down the other arm. It was unimaginable that the writhing thing beneath him was his son. The boy was snarling like an animal and he smelled of blood.

"You are a fool!" shouted Jonathan, spittle following the words from his mouth and striking Neal in the face. "How dare you raise your hands to ME?"

Neal knew he couldn't hold the boy down long. His strength was unbelievable. Neal felt like he was holding down a grown man *twice* his size. If he could just get the gun from him...

"Away!" Jonathan shouted, lifting his knee and ramming it into Neal's stomach. Neal felt his breath leave him and pain erupted in his gut. Another blow followed, this time from a small fist. It smashed into Neal's chin, knocking him to the ground beside the boy. The hold that he had on Jonathan's gun hand broke free.

"You'll not last long, Neaaalll." Jonathan laughed, standing up. "Time for your payment has come."

Neal was dazed from the punch but not so much that he couldn't see Jonathan lifting the gun again. He had to think of something damn quick or he would be dead.

So would Tiffany. . . . if she wasn't already.

Jonathan was taking aim when Neal swung his left leg around in an arc, catching the boy right behind the knees and laying him out flat on his back. The gun dropped from his hand and landed in the dirt. Neal immediately began to crawl on his hands and knees toward the gun, trying to reach it before the boy did.

Averting his eyes from for only a few seconds, Neal never even saw the boy pick up the metal gas can that was still lying right where it had fallen. He was just about to reach the gun when something solid and heavy struck him across the back of his skull, knocking him to his stomach and driving his face into the earth. He tried to get back up, but the world had begun to spin. Jonathan was standing over him, the gas can he had just used as a weapon still in his hand.

"I have wasted enough time with your miserable ass."

Jonathan grabbed Neal by the collar of his jacket. Using only one hand, he began to drag him toward the Durango.

"Doctor Bitch told you that the fields once glowed with fire on All Saint's Eve," the boy said. "So shall they glow tonight!"

Jonathan was pulling Neal's one hundred and ninety-pound frame along like it was nothing. He reached the truck on the passenger side. Neal had left the passenger side door open when he stepped out a few moments ago. Jonathan sat the gas can down, gripped Neal's collar with both hands, and hoisted him up from the ground. He threw him face first up into the truck's front seat and shoved him in the rest of the way.

"Join your friend in death, Neeaaall," the boy said. "You want to help him so fucking much, so you can keep him company for eternity."

Neal was aware of what was going on, but his senses had not come back to him yet. He put his hands on the seat beneath him and tried to push himself up, but he couldn't. It was like the part of his brain that controlled his motor functions was responding in slow motion. From the position he was sprawled in across the seat, he could see into the back. Wendy was still lying there. She was barely breathing and motionless.

Then, something splashed across the windshield.

Looking up, Neal saw liquid running down the glass. It poured through the bullet holes left by the Beretta and dripped down across Neal's face like rain. It ran down between his lips, stinging his skin. The odor filled his nostrils.

Jonathan was dousing the truck with gasoline.

"You'll burn, Neeeaall!" the boy shouted as he walked about the truck, the gas can in his hand. "Your flesh will roll from your bones and wither to a crisp! Oh, it will be glorious!"

He lifted the can and let the amber liquid pour across the Durango's hood, then moved around to the driver's side, splashing more against the door and side panels.

"Your weakling child has served me well!" he ranted as he poured. "I am pleased that the runt led me to him!"

Neal closed his eyes and opened them several times in a row, trying to get his bearings. Things were coming into focus a little better now, but it was taking more time than he had to spare. He put his hand down beneath himself again and managed to lift himself up from the seat a little. Pulling his knees up toward his stomach, he tried to rise up where he would be in a kneeling position on the seat. The steering wheel was right in front of him and he reached for it, using it to pull himself along.

Jonathan appeared in the open driver's door and covered him with gas. It hit him on his chest and soaked through his jacket, shirt, and jeans. He could feel it running down into his boots and drenching his socks beneath. Then, the gas was being splashed over the back seat. It seeped into Wendy's red gown and ran through her hair. Her eyes were mercifully closed as it poured across her small face and ran across the seat beneath her.

"St...st..stop!" Neal managed to shout. "Jonathan, don't do this!"

The boy kept to his task, dousing the rear of the vehicle now. "Jonathan is dead to you, Neaallll!" he shouted. "He is gone forever, as is the whore mother and mind fucking bitch doctor!"

Neal reached up and grabbed his head at the temples, placing his palms flat against them and pressing. He screamed out loud and closed his eyes tightly once more, trying with all his might to wipe away the stupor that had come from the blow with the gas can. When he opened them, his focus was still improving, but not entirely back to normal.

"Now all we need is a spark!" Jonathan shouted. "One tiny spark from a bullet from your own gun, Neeeaaal, and you and the runt will be nothing but ashes for me to drag my feet through!"

Jonathan turned and walked over to the spot where the gun had fallen from his hand, intending on firing one well-placed shot into the Durango's engine block. The resulting spark from the slug impacting with metal would set the truck and its occupants ablaze instantly. He stopped where the ground had been stirred up from their struggle, scanning the ground for the stainless steel barrel and black handle of the Beretta.

It was gone.

"Impossible," he said aloud to himself. "It was right..."

"DARIUS!"

The shout had come from his left, directly in front of the truck where the almost non-existent beams from the headlights faded out and the shadows began. He turned toward it.

Melissa stumbled out of the dark, the Beretta in her right hand and pointing straight at him. She was bleeding badly from her right calf. A trail of dried blood was visible running down the leg of her sweat pants and her white cloth shoe was a bright red. Her dislocated arm hung limply at her side and her auburn hair was strewn across her face. Stepping slowly forward, she kept the guns sight on Jonathan. Her hand was trembling terribly and her breath was coming out almost in gasps.

"Darius," she said, her voice stern and demanding. "I want you to stand right there and not move."

The boy grinned at her and sat the gas can down beside himself. "And what will you do if I don't, Doctor Bitch?" he asked, raising his eyebrows questioningly.

Melissa stopped six feet in front of him. "I'll blow your goddamn head off," she said. "Good enough?"

Jonathan pointed at her with a blood covered filthy finger. "You aren't screwing with me, are you, Doctor Bitch?" he asked. "I mean, after all, you *do* make a career out of screwing with people, right? How do I know you aren't full of shit?"

"Try me." she said.

The boy made a fist with the hand he had been pointing at her with, closing it so tightly she could hear his knuckle joints cracking. "I'll crush you, Doctor Bitch," he said. "I'll crush you into dust."

It was then that he moved…and he moved quick, launching himself with the agility of a panther straight at her. Melissa squeezed the trigger as soon as she saw his feet leave the ground, the shot ringing loudly in her ears. The boy had moved so fast that the bullet had to have missed. His forearm caught her across the stomach and she doubled over, dropping to her knees as he passed by her. Her wounded leg and arm throbbed with searing pain from the jolt of hitting the ground. It was intense enough to bring tears to her eyes. Holding her good arm across her stomach, she was amazed that she managed to hang onto the gun.

She sat there on her knees and waited for the boy to deliver a blow from behind her. There was no way she could turn around and get another shot in time to stop him from attacking again. Not in the pain she was in. Perhaps he would just break her neck and end it quickly.

I tried, Conner. I'm so sorry, Neal…. Tiffany…I did my best she thought to herself, anticipating the impact of a fist or whatever other weapons the boy might have up his sleeve.

What came instead was an angry cry of "BITCH!"

She turned her head slowly to look behind her, the sight before her the last thing she thought she would see.

Jonathan was sitting on the ground a few feet away. He was holding his right knee. A dark stain was growing steadily larger on the dirt beneath it. Pulling his hands away from it, he held them up to his face, palms open. They were covered in blood.

Holy shit, I hit him! Melissa thought.

"You miserable, brain twisting, worthless bitch!" Jonathan shouted, glaring up at her.

She rose to her feet, the gun still in her hand and hanging alongside her. The wave of pain in her stomach from where the boy had struck her was slowly subsiding. From where she stood, she saw the hole in the blue fabric of Jonathan's costume. The bullet appeared to have gone in barely an inch above the kneecap. It had to have severed muscle or tendons for sure. The exit wound was no doubt larger, but she couldn't see it because of the boy's position.

She still couldn't believe she had *hit* him. He had moved so fast that she didn't even have time to *aim* at him.

Jonathan tried to stand. Using his left knee and hands, he lifted himself from the gray dirt of the field and made an attempt to step toward Melissa. As soon as he put his weight on the right leg, it buckled and he collapsed right in front of her. She stood there and watched, the pain in her arm and calf taking a backseat to the shock of what she had just done.

"You think you have stopped me, bitch?" the boy asked, struggling to stand again. "It will take much more than one lucky shot."

He fell again, this time nearly face first. As soon as he hit the ground, he immediately began to struggle to stand again. Melissa just stood and watched as he went down a third time, her mind recalling certain things that Conner had told her tonight. One phrase repeated itself to her over and over.

Father is strong. He needs a host that will provide him with the physical ability to carry out his task.

She recalled her own words as well. The very words she had spoken to Neal before the gunfire had started.

Conner's physical limitations seem to be the same as Wendy's.

Jonathan was still straining to stay on his feet. Melissa could see the blood seeping from the wound. She began to back away from the boy, who was determined to reach her, even if he had to crawl.

"I need only to get my hands on you, Doctor Bitch!" Jonathan said from between gritted teeth as he kept dragging himself forward. "My leg may now be useless, but my grip is still powerful enough to rip the spine from your back!"

Inside Melissa's head, the mental tape recorder she had learned to develop for her chosen profession was still on replay.

Don't you see? He's only capable of doing what her body is capable of.

She began to realize what the bullet she had put in Jonathan's knee had done.

Wendy can't walk. She can't run. Neither can Conner.

The same rules would apply to Darius Weatherford and Jonathan Fowler. They had to. She had just incapacitated the body that Darius was within. If Jonathan could not rise to his feet, neither could Darius. It was that simple. The rest of what Conner had told them to do would be the hard part.

209

Burning the host body after it's been incapacitated is the only way to destroy the control-
ling spirit.

The bloody thing that was pulling itself toward her began to laugh as she kept backing away. "Where are you going, Doctor Bitch? Surely, you won't leave Neaaal and the mother whore to die. Or *would* you? And what about the runt and the girl - could you *live* with that?"

Melissa's heel bumped into something. She looked down and saw that it was the gasoline can that the boy had placed on the ground a few moments ago. She knew that she could simply pick it up, cover the boy in gas...and then...

No. She couldn't burn the child. She just...couldn't.

"You are a weakling, Doctor Bitch!" Jonathan laughed from the ground in front of her. "You have no nerve! Because of this pitiful excuse of a child I choose to serve me, you have let your emotions become your death warrant!"

She shakily raised the gun and pointed it at Jonathan's good leg. It was not what she wanted to do, but she had to make sure that he didn't get to his feet. He was only inches from her now, his blood soaked fingers reaching out and digging into the gray dirt to pull himself along. His thick brown hair was matted down across his forehead. The freckles on his cheeks were not visible through the thick layer of filth that was smeared across his face. The deep, rasping breaths he took sounded like that of a wild animal.

His eyes had to be the worst of all - they were black and lifeless, like those of a doll.

"Darius, I don't want to...have to shoot this boy," Melissa said, her voice trembling. "Please...don't...make me have to."

Jonathan stopped and looked up at her, grinning. He raised himself up on one knee and spread his arms out wide to both sides of him. "Why go for the leg, Doctor Bitch?" he shouted. "Why not the heart? If you're going to do it, do it right! Blow the little fucker's heart right out!"

Melissa's hand was shaking so badly that she thought she would drop the gun at any minute. Trying to keep it trained on Jonathan's leg, she curled her finger around the trigger.

"Darius...I beg you. Please, don't make me harm this child!" she said.

Jonathan kept his arms spread. "You can have the useless bag of bones if you wish!" he cried out. "Shoot him! I don't give a shit! I am nothing more than a passenger, riding on a worn cart! What makes you think there won't be another?"

Then, the boy lunged forward and grasped her wounded calf in a vise-like grip. Before she realized what she was doing, she had squeezed the trigger on the Beretta.

Click.

The clip was empty.

"Down, bitch!" screamed Jonathan, pulling her feet from beneath her as easily as pulling a tablecloth from an empty table. She landed hard on her back, pain shooting through her leg and arm. Having closed her eyes instinctively when she made impact, she opened them and found herself staring straight up into the night sky and disoriented. Dust was settling all around her and the stench of gasoline filled the air, so strong that she felt like she might vomit. The empty gun had dropped from her hand. Her cigarette case and house keys had flown from her jacket pocket, landing in the dirt beside her with a jingling thump.

Then, something moved near her feet.

She pulled herself up onto her right elbow, keeping her hurt arm close to her body. Peering into the darkness in front of her, she tried to hold back a scream when she saw what was coming.

Jonathan had crawled back to the gasoline can and grabbed it. Now, he was pulling himself back toward her with it in tow. His black eyes seemed to glisten as he approached.

"Oh, how you'll burn, Doctor Bitch," he said. "You'll burn and you'll burn. You'll scream too - quite loudly and for a looooonngg time."

The boy was already close enough to reach out and grasp her shoe. She tried to pull away and kick, but he had grabbed the leg he shot her in. The slightest movement caused her leg to go into spasms of pain. He drug himself close enough to her that he could prop himself up on his good knee. Hefting the gas can up in front of him, he began to tilt it toward her.

"Your time for payment has come!" the boy exclaimed.

Melissa was waiting for the stinging gas to wash across her face when movement exploded above her. Something hit the boy hard, sending the gas can rolling across the field. Then, the sound of what could only be bodies hitting the ground reached her ears. The resulting cloud of dust made it hard at first for Melissa to see through. Then, she heard the shout and smelled the gasoline soaked clothing.

"I want my boy back, you son of a bitch! I want him back NOW!"

It was Neal. He had regained his senses and waited for Jonathan to get so involved in his confrontation with Melissa that he wouldn't see him coming. The second he saw the boy raise the gas can, he charged him. He had hit him on the run, jerking him up from the ground and away from Melissa, only to stumble and send them both down into the field. Jonathan fell from his arms and landed beside him.

"Give him back to me, Weatherford!" Neal shouted, reaching out to restrain the boy.

Jonathan lashed out with a small fist, opening up a cut over Neal's right eye. He followed with another, catching him across his cheekbone. The blows sent Neal right back into the dirt on his back. Shaking them off, he hurriedly scrambled to his feet and dove for Jonathan, his hands out in front of him so that he could grab him. He felt the contact of his palms around the child's shoulders and then he was on top of him.

"Give him back, Weatherford!" Neal screamed again. "Give my wife and I our child! He's not yours anymore!"

Neal began to slap the boy. Once…twice…three times. Jonathan did little to resist, laughing each time Neal's open hand passed across his face. Neal stopped and stared deep into the child's black eyes, pulling him close to him.

"My son," he said, this time in a voice that was on the brink of break-ing down. "Please."

The boy just sat there letting Neal manhandle him. He ceased laugh-ing, and smiled at Neal with the same demonic grin he had worn all night. "A pity that you would go through so much pain for a worthless child, Neaaaaallll," he said. "Your weakling piss ant of a son isn't worth such trouble."

Neal shook the boy violently, screaming aloud into the night. The sound carried on the wind across the gray fields, vanishing amidst the trees near the highway. He could take no more. The boy just sat there watching with dead and dark eyes. Neal hung his head and tried to calm himself. After a few seconds, he looked back up at the child.

"Wendy and Conner are dead, Weatherford," he said. "There's no need for you to bother with them now. I ask you…to please spare my son. Please give him back to me. Give him back…to Tiffany."

The boy, still grinning, glanced back toward the Durango. "The girl's body may be dead, Neaaaalll," he said, "but the bastard-runt's spirit has not been burned from her flesh. Unless that happens, his spirit will seek solace elsewhere."

Melissa lay where she had fallen earlier, listening to the exchange between father and son.

"No, Weatherford," Neal said. "Conner doesn't want...to run anymore. He is ready to rest at...last. Wendy is dead...and Conner isn't leaving her. He is *ready* to burn; knowing that if at least one of us makes it.... out of here alive tonight, his remains will be placed alongside the others you murdered. He knows he will be.... at peace."

The boy's smile faded and his lips drew back from his teeth like that of a mad dog. "You LIE!" he shouted. "You lie to save your own worthless hide!"

Neal shook his head. "No, Weatherford. I do not. Conner is beyond your torment now. If nothing else...we *have* accomplished that."

Jonathan's face became a portrait of pure hatred. His eyes narrowed almost to slits. The veins in his neck began to pulse beneath the skin. The only sound that could be heard was their breathing and the occasional sound of the leaves racing across the field on the wind. Melissa stood and began to head toward them, limping along as best she could. The voices of father and son grew louder in her ears as she moved closer.

"You want the child?" Jonathan asked. "He's all yours. My need for him has passed."

Neal stood from the kneeling position and jerked the boy up with him. He raised him up to face level, shaking him hard again, his small feet dangling at Neal's waist. He would not let him go. He would not run. Not until he got his son back. He would sacrifice everything just to...

Suddenly, Jonathan burst into tears.

Melissa stopped in her tracks, the sound of the boy crying startling her. Neal could only stare, the anger that had taken him over dissolving. Excitement coursed through him when he saw the tears rolling down Jonathan's cheeks. Then, the child opened his eyes long enough for Neal to see that they were no longer black and filled with evil. They were Jonathan's eyes. Though they were red and filled with tears, they were a wondrous sight to behold.

"Thank you, thank you, thank you." Neal found himself repeating over and over. He pulled the boy tight to himself and pressed his face to his, feeling the warmth of him. Neal himself felt hot and dizzy, but he knew it was most likely due to the adrenaline coursing through his veins after all that had happened. How he felt didn't matter now. He had his son back.

"It's okay, it's okay, ssshhh," Neal said, slowly sitting down and rocking the crying child back and forth. "Daddy is right here. He's right here and he loves you. He loves you, Jonathan, he loves you."

Melissa watched the scene unfolding before her from where she stood. Weatherford had said something to Neal a few moments ago that she wasn't comfortable with - something that frightened her. Right now, Neal was holding Jonathan against him as if he would never let him go, gently rocking and soothing him. She would give them just a little longer before she went to them.

Jonathan lifted his head from his father's shoulder and rubbed his eyes. His nose was running and the tears had cut paths in the dirt on his face. He began to sob again and reached for his leg.

"Daddy, my leg hurts." he cried.

Melissa knew the child was feeling the pain now from the bullet she had put in him. She imagined he must feel as if he had awakened from an awful dream, the burning sensation of the gunshot arriving when the dream reached its end. She stood and watched as his father tended to him, listening to them intently and trying to figure out what it was about Weatherford's words that had bothered her.

Neal slowly laid him down on the ground. Telling him to lay flat, he ripped the blue fabric of his Halloween costume from the bottom of the leg up to the knee. There was a small hole just above the kneecap. Whether the bullet was still there or had passed through, he didn't know. He *did* know that there would be surgery and probably a permanent limp.

As long as his son was alive, he didn't care.

Tearing the fabric into strips, Neal wound it tightly around Jonathan's upper thigh. He grabbed a strong stick from the ground nearby and inserted it in the fabric, twisting it tightly to prevent any more loss of blood. Jonathan screamed with pain, but Neal knew it had to be done.

"Almost done, little man," Neal said, giving the stick one last twist. "Now we have to go and get your mom."

Jonathan's crying subsided a little at the mention of Tiffany. He looked at his father and asked "Where is she?"

Neal looked over at Melissa. She was standing there silently. He realized that she was allowing him his time with Jonathan. He prayed that Tiffany was still alive, looking down at his watch. Though it had seemed like forever, barely fifteen minutes had passed since they had made their getaway from the barn.

As Neal turned his attention back to his son, Melissa's thoughts were leading her to a silent and awful realization. Her eyes grew wide as the words she had been trying to recall ran through her mind.

Your weakling piss ant of a son may as well be dead, too. He's useless to me now.

She felt a sinking sensation in her stomach.

I am nothing more than a passenger riding on a worn cart.

The present words passing between Neal and Jonathan diminished to nothing but a distant whispering as more of their earlier conversation came rushing back to her.

What makes you think there won't be another?

"Neal!" Melissa called out, stepping toward them. "Neal, get away from him!"

He looked up at her as she approached. "What is it?" he asked.

Before she could reply, Jonathan repeated the question he had just asked of Neal.

"Where's mommy at?"

"Mommy is waiting for us in the barn," Neal said. "She has a hurt place just like you and you can both go to the doctor together."

Jonathan wiped his eyes. "Will you be with us? he asked.

Neal reached down and gently stroked the little boy's hair. "I'll always be with you, Jonath..."

He stopped in mid-sentence and grabbed at his head.

"NEEAAAALLL, NOOO!" Melissa screamed.

The hot flash that Neal had felt moments ago now returned to consume him. He felt drugged, as if he had been injected with morphine and was slowly fading away. Then, the feeling of weakness was replaced by one of vigor and strength. His mind was suddenly clear and focused. Then, just as quickly, he was dazed again and pouring with sweat.

"Oh, Jesus." said Melissa, running to reach Jonathan. She kneeled down and grabbed the boy as Neal stood crouched over just a few feet away. Jonathan realized that Doctor Melly had him now, but he had no idea what she was doing out here in this dark place with his daddy. She was carrying him and running *away* from daddy and he didn't understand that either. The pain in his leg stabbed at him each time it bounced with Doctor Melly's strides, and he tried not to cry in front of her.

"Damn you, Weatherforrrrrd!" screamed Neal into the night. He reached into the sky and grabbed at the air, madly clawing at something that no one could see. He ripped at the throat of his sweatshirt beneath his jacket, bursting the stitches. Then, he grasped his head once more and began to spin about. Losing his footing, he fell to the ground, still screaming and cursing the name of Darius Weatherford.

"What's wrong with my daddy?" asked Jonathan as Melissa rested him on the ground several yards away, just on the other side of the Durango. She looked at him and had a sudden realization; for the very first time in her life, she didn't know what to say to a child.

Neal rose to his feet. He stopped screaming and staggered as if he were drunk. Then, he seemed to shake the unsteadiness that had overtaken him. He slowly began to turn his head back in Melissa and Jonathan's direction.

All Melissa could do was sit there and comfort the boy, wondering what in the hell she was going to do while the prophetic words of a child long dead echoed in her ears.

Seek solace in another. . .. Seek solace in another. . .in another. . .another. . .

"You see, Doctor Bitch?" said a voice from the field. "It takes more than a bullet to take down the likes of me!"

The words were Weatherford's. The *voice* was Neal's.

"Please, Lord, no, no, no, no." she whispered to herself. Jonathan tried to sit up, but she restrained him.

"It's my daddy!" he cried out. "Lemm'e go!"

Melissa held onto him, her eyes never leaving the dark form that was now stepping toward them.

"It's not your daddy, sweetheart. It looks like him, but it isn't him."

"Who is it, then?"

"It's the bad man, Jonathan. The bad man who took you away and made you hurt people."

Jonathan looked up at her, his eyes suddenly showing fear instead of innocence. "The man who wanted to hurt the little boy who talked to me at night?" he asked.

"Yes, it is, honey." she told him. "He's sent your daddy away and now he wants to hurt us too."

Jonathan tried to pull free from Melissa again, but she wouldn't release him. "No, it's my daddy! It's my daddy!" he began to cry out.

Neal was so close now that his face was visible. He was grinning as he approached - the same grin that Jonathan had worn earlier. Though it was horrible to look at, his grin didn't disturb Melissa anywhere near as much as his eyes did. They had, as Jonathan's had before, become dark and lifeless - the eyes of a dead man.

He stopped in front of her, staring down upon her and Jonathan. Then he laughed, throwing his head back as he did so. His gasoline soaked and dirt-matted hair fell across his eyes and he brushed it away with a filthy hand.

Melissa pulled Jonathan closer to her. "You failed, Darius!" she shouted after him. "Conner knows that his bones will be found now. He *knows!*"

Neal's expression slowly changed into a horrific scowl, his lips drawing back and his fists clenching. The gasoline stench from his drenched clothing was almost overpowering.

"Even so, there will be *no one* to lead anyone here if I and I alone walk out of this field tonight, Doctor Bitch!"

Then, he lunged at her, his hands opened as if they were talons about to shred prey.

Melissa and Jonathan began to scream.

He hit her with his hands locked around her throat, already starting to constrict her breathing as she fell back against the ground and he landed on top of her. The blow had knocked Jonathan from her arms, sending him rolling over on his side in the dirt. His screaming went on and on, driven by pain and the fear of what was happening. Melissa half gasped, half screamed to him as he sat up and turned toward them, watching through his tears.

"Jonathan, run! Run...as fast as you can! Go *now!*"

Then, Neal took one hand from her throat long enough to strike her in the mouth. The punch caused her eyes to fill with water and she felt blood against her tongue. He had split her lip. The next blow would probably do worse than that.

"Shut your fucking mouth!" he yelled down at her. "It will do neither you nor the boy any good. It's over, Doctor Bitch! It's the end of the line for you and the worthless spirit-child!"

In the background, Jonathan had gone silent.

She reached up and grabbed Neal's face, trying to at least get her nails into his skin. Her hands fell across the wound on his cheek where the bullet had grazed him earlier. She jammed her index finger into it, scraping across the interior of it with her nail. He screamed with pain but would not relinquish the grip he had on her. She felt like her windpipe was about to collapse. She felt dizzy. As the terrible pressure increased and increased, she started blacking out. The way that he had spread his body out atop hers and pinned her, she knew she had no chance of throwing him off of her.

As she gave up struggling and waited to die, she prayed to God that Jonathan had done as she asked and ran. She hoped that he had run far away. Far from the clutches of the beast that was atop her now.

Then, she heard a sound.

Click!

The sound came from her left and was accompanied by a brief flash of light. Then, the most awful shriek of pain she had ever heard came from above her.

It was Neal.

He released her throat, rolling onto his back in front of her and madly thrashing about on the ground. She lifted herself up and tried to see what was going on. Dirt sprayed across her face as Neal screamed and writhed just inches from her feet.

His jacket was on fire.

Melissa scrambled to stand up as quick as she could, instinctively reaching for her throat and holding it as air began to return to her lungs. She looked to her left and saw Jonathan standing there in the darkness. He was trembling violently and it wouldn't have surprised Melissa if the boy were in shock. She saw that he was holding something between the thumb and forefinger of his right hand - something small with a shiny top that reflected the flames.

It was her lighter — her silver Zippo that had fallen from her jacket earlier with her cigarette case and house keys.

Jesus she thought to herself. *He found the damn lighter and….*

Neal's screams interrupted her thoughts. The smell of burning gas and hair reached her nose as she looked back to see that the flames were climbing dangerously close to his head. The entire back of his leather jacket was almost gone, the fire now starting to creep down his arms. He lay flat on his back and began to grind his back into the dirt, trying to extinguish the flames. Jonathan never took his eyes from him.

"Daddy..." he said softly.

Melissa heard a ripping sound as Neal pulled the burning jacket from his body and threw it, dropping to the ground and burying his hands in the dirt to extinguish the flames that had ignited on them. She limped her way over to Jonathan and pulled him close to her. He was still gripping the lighter as tightly as he could and watching his father.

Neal pulled his hands from the gray soil beneath him. His flesh had been burning. Melissa could smell it. His lower jaw and entire neck were reddish, pink color from the flames that had licked at him seconds before. His hands were shaking as he held them up in front of him to study them. They were burned, but not to the bone. The skin was raw and beginning to bubble in several spots. He looked up at Melissa and Jonathan, managing a staggering step toward them.

Then, he dropped to his knees and hung his head, putting his face down into his burned hands. He kept it there, his breaths coming in heaving gasps and his body beginning to tremble all over.

Melissa had her hand on Jonathan's shoulder. She had been so engrossed in what was happening before her that she didn't even realize he had started to slip from beneath her touch until it was too late. He walked straight toward Neal.

"Jonathan, no, you..."

He was already over an arm length away from her by the time she got the words out of her mouth. Within seconds, he was standing in front of the kneeling form of his father.

God help us, she thought. *Please don't let this be happening.*

She knew she should go and pull him away from the demon that hid within Neal's body. That she should save him from the danger he had just placed himself in. It was an all-consuming urge that she nearly acted on...until a strange calmness suddenly settled over her. A calmness that seemed to tell her that everything would be okay and she need not worry anymore. She had no idea where it had come from or why it had suddenly wrapped its soothing embrace about her, but she knew that whatever it was, it was welcome.

Then, she heard Jonathan speak.

"I....I'm sorry, daddy."

The kneeling man in front of him slowly lifted his head. He opened his eyes and looked at the boy, reaching out with both of his shaking hands and placing them on each small shoulder. Melissa stood her ground and listened as he opened his mouth and spoke to Jonathan, the words surprising her, yet breaking her heart at the same time.

"I love you, Jona...Jonathan. Please don't for...forget that. I love y...you."

The boy reached out and put both of his arms around his father's neck. Neal's hands dropped from his shoulders and hung limply at his sides as the boy embraced him. He felt burning pain as the little arms pressed against his charred skin, but he knew he wouldn't be able to fight much longer.

"Jonathan," he said, hearing the boy start to cry. "I'm going away... and I won't be...coming ba...back."

"Why not?" cried the child, tightening his hold. "Why, why, why, why?"

"Because, son, I just.... have to. I can't..... hold him off of me. He's too...strong. Any second.... now...he'll have me again and he'll make me..."

"Is it the bad man?" Jonathan asked, slowly letting go of Neal and stepping back to look him in the eye.

"Yes it is, Jonathan. It's the b...bad man, and he wants me to hurt people. He wants me to...hurt you and Doctor Melly."

Melissa heard Neal start to sob as he spoke.

"I'm sorry for...not believing in you, son. I'm sorry...for thinking...that all those nights were just...bad dreams. I know now...that they weren't. I'm so...sorry."

Jonathan reached out and wiped his father's tears away, then wiped his own. His lower lip was protruded in the pout that Neal knew well. He looked down at the silver lighter in his hands and slowly began to turn it over and over again.

Neal reached out and placed one badly burned hand across Jonathan's - across the one that held the lighter. He lifted it up between the two of them and flipped open its top. His pleading eyes looked as if they were almost back to normal.

"Please," he whispered. "I beg you, Jonathan. It's the only way."

The child shook his head. "No, daddy, no!" he cried, the tears coming again.

"It's...the only way to make the...bad man leave daddy alone."

Jonathan looked at the lighter, then back to his father, still shaking his head.

Neal removed his hands from Jonathans, letting his arms fall limply to his sides. He looked over his son's shoulder and saw Melissa standing there watching. They made visual contact for just a second, and Melissa found herself looking into eyes that were once again Neal Fowler's, if only for a few more seconds. Somehow, she realized, he had suppressed being dominated by Weatherford just long enough to say goodbye.

"Jonathan," he said. "Please tell your mother...that I love her...and that I did my...best."

The boy stood there listening.

"And you...you will always be...my little man."

Hanging his head once more, Neal began to cry freely, the sobs wracking his body. He was shaking violently and he began to cough. His crying began to slowly change into a moan of pain. It started out low and began to build until it was almost a scream.

Jonathan slowly extended the lighter to just beneath his father's chin. Though his small hands were still trembling, he managed to place his thumb on the lighter's striking wheel.

"Please son." he heard his father say.

Click!

CHAPTER 30

By dawn the next morning, the numbers of the dead were many.

Sumter police had a death toll of thirty-two and still counting at around one o'clock in the morning. Of the thirty-two, eleven were between the ages of five and fourteen.

A retired security guard shot little Zachary Welch over on Willow drive. The old man had caught him trying to break through his kitchen door out back. He said that the boy had damn near ripped the outer screen door off by the hinges by the time he was able to get to his gun. After firing four shots through the door, the old man opened it to find Zachary lying on his porch in a pool of blood. He never had even the faintest notion that it had been a child out there in the dark, tearing his house apart like an animal.

Aimee Jacobs was run down in front of the Swan Lake Park by a city police car. The twenty three-year-old cop who was driving felt awful about it, but only moments before, the tiny little girl had leaped onto the vehicle's hood as he pulled away from a stoplight and smashed the windshield with her fist. When the young officer hit the brakes, she was flung into the path of an oncoming pickup truck.

The owner of an animal hospital out on the 378 frontage road shot three unidentified boys. The vet had come in to check on the dogs he had been keeping in the pen out back overnight and found them in a frenzy. When he flipped on the floodlights, the boys were already halfway over the fence and charging him. In their hands were knives that they had taken from home. The vet was pocketing a thirty-eight and he used it after he had already been slashed three times.

Out on 76 headed toward Lynchburg, a four-year-old girl was trying to hack her mother to death with a bush ax she had brought in from the garage. She died when she fell from the front porch steps and landed on the blade, but not before she managed to hit her mother with it twice.

Not far from Shaw Air Force Base, Milton Carter stumbled out of Scooter's Lounge after several drinks and came face to face with a nine-year old Asian girl who managed to cut him across his femoral artery with a piece of a broken beer bottle. Milton immediately sobered up enough to defend himself, cutting the girl's throat with a switchblade he had carried since the sixties. Unfortunately, he bled to death right next to her in the parking lot.

On Church Street, a seven-year old boy set his family's home on fire by throwing their still burning jack-o-lantern against the living room drapes. His father snuffed out the blaze with the fire extinguisher from beneath the kitchen sink, and then he fractured the boy's skull with the empty canister trying to defend his wife and himself.

The scenario repeated itself throughout town that night. Sumter Fire and Rescue received a flood of 911 calls up until well past midnight. Most were from adults who had either witnessed or been a victim of their own or someone else's child. Around one a.m., many of the callers started becoming hysterical children, crying that they had woken up and found their families butchered. On the streets, children suddenly found themselves not knowing why or how they had gotten there. They called for their families and cried into the night. Moments before, they had walked in a murderous horde. Now, they were nothing more than lost, confused, and afraid, their clothes covered with someone else's blood.

The fire in Weatherford's field was just one small part of the chaos that went on in the town of Sumter that Halloween night. It had been spotted from Highway 76 by a passing motorist who called it in on his cell phone. Trucks and an ambulance arrived to find a burning sport-utility vehicle and the charred remains of its driver not far from it. Though they responded to the call fast, by the time they got there the truck was nothing more than a burned out shell. The smell of gasoline hung heavy in the air, telling attending volunteer firemen that this was no accident. It appeared that the truck and the driver were both soaked with it. The body was unrecognizable at the scene, but it would soon be identified as that of Neal Fowler who lived up on the highway just outside of the city limits.

Further investigation resulted in finding the burnt corpse of little Wendy Crenshaw in the truck's rear seat. She was lying flat on her back in a resting position, as if she was dead before the fire ever started.

There was also a woman and a boy, both pretty beat up and with gunshot wounds. Neither one wanted to offer any insight on what had happened, both clinging to each other tightly as they were wrapped in blankets by one of the paramedics. The ambulance had arrived first and found the two standing in the old Weatherford barn doorway, tending to another woman who was lying on the ground and bleeding badly from an apparent gunshot wound.

Sumter Hospital's Emergency Trauma staff got the call that two women and a young boy were on the way in. The older woman and the boy were said to be in a mild state of shock and weren't talking. Given the present state of what was happening all over town tonight, the paramedics instructed the waiting staff to have the authorities hold off on swarming the two with questions as soon as they arrived.

The woman who had been shot wasn't expected to make it to the hospital alive.

CHAPTER 31

It was mid-November when the funeral service took place in Camden Memorial Cemetery. The afternoon was cold and rain clouds loomed above the treetops as the two caskets were lowered into the earth.

Nearly two weeks had passed since the events of that night. The bodies had been autopsied and held until authorities would permit the burial. Several such burials were taking place in and around the town of Sumter, as well as in Bishopville, Maysville, and Lynchburg.

The burial plot at Camden Memorial had been in Tiffany's family ever since she had been a child. Neal had told her and her parents that he would be honored to rest there among them and beside his wife. Most of his own family had already passed on, and he often told Tiffany that his place on earth was *with her.* He saw no reason why he shouldn't be beside her in the *next* world as well. Tiffany would always tell him how much of a romantic he was.

As cars filed out of the cemetery under the gray sky, drops of rain began to fall. Melissa Grayson felt them on her face as she sat in her wheelchair by the gravesite, looking down at the two caskets in their vaults. She was wearing a knee length black dress and a matching black jacket, the dark blue sling her arm was in hardly noticeable against it. The bullet that the doctors had removed from her leg had fractured the bone and torn through her calf muscle. It was still painful to put much weight on it, so she was to use the chair for a couple more weeks and then graduate to a cane. The bruises on her face had almost healed, fading away a little bit more with each passing day.

Beside her, Jonathan was standing with Tiffany's mother and father. He sobbed quietly and turned to press his face into his grandfather's pants leg. His grandmother kneeled down to comfort him, pulling a handkerchief from her purse to dry his eyes. He turned to her and embraced her as best he could, the brace on his wounded leg and small crutches he stood upon making the hug quite awkward.

Melissa sat there and closed her eyes, listening to the boy as he grieved. She thanked God that the shot she had put into his knee had not severed a major artery. It had, however, shattered his kneecap and re-constructive surgery. He had thought it was *"cool"* at first when he learned he would have a steel kneecap put in to replace his damaged one. Then, after the numerous surgeries, the pain and the limitations put on him by the doctors began to frustrate him. It would all pass soon, as would the memories. He was *alive*, and that was all Neal and Tiffany Fowler ever wanted.

Beyond the cemetery walls, the town of Sumter was beginning to recover, though no one had offered a logical explanation yet for what had happened. The talk of Darius Weatherford returning from the dead made its rounds, but it was dismissed by many as an overblown campfire tale. Still, such talk would instill the idea in the community that something evil was at work that night.

It was a dark time, one that many would eventually refuse to talk about in the years to come. The press and the television cameras would be around for a few months, as would the State Police, paranormal investigators, psychics, and curious day trippers who would travel from all over the Carolinas and surrounding states to see the town where *it* had happened - the town where children had gone insane.

Soon, the dust would settle. After a substantial amount of time went by and all of the dead were laid to rest, it would become a part of the town's history that people would preferably block from their minds. Some would say that the town lived in a state of denial, refusing to confront their fears about what had really happened, though it mattered little to those who had lived through it.

It was best to let old ghosts simply fade away.

CHAPTER 32

"Higher, Doctor Melly, higher!"

Jonathan's voice was filled with excitement as the kite soared upward, dancing against the backdrop of blue sky and white clouds. Melissa released another few feet of string from the spool in her hands and watched it climb a little more.

"I think it's about high enough, don't you?" she asked, watching him as he slipped down from the wooden split rail fence he was sitting on and began to run toward her across the lawn.

It was a joy to watch him run again. He had a noticeable limp and he favored the leg a bit when he ran, but at least he was acting like a normal eight-year-old boy again.

Almost two years had passed since that Halloween. Things were better now. Melissa's wounds had mended rather nicely, and her practice was thriving. She refrained from working for about six months following the incident, but now she was back at it full steam ahead.

Jonathan was still her favorite patient.

He had hardly spoken a word for weeks after the night in Weatherford's field. Other than the crying, he never uttered a single word at the funeral service. She really thought that the child had lost his mind. Fearing that he would wind up in a mental facility like many of the other children had, she had pleaded with her doctors to allow her to sit with him in his room while he recovered from the many surgical procedures on his knee. There, she talked with him, comforting him as best she could. She talked with him about his mother and father. She talked about the little boy and the bad man who wanted to hurt him, and everybody else too. Trying to explain such events to a child of six was hard, but she sat there and tried to answer all of his questions in the best way she knew how. It had been a long road from then until now, but at some point over the last few months, he had let go of the whole experience. He was just a typical little boy again, one who loved racecars, action figures, cartoons, and G.I. Joes.

Jonathan had been living with his grandparents in Camden ever since he came home from the hospital. Their brick ranch style home was situated on the outer edge of the sub-division, and a split rail fence separated it from a large grass lot next door. It was a perfect open space for Jonathan to play in. There were other kids his age in the neighborhood as well, so finding a playmate was never a problem. They would toss their Frisbees and play football for hours on the lot beyond the fence. There was no place better in the world for the child to be.

Melissa spent lots of time with Jonathan now. Not having his mother and father around was extremely hard on him at first. She had driven over to see him on several nights when his grandmother had called her, telling her that he was asking for *Doctor Melly* in his sleep. She had been willing to do anything to help him on his road to recovery. Besides, she knew what losing someone could do to a person, especially a child like Jonathan.

She had put the past behind her as well. Life was good again. The look on the child's face as he ran to her side made everything seem so much better.

"Lemm'e fly it now, Doctor Melly. Lemm'e."

"Okay, okay, here, take it."

She handed him the string and watched as he took off in a run, headed across the grass toward the back of the property. The kite looped and dove as he pulled the string in every direction imaginable, excited over what trick he could make it do next.

The day was only mildly hot, not bad at all for September. She had woken this morning and decided to come out and visit for the day. Sunday could be extremely dull just sitting around the house. Jonathan would certainly keep her busy. The moment she had pulled into the driveway an hour ago, he was already bounding out the front door waving the kite.

Now, as the boy played, Melissa sat down on the ground and hugged her knees up to her chest. Luckily, she had worn what she called her "Camden Clothes," consisting of faded jeans, worn out tennis shoes, and an old T-shirt. Afternoons with Jonathan could be quite a dirty and grass stained affair at times, though well worth it. She pulled a pack of cigarettes from her pocket and considered lighting one. After sitting there and holding it for a moment, she decided not to. She had been trying to quit for about two months. She still kept a pack on her most of the time, just in case the urge got too strong and she decided to throw in the towel, but she had made it this far. No sense in blowing her record now.

Closing her eyes, she leaned her head back and let the breeze dance through her hair. Such a simple pleasure - one that most people would overlook. She was thinking about how good it felt when she thought she heard light footsteps coming across the lawn behind her.

"You have no idea how much these visits mean to him, Melissa."

Melissa turned her head toward the voice and smiled. Sitting down on the grass next to her was Tiffany Fowler. She was wearing an oversized T-shirt that hung to her knees, jeans, and was barefoot. Her long hair was pulled back away from her face and tucked behind her ears. She looked relaxed and at peace with herself. Sliding up next to Melissa, she sat Indian style. It had always been her and Jonathan's favorite television watching position, and she had grown accustomed to it.

"Look, mom, look how high!" shouted Jonathan, having spotted Tiffany. He was pointing at the soaring kite.

She smiled and waved. "I see, I see!" she yelled to him. "It's as high as an airplane!"

Jonathan turned his attention back to the task at hand, reeling out a few more feet of string and taking off in a run toward the other side of the lot.

Melissa thought that Tiffany looked wonderful. It was an absolute miracle that she was even here after losing so much blood in Weatherford's barn that night. The slug had basically gone right through her, entering her body in the fleshy part of her stomach and exiting through her lower back at a slight angle. The wound it left behind and its aftermath, however, had been horrific. Tiffany had already lost a vast amount of blood by the time that the paramedics arrived that night. So much, in fact, that no one thought she would survive the ride to the emergency room. Astoundingly, she made the seven-minute trip fully conscious. Only when they rolled her into the Trauma Unit did she begin to black out.

Transfusions had begun immediately as doctors evaluated her wound. There was no bullet, just its path. A ghastly pale when she arrived, color began to return to her cheeks. For the first twenty-four hours in I.C.U., she was considered stable, but serious. Then, an infection set in that turned out to be more life threatening than the gunshot. For weeks, she lingered as it slowly poisoned her body. Her parents were in constant contact with the I.C.U. nurses, or were at the hospitals themselves during the whole process. Once Melissa was well enough, she joined them. When Jonathan inquired about her and asked when she could come home, no one knew quite what to tell him.

After six months of antibiotic treatments, pain medicine, and hospital food, Tiffany came home to her parents' place in Camden. Jonathan was ecstatic about her return. They were totally inseparable, and still were most of the time.

The house in Sumter was sold to a couple from Raleigh, North Carolina. Tiffany walked away with a little money from it, but not as much as she would have if she hadn't dropped the price on it. Following all that had happened, she was in no mood to haggle about money, and especially over a home that signified the beginnings of that awful night. She was more than ready to do what she had to do to part with it.

It had taken a long time, many sleepless nights, and countless tears, but for her, Jonathan, and Melissa, life had returned to as close to normal as possible.

Tiffany watched as her son ran and laughed, the kite sailing above him. She plucked a tall blade of grass from the ground beneath her, twirling it between her fingers. Melissa put a hand reassuringly on her leg, knowing what was on her mind.

"Been thinking about him today, haven't you?" she asked.

Tiffany let the grass fall from her hand, watching as it spiraled down to the ground. She looked over at Melissa, sadness in her eyes, but smile still on her face. "All day long," she replied. "It hits me like that sometimes."

"It's okay, Tiff. You're supposed to miss him. How about Jonathan? Any bad dreams?"

Tiffany turned her eyes back to the boy again. "No. Not lately. It's been at least three or four months."

"And yourself?" Melissa asked with a smile, raising her sunglasses so Tiffany could see her raised eyebrows.

"I'm fine. Really. No bad dreams for a long time. Just…ones that make me sad. That's all."

"Dreams of Neal?"

Tiffany looked up into the clouds. "Yes. I dream of Conner, too. It's odd that I dream of him, because other than that old photo of yours, I really never knew what he looked like. I dream that…he's alive and that he's with other children somewhere. And sometimes, Neal is there too, standing with him. Sometimes when they talk to me…it seems so real that I wake up expecting them to be right there with me…but they aren't."

"No, they aren't." said Melissa. "They exist now only in our hearts and minds, Tiff. I think of them too, believe me. I think of how wonderful a father and husband Neal was to you and Jonathan. About Conner and what would have happened to all of us if he. . ."

"Hadn't spoken to us in the lot or in the barn?" asked Tiffany, finishing the question for her.

Melissa nodded. "Yes. The lot. The barn. And later, in the field. I could hear him. . .trying to reach me."

"We all heard him, Melissa. The first time it hit me was in the barn, when we thought he was dead. Couldn't you *feel* it? It was overpowering, like a wave washing over my body. I knew he was alive. He was telling me. He was telling all of us so we wouldn't give up."

They were both silent for a moment, Jonathan's distant laughter and the singing of the birds the only sounds present. After a little while, Melissa spoke again.

"You know, Jonathan says that. . . . Conner told him where the lighter was that night, Tiff. He told him that I had dropped it and exactly where it was. Did you know that?"

"Yes. He talked to me about it. He told me that the little boy who came to him at night told him that if he didn't. . .get the lighter and. . . .. do what he did, that his daddy would be taken by the bad man and that his mommy and his Doctor Melly would all die."

"We would have."

"I know."

Tiffany gazed off into the distance toward the main highway that led up to I-20. Her thoughts traveled along it as they often had, twisting and turning along the pavement, heading across the overpass and down country roads until Camden Memorial came into view. She found herself staring down at her husband's headstone, fresh cut flowers standing in vases on both sides of it. The inscription she had asked for was as much a part of her memory as it was of the stone it was engraved in.

Neal Thomas Fowler

May 8, 1965- October 31st 2002
"Beloved Husband and Father"

Beside the stone was another. Somewhat smaller, it was adorned on its curved top by the carved figure of a young lamb at rest. Tiffany had thought that the figure represented all that would ever need to be said about whose grave it marked.

Conner

She had asked that the stone be simply inscribed with the child's first name only. He wouldn't have wanted Weatherford.

There had been no one to claim him. The location of the graves of the other children had turned out to be a mystery. Most said that they were unmarked, forgotten, and could be anywhere in the countryside surrounding Sumter. Tiffany, with the approval of her family, had Conner laid to rest beside Neal. Until the other children were found and she could fulfill the promise, she thought it was where he would want to be.

She would make sure that he was not forgotten. That people would know that someone cared.

"Tiffany?"

Melissa's voice startled her back into reality.

"Sorry," Tiffany said, laughing a little. "Just…. lost myself for a minute there. I was thinking."

"I see that. You were zoning out on me, hon."

Tiffany leaned back on the grass and rested on her elbows, putting her feet out in front of her. "The zoning out champ, that's me," she said. "Sorry."

Melissa leaned back on the grass also, facing her. "No need to be. Hell, I find *myself* doing it from time to time, and I'm a psychologist. What's wrong with that picture?"

Tiffany laughed softly again. "I guess nothing. Thanks for making me feel not quite so crazy."

"We aren't crazy, Tiff. We're just trying to go on. To live with what happened and to be there…for Jonathan."

"I know, and I appreciate that. I guess he's a lucky little guy. He's practically got two mommies now."

Melissa smiled at the comment. "Well, I appreciate *that*. More than you know."

Tiffany looked down and began playing in the grass again with her fingers. "You think that maybe we could all take a ride...to the cemetery today?" she asked. "I haven't been in a while and I feel like I need...to go."

"Sure," Melissa said. "Just say when."

Looking back up at Melissa, she smiled again.

"Thank you," she said. "Thank you so much."

Tiffany looked back out across the lot, watching as Jonathan ran on and on with his kite. She turned her face toward the sun and lost herself in the sound of his laughter as it drifted back to her on the warm summer air.

She hoped that Neal, from wherever his soul now called home, could hear it along with her.

God, he had loved the boy so.

ABOUT THE AUTHOR

Robert A. Howell was born December 21, 1964 in Florence, South Carolina. Developing an interest in fright films and literature at an early age, he began to write his first short stories while still in grammar school at Roy Hudgen's Academy, often illustrating them as well. While still in his teens, Howell became an avid fan of authors such as Dean R. Koontz, John Saul, Clive Barker, and Stephen King. At present, he still enjoys their work, alongside the works of Richard Laymon, Robert R. McCammon, and Steven Alten.

Howell is a published artist, columnist, amateur filmmaker, and horror fiction and film enthusiast. He is the founder of Carolina Moon Publications. Currently, he is developing "Night Roads," a collection of original horror tales set once again in his home state.

Howell currently lives and writes in the small community of Sardis, South Carolina.

Contact the author via Carolina Moon Publications at:

cmoonpub@earthlink.net

ACKNOWLEDGMENTS

Many thanks go to Pamela Denise White, without whose meticulous editing skills and suggestions, this book would not have been complete. To Margaret Shelton, my friend and mini-agent, who tolerated me when I bombarded her e-mail inbox with questions day after day. And to the residents of Sumter, South Carolina, who will surely spot every artistic liberty I took involving street names and/or local history. May your town never experience an All Saint's Eve such as the one which occurs within the pages of "Voices Carry."